POLISHED EBONY

"Hearin' you is the easiest thing they is."
Page 288.

POLISHED EBONY

BY
OCTAVUS ROY COHEN

ILLUSTRATED BY
H. WESTON TAYLOR

Short Story Index Reprint Series

 BOOKS FOR LIBRARIES PRESS
FREEPORT, NEW YORK

Copyright © 1919, 1947 by Octavus Roy Cohen

Reprinted 1970 by arrangement with Dodd, Mead & Company

INTERNATIONAL STANDARD BOOK NUMBER:
0-8369-3616-7

LIBRARY OF CONGRESS CATALOG CARD NUMBER:
74-128725

PRINTED IN THE UNITED STATES OF AMERICA

To
My Wife

CONTENTS

	PAGE
ALL THAT GLITTERS	3
POOL AND GINUWINE	47
THE AMATEUR HERO	93
TEMPUS FUGITS	119
NOT WISELY BUT TOO WELL	145
BACKFIRE	181
A HOUSE DIVIDED	213
POPPY PASSES	243
PAINLESS EXTRACTION	275

ILLUSTRATIONS

"Heahin' you is the easiest thing they is" . . . . *Frontispiece*

PAGE

"Semore," she murmured with downcast lids, "I — I — is totumly misundumstood you" 28

"Elias' face was pathetic. He stood in his tracks, back against the door, eyes rolling wildly and showing white" 110

"He crossed the room and hammered on the board wall until it shook" 214

ALL THAT GLITTERS

POLISHED EBONY

ALL THAT GLITTERS

URIAS NESBIT paused with his hand on the knob of the front door. From the rear of his cottage there was wafted to his ears the rhythmic swish-swash of soapsuddy lingerie caressing a rubbing board.

Urias nodded grimly and entered the three-room mansion. He proceeded to the bureau, opened the top drawer, *tchk'd* petulantly and strode through the kitchen into the yard.

Elzevir heard the slam of the door and straightened her shapely body. Her plump, rounded arms were soapy to the elbows. She sensed the captious antagonism of her husband and carried the war into his country. "Wha's troublin' yo' min' now, 'Rias?"

He frowned with dark disapproval. "Whar yo' di'min' ring is at?"

Elzevir mechanically raised her left hand and glanced at the ringless third finger. Then her teeth clicked together. "You is some naggin' man, 'Rias. You know puffectly well my ring is in the top bureau drawer."

"Yeh," he retorted with biting sarcasm. "Tha's jes' the trouble. I knows whar tis at. I is tol' you a thousan' times a'ready, Elzevir, an' Ise tellin' you again — if'n you leave that ring in yo' bureau drawer 'stead of lockin' it up in yo' trunk when you washes, it's gwine be stold jes' sho's hell's a fishpond."

"Huh! You is been sayin' that for a yeah. Tain't been stold twell yet."

"They's folks dyin' ev'y day, Elzevir, which aint never died befo'!"

He turned away and was safely within the house before a fitting retort came to her lips. He made his way once more to the bureau drawer and took therefrom a diamond ring of scintillant brilliance.

For sixty-three weeks Urias Nesbit had paid on that ring. One hundred and twenty-five dollars had been expended for the stone in instalments of two dollars each Saturday afternoon. That had been in the days when the elusive coyness of the regal Elzevir bade fair to put Urias permanently into the matrimonial discard. The ring had won her. And so they were married.

That diamond ring was the guarantee of Elzevir's social eminence. At first there had been skeptics — numbering legion — who questioned the genuineness of the stone, but they had been effectively squelched by the triumphant Elzevir who invariably convoyed them to a jeweller of unimpeachable integrity for an appraisement. And as there wasn't a jeweller in the city who did not instantly value the ring at anywhere from a hundred and twenty-five to a hundred and fifty dollars, its reputation quickly spread and by her diamond Elzevir became known.

But the diamond was the lone sign of affluence about the Nesbit ménage. Somehow work and Urias didn't get along very well together. The best he had ever been able to do was seven dollars a week — some weeks. The instinct of self-preservation had driven Elzevir to take in two family washings per week at one dollar and a half each. To her surprise she did not lose caste. Other society queens had been dethroned for less. And Elzevir correctly guessed that because she was possessed of a hundred-and-twenty-five dollar diamond ring, the taking in of a couple of washings was catalogued among the justifiable eccentricities of the wealthy.

She paid the diamond full homage. The Tiffany setting was kept immaculately clean. The stone itself sparkled elegantly from the brown background of her finger. It was the supreme joy of her existence, the fetich to save which she had more than once cheerfully faced hunger. Once, during a long, jobless period, Urias had insisted that she pawn the gem. "Di'min's is all right, Elzevir, but they is no good if'n you is sta'vin' to death."

"This heah ring gwine stay whar it is at — which is on my finger, 'Rias. If'n I die fum starvin' because you is too lazy to wuk — then I reckon it'll look gran' on my corpse."

But all of her passionate love for the ring could not emancipate Elzevir from her cardinal weakness. She was careless. For instance, she had for months been cognizant of the fact that one of the prongs was badly worn and that there was grave danger of some day losing the stone. For months she had conscientiously meant to see a jeweller and have a new prong installed — but a thousand and one things had prevented.

Again, during the arduous hours of her twice-weekly washing seances she invariably slipped the ring from her finger and placed it in the top drawer of her bureau: a drawer the lock of which had long ceased to be of any save ornamental value. Her husband had scolded her about it — chided her so frequently and earnestly that his criticism had degenerated into mere nagging. According to his views the treasure should, on wash days, be carefully locked in her trunk: a trunk being to the negro what a steel deposit vault is to his more Caucasian brother.

And Elzevir meant to do it. She always meant to do the right thing. But the bureau drawer was handy and she was regularly a half-hour late in starting . . . and the ring was inevitably dropped carelessly into the bureau drawer.

Urias's fears for its safety were well grounded. The ring was famed in coloured social circles and he realized that the neighbours must know that when washing for the white folks, Elzevir was without it. He knew, too, that while she was washing clothes in the back yard any larcenous individual could enter the front door, conduct a thorough search, find the ring and extract it from its hiding place and vamoose undetected.

"Jes' like'n to a woman," he soliloquized bitterly. "She ain't never gwine re'lize what that ring is ontil it's stold fum her."

He left the house in high dudgeon and traced his steps downtown. Near the L. & N. crossing which divides the north and south sides of the city he almost collided with a young overalled negro who pulled up short, grinned with delight and clutched his arm eagerly. " I is been lookin' for you ev'y-where, 'Rias."

" Is you? "

" Sho' is. Got a few minutes to spare? "

" Spare time," answered Urias gloomily, " is the on'y thing I ain't got anythin' else but."

" You ain't wukin'? "

" No."

" How come? "

" Me'n my boss ain't been gittin' 'long so well for some time so I thought I better quit."

" 'Rias," interrogated the other intensely, " how'd you like to make a hund'ed dollars cash 'thout doin' no wuk? "

Urias glared severely at his companion. " Cass Driggers, you might's well on'erstan' I ain't in no jokin' humour."

" Nor neither I ain't. Ise plumb serious."

" Huh! When you makes talk like what you is doin', you is plumb foolish."

Cass's voice took on a nuance of pleading earnestness. " 'Tain't so, 'Rias. They's a chancst for I an' you to make a hund'ed dollars each — easy. 'Thout doin' no wuk a tall. An' seein' as I an' you is good frien's, Ise lettin' you in fifty-fifty."

" Splain it, Cass — an' if'n you ain't want me to git pow'ful mad, you loocidate it tho'ough an' complete."

" Heah's the how of it, 'Rias. For th'ee months sencst I been wukin' as a mechanic down to the 'Celsior gyrage I is been teachin' a white gen'leman name of Cap'n Zacharias Foster how to run a new flivver which he done bought. It been jes' about a hopeless job 'cause'n he's one of them they men which jes' wa'nt bohn to run no autymobile. This mawnin' I gits a telyphone call fum him. He says he's out on the Potterville road — him an' what's lef' of the flivver. I got the wreckin' car an' driv out. They was jes' 'bout as much lef' of his clothes as they was of the car — an' he was most nekkid. I prized him up an' driv him in.

"If'n yo'd ever wukked 'round a gyrage, 'Rias, yo'd know they is two kin's of men whut owns autymobiles. One kin' loves 'em an' t'other kin' hates 'em. They ain't no inbetwix'. I is seen 'em all but I ain't nev' saw no man so sick of autymobiles as whut Cap'n Zacharias Foster was this mawnin'.

"'I'd sell that ol' junkpile for sevumty-five dollars,' he said.

"'Huh! Cap'n,' I comes back. 'You is the jokines' man!'

"With that he swears the mos' elegant I ev' did heah. 'I mean it,' he growls.

"'Bet'n you woul'n't put that in writin',' I says.

"I knowed he was a pow'ful sot feller an' sho nuff he pulls out a notebook an' writ out a 'greement to sell me that car for sevumty-five dollars if'n I perduced the cash in fohty-eight hours. An'," as Urias showed symptoms of interrupting, "that ain't noways the all of it, neither. 'Rias — I is got that car sol' for th'ee hund'ed dollars soon's I fix it up a bit."

Urias turned toward Cass Driggers a face wreathed in superlative contempt. "What is I got to do with all this?"

"You is the feller," explained Cass blandly,

"what is gwine put up the sevumty-five dollars!"

"Haw!" returned Urias with ponderous sarcasm. "You is foolish as you look. How come you to git the idee in yo' haid I is got sevumty-five dollars?"

"I ain't. But you is gwine git it."

"I ain't nev' yit been in jail, an'—"

"Lis'en heah, 'Rias: they ain't no trouble 'bout me gitten the money. Reckon Flo'ian Slappey'd lemme it if'n I'd take him in on the deal, or I could git Semore Mashby to do it —"

Urias clutched his short, dumpy friend by a greasy shoulder. "If'n you was ev' to give Semore Mashby the oppomtunity to make money, Cass, I'd plumb ruint you. That ol' jack-face' monkey is so tight 'bout'n money he ties chains to his dimes. Semore Mashby, Cass, is a discredick to the coloured race — an' sides, he is got too much money a'ready."

Cass nodded vehement agreement. "Ise with you in all what you says bout'n Semore Mashby, 'Rias. I woul'n't enter into no business deal with that man on'y if'n I had to. But I is sayin' I c'n git the money a' right. They's Flo'ian Slappey: he's the on'y an' original take-a-chancst feller, an' fust off I thought I'd go to him, but I says to myse'f: 'Cass Driggers,' I says, ''Rias Nesbit an' you is been buddies sencst you was kids an' if'n they's more'n two hund'ed dollars profit gwine be divided up seems like you owes him a slice of it.' Tha's jes' zac'ly what I says to myse'f, 'Rias, jes' like that — which is how come I to decide I an' you is gwine split up them they profits."

Urias shook a perturbed head. "You is speakin'

silly. I ain't got no sevumty-five dollars an' you know it."

"Sho' I does. But worser men'n you is made money what they ain't nev' had befo'."

"I got zac'ly th'ee dollars, fo' bits an' a dime, Cass. I ain't hahdly prospec' tha's enough to buy no autymobile."

"Woul'n't Elzevir like bout'n a hund'ed dollars?"

"Her! If'n Elzevir ev' seen that money all to oncet I'd be a widdier."

"Sho' nuff. Tha's jes' what I says to myse'f. I says: 'Cass Driggers,' I says, "'Rias is yo' buddy an' Elzevir is his wife, an' Elzevir is a broad 'ooman —"

"Crost the hips mebbe. But if'n you is makin' talk 'bout gitten Elzevir interes' in 'vestin' sevumty-five dollars . . . anyways, Cass — she jes' ain't got it!"

Cass lowered his voice discreetly. "She is got it, too!"

"Elzevir?"

"Uh-huh!"

"Sevumty-five dollars?"

"Yeh."

"You is absotively an' ontirely crazy, Cass Driggers. If'n autymobiles was sellin' for ten dollars apiece each me'n Elzevir between us coul'n't buy a puncture. Whar you git that notion 'bout Elzevir havin' sevumty-five dollars?"

"Her di'min' ring!" sibilated Cass eagerly. "Ol' Semore Mashby is a lookin' man when it comes to good s'curity an' he'd easy leave us have sevumty-five on that ring, an'—"

"They's a train leavin' fum heah in twen'y minutes, Cass," remarked his tall friend with heavy irony. "Bes' thing for you to do is to take that train, git off at Tuscaloosa an' enter right into the 'sane asylim. If'n they balks 'bout lettin' you in, you jes' tell 'em you got the idee Elzevir'd let that ring git away fum her — even for a minute . . . tell 'em that, Cass, an' they is gwine make you they stah bo'der."

"But they is a hund'ed dollars cl'ar profit for you, 'Rias. Ain't you hankering none a tall for a hund'ed dollars?"

"Hund'ed dollars ain't no good to a daid man."

"You is sho' Elzevir woul'n't —"

"I is sho' that if'n I was to siggest it to Elzevir they woul'n't be nothin' lef' on my shoulders but a li'l piece of neck."

Cass shook his head dolefully and tramped along in sombre silence. "I — I kinder sispected yo'd take it thisaway, 'Rias — an' so I done had another idee."

"If'n tain't no better'n that fust one yo'd better leave it stay whar it is at."

"It's a good idee, 'Rias — an' it'd wuk if'n you was a man with any cou'age — jes' even a li'l bit of cou'age. . . ."

"I ain't nev' been no coward, Cass."

"Bout'n some things you is."

"Name which?"

"Elzevir!"

"There you goes ag'in —"

"Lis'en heah to what I is sayin', 'Rias. Elzevir's got a di'min which is wuth a hund'ed an' fifty dollars, easy. If'n we was to try an' pawn that ring we coul'n't git more'n fifty dollars or mebbe fohty. But Semore Mashby'd let us have sevumty-five —"

"Goo'-bye, Cass. I gits ne'vous when I talks with a crazy man."

"Wait a minute. Heah me th'ough. Me'n you is buddies, 'Rias, an' if'n somebody is got to git a hund'ed dollars off'n me, I'd a heap ruther it was you. Now I got it all figgered out how we c'n raise that sevumty-five dollars an' if'n yo'll lemme splain —"

"Go ahead," commanded 'Rias with weary hopelessness — in the grip of a desire to humour his friend's infirmity, "but be sho' you splain it tho'ough."

Cass perked up with enthusiasm. "Heah's the how of it. A di'min' ring is a di'min' ring, an' if'n a 'ooman is got one she is salisfied. Now my idee is that we is gwine borry Elzevir's di'min ring on'y she ain't gwine know nothin' about we is done so!"

"Tha's a fine idee, Cass. An' w'en we finishes doin' that mebbe we is gwine borry the Chinnerses baby off'n Truman an' Orpha an' they ain't gwine know it, neither."

"Babies is diff'ent fum di'min's, 'Rias. We is gwine borry yo' wife's di'min' but she ain't gwine know it because we is gwine put another di'min' back in the place of the one we borries!"

"If'n you is got a di'min' a'ready what you wants with mine?"

"Ain't got one yit. We is got to buy it fust."

"With my th'ee dollars?" sarcastically.

"Yeh. They on'y costs two dollars an' a halft."

ALL THAT GLITTERS

"Reckon you ain't know no more bout'n di'min's than what you does 'bout wifes."

"Les'n heah to what I is sayin', 'Rias. We is gwine downtown an' buy a immytation di'min' fum off'n that feller on Secon' Avenue. It's glass in course, but they ain't nobody less'n a jooler could tell it, 'cause it's set in ten yeah gol' plate.

"Then," he continued radiantly, "we is gwine to yo' house tomorry while Elzevir is doin' the Carruthers' washin'— I is hea'd you scol' her a-plen'y bout'n she leaves her ring in the bureau drawer w'en she washes. We is gwine borry her ring an' leave the immytation in the place of it. An' seein' as they looks jes' alike she is gwine put it on an' nev' be no wiser. Tha's where rings is diff'ent fum chillun." Cass paused to inspect the face of his friend and noted with satisfaction that he had made a vast impression. He drove his advantage home in sledge-hammer fashion.

"I is gwine take that ring so's you won't be mixed up in it none a tall an' borry sevumty-five dollars fum off Semore Mashby on it at five dollars int'res'. Then Ise gwine buy that flivver off'n Cap'n Zacharias Foster an' fix it up, the gyrage givin' me credick fo' the twen'y dollars wuth of materials I need. I ain't gwine cha'ge you nothin' for my labour. Then I gwine sell the car for th'ee hund'ed dollars, pay Semore Mashby the eighty what we is gwine be owin' him, settle with the gyrage, split the diff'ence with you an' sneak Elzevir's ring back ag'in. You think it over, 'Rias, an' see if'n I is as crazy as what you thought I was."

Urias thought it over. The scheme was flawless. "You is sho' you can sell the car?"

"*Sho'* ain't even the word, 'Rias. I can sell it for th'ee hund'ed easy. They is somethin' 'bout a secon'-han' flivver, 'Rias, which gives white folks the itch in they money pockets. Reckon they think they is gittin' nothin' for less. I asts you for the las' time — is you with me?"

Urias didn't have a chance. He battled desperately with his conscience and his ingrained terror of a militant spouse. Arrayed on the other side was his passion for money and plenty of it — and a hundred dollars all in one luscious lump was more than he had dreamed of in his most avaricious mental orgies. And finally — albeit tremblingly — he informed Cass Driggers that he was with him. The die was cast — and if Urias felt like unto the trembling surgical victim who fearfully inhales his first paralysing whiff of ether while eyeing a glittering array of knives and clamps, he did not show it by other than a slight greenish pallor under his rich brown skin.

He voiced only one doubt. "You — you ain't gittin' me into nothin', is you, Cass?"

"Meanin' which?"

"They ain't possibly gwine be no slip 'bout sellin' that car?"

"Huh! You is just makin' sounds with yo' voice, 'Rias. You ain't talkin' a tall."

They proceeded to an almost-jewelry store on Second Avenue where for twenty minutes they pottered around purple velvet trays. They laid aside a half-dozen "as good as the real thing — only an expert can tell them" diamonds, and from that half dozen made a choice.

The brummagem brilliance of the ultimate selec-

ALL THAT GLITTERS 15

tion allayed to some slight extent the doubts which clung, fungus-like, in Urias's congenitally guileless breast. He was forced to admit that he couldn't, to save his life, have distinguished the imitation stone with its plated setting from the genuine bluewhite and its fourteen-karat mounting.

"Think Elzevir'll know the diffe'nce?" demanded Cass triumphantly as they left the store.

"Not less'n she's a wizzid," answered the considerably relieved Urias.

Knowing that he was on the eve of borrowing — without her consent — the gem which headlighted her way along the topmost social stratum, Urias Nesbit was unusually considerate of his wife's feelings that night. They walked to town and howled deliriously through four acts of a moss-eaten farce which was playing a two-day visit to the city. Their two tickets had cost all of four bits and their seats were in the front row of the supergallery which does not exist in the north and which is known south of the Line as Buzzard Roost or Nigger Heaven.

The following morning Urias hung doubtfully around the garage where Cass Driggers was employed. Cass was labouring skilfully over what had once been a proud and valiant flivver. About eleven in the morning a distinguished, hatchetfaced gentleman swung into the repair shop and stood eyeing the wreckage with a baleful stare.

"What are you doing, Cass?"

Driggers straightened and bobbed his head — an inherited courtesy which he reserved for those especially distinguished southern white folks in the light of whose approval he desired to bask.

"Howdye, Cap'n Foster. How you is feelin' this mawnin', suh?"

"As miserable as that mess looks. I'm through with automobiles, Cass."

"You is gwine git ov' that feelin', Cap'n Foster. They all does!"

"Not I. I wish I could sell the thing for junk."

"You is gwine sell it, Boss-man. An' I is gwine buy it. 'Member our 'greement bout'n that sevumty-five dollars?"

"You don't mean you contemplate paying seventy-five dollars for that bunch of tin?"

"Sho' is, Boss; by tomorry afternoon."

Mr. Zacharias Foster withered Cass with a glare of supreme contempt. "Cass Driggers," he snapped. "You haven't the sense of an ape!"

After he had left Urias took his place near the repair pit and gazed upon the ex-automobile. "You reckon you c'n r'illy fix her up, Cass?"

"Huh! 'Rias, these heah cars is like snakes. You c'n cut 'em in half but they goes right on. Hones', it takes th'ee wrecks to get 'em goin' good."

Urias was sceptical. During lunch he kept his eyes away from the brilliant ring which shone splendidly from the finger of his consort. He was gradually becoming alive to the fact that if anything went wrong he was holding the bag. He admired his friend's loyalty in wishing to donate to him one hundred dollars, but he was acutely conscious that Cass Driggers was risking nothing.

When he reached the garage at two o'clock he was aflame with open rebellion. But his mistrust disappeared like magic at sight of the reincarnation which confronted him.

ALL THAT GLITTERS 17

Cass had worked fast and expertly. Bent fenders had been straightened, an axle treated likewise, a new wheel provided, one casing vulcanized, new lenses placed in the headlights (Cass confided long afterwards that he had used window-glass), the car had been washed and polished and the top put up and dusted. "One graham cracker an' a glass of milk in 'er radiator an' she'll be better'n new," exulted Cass.

Urias was converted. In the face of his friend's mechanical legerdemain he hadn't the heart to withdraw. The glittery beauty of the car impressed him vastly. "Ought to git fo' hund'ed for that," he muttered.

By three o'clock the conspirators reached the neighbourhood which Mr. and Mrs. Urias Nesbit graced with their presence. Urias reconnoitred meticulously, ascertained positively that his wife was engaged in divorcing certain pieces of Carruthers linen from more or less dirt, and pussyfooted nervously through the front door.

He opened the bureau drawer. The real diamond sparkled a welcome. He acted swiftly — speed being a virtue. The fake diamond was substituted and Urias retreated precipitately. From the corner he paused to observe the swaying form of his wife who laboured earnestly over the washtub.

Cass relieved his friend of the ring and departed joyfully townward. "Gwine see Ol' Semore Mashby an' raise that sevumty-five dollars," he proclaimed. "Yo'd better not come with me if'n you ain't want Semore to sispec' whar I got this heah ring at."

Urias parted from his friend and his ring reluctantly. He gloomed down the street to Bud Peaglar's Barbecue Lunch Room & Billiard Parlour and was soon immersed in a free-for-all game of Kelly Pool at two bits per player. He won two of the first three games and temporarily forgot to worry about the diamond.

But at the very instant that Urias pocketed — with much gusto — his own eight ball, collecting therefor a net profit of one dollar and forty cents, things were happening at his home.

Elzevir had finished her washing. She entered the house, changed her waist and applied a guaranteed-to-make-kinky-hair-straight tonic to her raven tresses. Then she opened her bureau drawer and reverently picked up the ring which glittered adorably in its nest. Idly she slipped it on her finger.

It got as far as the bony knuckle!

And there it balked!

A slight frown corrugated her chocolate forehead. She pushed the ring. It cut into the flesh but obstinately refused to proceed beyond the knuckle. A tremor of apprehension shook her shapely form.

Urias Nesbit and Cass Driggers had slipped. They had expended a vast amount of mental effort in selecting a ring which was the apparent duplicate of the one which they borrowed. But to them a ring was a ring. They had totally forgotten that rings have sizes and that the one they had substituted was about three sizes too small for Elzevir's finger!

The knuckle refused passage to the ring. **Tiny**

ALL THAT GLITTERS 19

beads of perspiration appeared on Elzevir's brow. She inspected the ring closely and her most awful fears were confirmed. Her ring boasted a sadly worn and defective prong. The prongs of this usurper were new and flawless. Elzevir dropped limply into a wicker chair.

"Oh! my Gawd!" she groaned. "My di'min' is done been stold! Ol' 'Rias is gwine give me the devil an' some, sho' nuff!"

It was all very plain to her. In some way news of her carelessness with the family Koh-I-Noor had become bruited about. Perhaps Urias himself had told of it. A covetous, unscrupulous gentleman had thereupon stolen it, substituting an imitation in order to postpone discovery as long as possible.

The gloom of the ages descended in one great gob on the shoulders of Elzevir Nesbit. She bowed supinely under the burden of woe which had been heaved at her. That Urias was the culprit she never dreamed. He, like Cæsar's wife, was miles above suspicion. Besides, she knew that he didn't have the nerve.

As the horror of the situation banged itself with trip-hammer blows into her consciousness she saw one fact staring her in the face. Urias must not know of the loss! He must, at all hazards, be kept in ignorance. For the first time in her married life Elzevir knew fear of her husband.

She thought it over from every conceivable angle. She reinspected the ring. It was a beautiful ring: even she in her misery gave credit for that much. She knew that if it could be made to fit her finger, Urias would never suspect the substitution. She was a woman of action. Twenty minutes later she entered a second-class downtown jewelry store. She laid the ring on the counter: "Wha's that wuth, white folks?"

The expert flipped it contemptuously. "Dollar and a half — probably."

"How much'll it cost me to delarge it to fit my finger — right now?"

He named his price and she nodded grimly. Forty minutes later she left the store with the cut glass glowing in noble camouflage from her finger. She felt slightly better. But even yet the future was drab with the sadness of irrecoverable loss, although Elzevir was concerned principally with the present and its chances of detection. For the moment she seemed safe.

If only Urias hadn't been so passionately persistent with his warnings. If only his fervid diatribes on the subject of her carelessness had been less frequent. In that event she might have dared the truth. But now she knew that at any cost he must be kept in ignorance.

She was safe socially. So often had her ring been professionally appraised in the presence of sceptical witnesses that there remained no conscientious doubters in darktown. And so she determined upon a career of deception, hoping that it might exist until it became a habit. Should Urias learn of her loss, her tenure as head of the family would be at an end. Elzevir set her lips, stifled her grief and went home to prepare dinner.

Meanwhile Cass Driggers was progressing very well indeed with Semore Mashby.

Semore doubted the genuineness of Cass's proffered security. Cass conducted him triumphantly

ALL THAT GLITTERS

to the best jewelry store in town and had the most expert expert in that store appraise the stone. "Hundred and fifty dollars," was the instantaneous verdict. Semore was convinced. He produced the seventy-five dollars from a capacious wallet, wrote a receipt and an I. O. U. for eighty dollars — payable in thirty days — and pocketed the ring.

Both men were content. Semore was happy because there was more than an even chance that Cass would not redeem the ring and also because even if he did Semore would have profited at the rate of eighty per cent per annum, which is slightly more than is allowed under the Alabama usury laws.

Cass was happy because with Semore's loan he stood to clear two hundred dollars for himself and his pal . . . and he chortled with glee as he contemplated the day of the money's return, at which time he would tell Semore of the wealth begotten with his money.

Semore Mashby was about as popular with his coloured brethren as a policeman with a gang of crap-shooters. He was tall and angular and shifty-eyed — and had developed canniness to a high art. He loved to make money almost as much as he hated to see others do likewise. He was misanthropic and miserly. Each dollar that dropped into the pocket of his frayed coat clinked twice — once for itself and once for the dollar it was destined to earn.

But as heartily as Semore was disliked, just so heartily was he feared. His wealth — by darktown standards — put that of Crœsus into the also-ran class. He was the last refuge of desperate darkies who needed money on any terms and didn't have collateral satisfactory to licensed pawnbrokers. Semore handled any collateral cheerfully, willingly lending on such stuff as came his way as much as fifteen per cent of the forced-sale value. Of course a diamond was different. That was high finance.

And so darktown hated Semore Mashby: hated him passionately and single-mindedly. If there was any unanimity of feeling among the negroes of the community it was in the desire to sting Semore for even a modest portion of his bankroll. "If'n I could once do Semore Mashby out'n a dollar," Urias had often articulated, "I'd be buried smilin'."

For the man who succeeded in parting Semore from any of his coin there was waiting a universal acclaim. Several had tried it — with results disastrous to themselves. But it was understood that there was open season on Semore's bankroll three hundred and sixty-five days in the year.

So much the public knew of Semore Mashby: so much and no more. He was looked upon as a dried fig of humanity, a bloodless entity from which all semblance of softness had been squashed. Above all, he bore reputation as a misogynist. And of all things in the catalog, Semore Mashby was not that.

Vistar Goins was her name, a delectable creamy-brown creature of luscious curves and full red lips; a vivacious, pert-tongued little thing whose *élan* set Semore's heart to thumping madly beneath his threadbare shirt.

Vistar was a woman of keen perception and nice

ALL THAT GLITTERS 23

discretion. She was dazzled by Semore's wealth but wary of his tight-fistedness. She realized that a wealthy husband is an asset only when his wealth circulates out as well as in.

Vistar had a sneaking desire to marry Semore. More than once she had been tempted to take a chance: not because he had awakened in her maidenly breast any grand passion but because he had the wherewithal to insure her physical comfort to the end of her days — provided he would. But she was afraid that after the rose-and-rapture period of the honeymoon she would find herself still engaged as maid-of-all-work at some fashionable South Highlands home with part of her weekly earnings swelling the considerable Mashby fortune.

"If'n I ev' seen that man spen' a dollar where they wa'n't th'ee dollars comin' back to him, I'd marry him quick," she had informed her best friend more than once, " but I is skeered to take chancsts. Semore ain't even a member of the Over The River Buryin' Sassiety —'cause even if it on'y costs ten cents a week he'd have to be daid to c'lect an' that ain't his way of doin' business."

However, the delicious Vistar was too adroit to let Semore go entirely. For a year she had kept him dangling disgruntledly. For a year his passion for her had mounted in inverse ratio to her unattainability. His shiny, russet-black suit — flapping about the skinny, angular frame like the clipped wings of a bald-headed buzzard trying to take flight, served as a warning. If he wouldn't buy himself a new suit it was self-evident that he would be chary of expending real money for wifely raiment. And fine clothes were as necessary to

Vistar's happiness and well-being as colours are necessary to the rainbow.

He called upon her the night of his little business transaction with Cass Driggers. He was at peace with the world. Only that day he had summarily foreclosed a chattel mortgage on some cotton which had been grown by an old-fashioned, painfully unbusinesslike darkey living a few miles from the city. He had promptly sold the two bales at a net profit on the deal of more than seventy dollars. He gazed upon Vistar with a warm and appreciative eye. His protestations of love were even more fervid than usual but there was a new note in his declaration of eternal and liberal affection.

Vistar Goins sensed that the answer she returned this night must be final.

"I — I reckon you wa'n't hahdly bohn to be a husband, Semore."

"Huh? Wha's the matter with me? Ain't I the richest nigger in this heah town?"

"Sho' is — I reckon. But they ain't nobody c'n prove it 'ceptin' the cashier at the bank."

"Tha's what makes good credick, Hon."

"Credick don' nev' git nobody nothin' if'n 'tain't nev' took adwantage of. You know, Semore, I is a pow'ful free spender."

"Tha's because you is single," returned Semore tolerantly. "A married 'ooman ain't got no use for fancy clothes."

"An' I reckon yo'd spec' yo' wife to wuk, woul'n't you?"

"Wuk," proclaimed Semore sententiously, "ain't never hu't no one. If'n you wan'ed to wuk I reckon I'd be broad-minded enough not to stop you."

ALL THAT GLITTERS 25

"But s'pose I di'n't?"

Semore smiled enigmatically. "Well, if'n that was the case—" Something in his smile decided her. It was at one time a concession and an iron warning. It seemed to threaten: "Once you is married to me you is gwine *want* to wuk!" Reluctantly—knowing that it was her last chance—Vistar took the plunge. She shook her head—

"Reckon I cain't do it, Semore."

It was the first time her refusal had been unqualified by some ray of hope. Semore bent skinnily forth in his red plush chair, gripping the battered arms with talon-like fingers. "You—you mean—you ain't nev' gwine marry with me?"

She sighed. "Reckon not, Semore. Me'n you wa'n't meant for each other."

A good deal of the calculating harshness disappeared. He was stunned by her refusal. It had never occurred to him that he would not eventually be accepted. He had fancied that the lure of his wealth was too much for any dusky damsel to resist. "Ise rich," he faltered.

"Guess so. But me—I is always said I was gwine marry for love. . . . Yo'd better go, Semore, 'cause this heah intumview is painful for the both of us."

He rose. "I is comin' back—"

"'Tain't no use. I ain't nev' gwine marry you."

"But, Honey. . . ."

"Goo'-bye, Semore. You is gwine fin' another gal soon what you will like her better'n me. Guess I ain't wo'thy of you, nohow."

He turned toward the door in a daze. He knew that her answer was final and he simulated a tragedy which he did not feel — however great a blow his pride had received. At that, he had really wanted to marry Vistar. She was a woman to do any man proud. She would be as great satisfaction as a first mortgage on city real estate. And she was turning him down.

He stood uncertainly before her, swaying like a great blackbird on the rundown heels of his enormous shoes. His ancient Prince Albert coat was pushed back, his fingers shoved into the pockets of his much-mended grey vest. His expression showed equal portions of lugubriosity and surprise. He had not expected this. " Nev' can tell bout'n wimmin. . . ." His fingers brushed against something hard. He frowned — then remembered the ring he had that day received as security from Cass Driggers.

He drew it forth and inspected it glumly. The light from the electric bulb struck it full and reflected dazzlingly into the popping eyes of Vistar Goins. Realizing that he was making his final exit from the list of Vistar's matrimonial possibilities Semore instinctively gave play to the theatric instinct of his race. He turned the diamond over and over, muttering miserably; scarcely conscious that Vistar's eyes were focussed covetously upon the stone's scintillant perfection.

" Reckon I ain't gwine have no use for this ring now," mourned Semore sadly. " Might's well th'ow it away."

" Wh-what's that? " faltered Vistar.

" Nothin'. Nothin' on'y jes' a hund'ed an' fifty dollar di'min' 'gagement ring."

" Whar you git it at? "

"Bought it. Ain't got no use for it now."

A tremor of misgiving smote Vistar amidships. Was it possible, she cogitated wildly, that she — in common with the general coloured population — had mistaken the consistency of Semore's heart?

"What you buy it for?"

"Huh! What you reckon a man usuamly buys a di'min' ring for w'en he's plumb crazy bout'n a gal an' is gwine ast her to be his wife?"

Vistar shook her head. She couldn't quite grasp the idea that Semore was capable of an affection strong enough to unloose his purse strings to the tune of a hundred and fifty dollars. "Is that a ginuwine di'min'?"

"Reckon they ain't nothin' countumfeit bout'n Semore Mashby."

"An'— an' you bought it for me?"

"Co'se."

Vistar's doubts were dispelled. Her heart flippity-flopped toward Semore. A surge of genuine affection accompanied realization of the fact that she had done the man an injustice. And if her sudden accession of ardour was influenced largely by the blue-white sparks which glinted from the diamond she was at least honestly unconscious of the fact. "O-o-oh! Semore!" she quavered.

He stiffened. Here was a nuance which he had never before heard from her luscious red lips. "Wh-wh-what?"

"Semore," she murmured with downcast lids, "I — I — is totumly misundumstood you. . . ."

"Vistar! You — you ain't mean that . . . that . . ."

She shook her head violently and sidled closer

to his skinny frame in maidenly token of surrender. Her left hand strayed upward and rested maddeningly on his frayed vest. "Oh! Honey...."

Better men than Semore Mashby have made greater tactical blunders in the embrace of soft round arms. He could no more have resisted the lure of the parted, upturned lips than he could have neglected to collect interest due him. He crushed her to him and quivered with the delicious novelty of a soul kiss such as had inflamed only a few of his wildest dreams.

When, two minutes later, they seated themselves on the sofa and entwined themselves again in each other's arms — the fourth finger of Vistar Goins' left hand flamed with the glory of Elzevir Nesbit's diamond!

Elzevir frowned as she massaged, with a hot iron, various rough-dried garments of the white folks.

She had plumbed the nethermost depths of misery — and she was scared: scared completely and thoroughly. During dinner the previous night she had intercepted countless glances directed by Urias toward her imitation ring. Conditions had been worse at the matutinal feast. It could mean but one thing: — Urias suspected the true state of affairs but was not sufficiently convinced to voice his suspicions.

Once before he had pursued such a course and been forced to retreat precipitately from the house pursued by a verbal barrage of terrible intensity. Elzevir knew that Urias was merely awaiting substantiation of his suspicions before loosing his initial tirade. The future seemed dark with impene-

"Semore," she murmured with downcast lids, "I—I— is totumly misundumstood you."

ALL THAT GLITTERS 29

trable blackness, the clammy gloom about the Nesbit house was thick enough to be sliced with a knife.

There came a light knock at the door and Elzevir called a "Come in" without turning her head. The door swung back and she heard a cheery, musical voice: "Mawnin', Mis' Nesbit."

Elzevir dropped the iron and squared her shoulders. She and Vistar had long and frankly confessed to a mutual antipathy and she knew that the visit boded some unpleasantness. "Mawnin', Miss Goins."

"Jes' dropped in for a minute. Le's sit on the po'ch."

Elzevir dropped into a wicker chair opposite her visitor. "Fine day, ain't it, Miss Goins?"

"Elegant. But I guess mos' ev'ything looks fine to me today, Mis' Nesbit."

"How come that?"

With downcast eyes and modest mien Vistar wordlessly extended her left hand. Elzevir gasped: "You is got a di'min'?"

"Uh-huh."

"How come that?"

"I is engage'," simpered the fair Vistar.

"G'wan. To which?"

"Semore Mashby."

"Semore. . . . Lis'en heah, Vistar Goins, is you tellin' me the Gawd's hones' truth?"

"Sho' is, Mis' Nesbit. Ain't that ring prove it? Semore give me that las' night."

Here was a draft doubly bitter. She knew that Vistar disliked her and had always been intensely jealous of the social pre-eminence which was hers by reason of ownership of a genuine diamond. And now Vistar had come to cut her social props from under, to smash her cosmic scheme in the solar plexus. How thorough a job she was performing, even Vistar did not know, for she did not dream that the ring which glowed from Elzevir's finger was born in a glass factory.

Elzevir was lavish in her praise. "Lemme see it, Miss Goins. I sho' does congratumlate you."

Vistar slipped the ring from her finger and passed it over, exulting in her triumph. Elzevir inspected it languidly — then suddenly her eyes narrowed, her lips compressed and every muscle in her body tensed.

She recognized her own ring!

There wasn't a doubt of it. The worn and battered prong, the . . . she spoke merely because she was afraid that by prolonged silence she might betray her emotional seethe to Vistar's close and exuberant scrutiny. "Sho' is a han'some ring, Miss Goins."

"My inten'ed ain't no piker, Mis' Nesbit."

Elzevir did not know how Semore Mashby had become possessed of her ring. She didn't particularly care. All that she did know was that by some kind act of a merciful Providence the missing ring was once again in her possession and there she intended to keep it. Her conscience was clear: the ring had been stolen from her. It had come home to roost. It was her property — and her property she intended it to remain. To her legal right of possession she intended to add actual possession.

"Elegant ring," she murmured absently, turning it this way and that in the sunlight. "Prettier than mine, I reckon."

ALL THAT GLITTERS 31

"Tha's nachel," cooed Vistar. "My fiansay is got mo' money than what yo' husband is got. He c'n fo'd ril fine stones."

"'Tain't no larger — lemme see," and Elzevir, a-tremble with inspiration, slipped the imitation diamond from her finger. She compared the rings carefully. She shuffled them deliberately. And finally she slipped a ring back on her finger.

But the ring which she returned to Vistar Goins was a gold-plated affair set with a piece of glass! The Nesbit crown jewel had been restored.

Vistar was pitifully unsuspicious of the substitution. She slipped the imitation on her finger and sighed with satisfaction. "I espec' I'll have sev'al more di'min's pretty soon," she commented idly. "Semore is so foolish in how he spen's money whar I is consarned at."

Elzevir knew that she was now safe from detection. Should trouble arise she realized that she could easily prove ownership to the ring she wore. And Vistar had rubbed it in just a little bit too strong.

"Semore Mashby ain't got no reppitation for bein' zac'ly what yo'd call a spen'thrif'," she remarked acidly.

"Whar I is consarned at —'tis diffe'ent," came the bland answer.

Elzevir's eyes narrowed. "You ain't happen' to show that to no jooler yet, is you?"

"What for?"

"Nothin'. Nothin' tall. On'y some immytation di'min's, Miss Goins, looks pow'ful like the ril thing."

Vistar rose indignantly. "Is you meanin' to 'sinuate, Mis' Nesbit, that —"

"I ain't 'sinuatin' nothin', Miss Goins. I is said what I is said. An' what I is said is that Mistuh Mashby ain' nev' th'ew no money away yet an' if'n 'twas me he give that stone to I'd be pow'ful sho' 'twas ginuwine befo' I went boastin' roun' wimmin what ev'ybody knows wears the ril thing. Tha's all what I is got to say, Miss Goins. Ise busy — doin' hones' wuk. Good day!"

It was ridiculous; unthinkable; absurd! Semore would never dare. But the seeds of distrust, so cleverly planted, insisted on sprouting.

An hour later she staggered from a leading jewelry store. Tears — part of stricken pride and part of fury — trembling in her eyes. "A dollar and a half," had been the jeweller's prompt verdict. "It isn't worth a cent more than that."

She walked dizzily toward her home, groping blindly through the wreckage of her air-castles. All the venom in her nature had concentrated against Semore Mashby; Semore the hopelessly tightwad whose fervently protested love for her had proved not sufficiently strong to master the plea of the dollar.

She was prostrated, abased, made a laughing-stock in the eyes of the society set. Nor was she labouring under any delusions. Elzevir Nesbit detested her and Elzevir knew that the visit of the morning had been for the express purpose of quaffing the nectar of superiority. Elzevir would not rise to heights of mercy. Not a chance. Nor would the story lose colour in the telling. The world had become a dark, drab place for the crushed

Vistar. Her pride had wenteth before her fall and the fall was exceeding hard.

Her first move was strictly feminine. She went home and cried it out. And with her cry came realization that, diamonds or no diamonds, Semore was not — and could never have become — her man. When she left home it was to walk swiftly to Semore's office, a dingy room in an ancient two-story red-brick building a half-block removed from the best business section of darktown.

She had been in the office before and never liked it. Now its noisome dankness smote her and filled her soul with loathing for the place and the man who sat hunched like a great skinny buzzard in his swivel chair. At sight of her Semore rose eagerly and started forward with arms outstretched. He caught the pale yellow gleam of cold fury in her eyes and paused. . . .

Vistar exploded. She ripped the offending ring from her finger and hurled it viciously. It struck a broken button on his vest and tinkled to the floor. Semore's lantern jaw dropped weakly. "Wha-wha's the matter, Hon?"

"I — I —" Vistar choked. She turned wordlessly toward the door.

"Vistar — Honey — Sumthin's wrong —?"

She whirled in a fury. "You is said sumthin', Semore. They is plen'y wrong!"

He cautiously rescued the ring from a dust-heap. "S'posin' you tell me. . . ."

"If'n I was to tell you what I is thinkin', Semore Mashby, you sho' would have me 'rested. I is thinkin' things bout'n you, Semore Mashby, which I cain't say 'thout fo'gettin' I is a lady. I is on'y gwine say this much — they is some wimmin you c'n fool with a fake di'min', but I ain't one of them!"

"Fake di'min'?" Semore stiffened. His parsimonious soul shrivelled before the possibilities contained in the accusation. "What you mean — fake?"

"Mebbe so I is got a price, Semore Mashby; but 'tain't no dollar'n a half! You go give that they di'min' to s'mother gal what ain't got sense enough to know yo'd fool her. Tha's all what I is got to say bout'n it. Goo'-bye! you ol'— ol'— rooster!"

The door slammed behind her, raising a tiny spurt of dust. Semore's head wobbled crazily on his thin neck. He passed talon-like fingers across a perspiring forehead. His chief terror, however, was not of his blasted love-hopes but of the certainty that something was wrong with his diamond.

He knew Vistar Goins: knew her very well indeed. And he realized that she was not of the type to theatrically fling real diamonds around his office. Therefore, she must *know* that the stone was imitation. *Quod erat demonstratum!*

But how? Twenty-four hours previously one of the best jewellers in the city had appraised the stone as worth not a cent less than a hundred and fifty dollars. He broke the world's middle-distance records in traversing the distance between his office and the jeweller's. He shoved the ring across the counter: "How much that is wuth, Cap'n?"

The white man glanced at the bit of glass and smiled. "About a dollar. Maybe two."

"Two dollars?" There were tears in Semore's

ALL THAT GLITTERS

voice. "Ain't they some mistake, Boss-man?"

"No. It is a cleverly-cut imitation and a fairly well made, plated setting. But it's intrinsic value isn't possibly more than two dollars."

Semore closed his eyes in horror. In the light of this certain financial catastrophe the loss of a prospective wife and a happy home seemed as nothing. "B-b-but," he stammered. "It wa'n't on'y yestiddy you tol' me that they ring was wuth a hund'ed an' fifty dollars!"

The jeweller shook his head. "Not that ring. That is not the ring I appraised for you yesterday."

"But Boss-man," wailed Semore, "is you sho' bout'n that?"

"Positive. The ring you showed me yesterday was a very pretty genuine diamond. This thing is plain glass."

"O-o-o-oh! Lawdy!"

"You haven't loaned any money on *that*, have you?"

Semore glanced at the ring. He raised pain-filled eyes to the face of his vis-a-vis. "No," he groaned, "I ain't loant nothin' on nothin'. I reckon I is jes' nachelly gave sevumty-five dollars to cha'ity!"

The stricken Semore lurched into the street and groped blindly toward his musty office. There he sank into a creaky chair and lighted a cigar butt which he spitted on a penpoint so that he might get the ultimate puff of rancid smoke. He tried to collect his thoughts.

He knew that the jeweller was above reproach. Some fiend of evil had stolen his real diamond and substituted this bit of glass. And yet — no one had possessed the ring save himself. It hadn't been out of his pocket —

He leaped to his feet and smashed a bony fist into the palm of his other hand.

"Me an' Samson," he roared, resorting to the Bible for a parallel, "we is both been done dirt by wimmin! Vistar Goins wukked me for that di'min' an' then double-crossed me!"

It was all quite plain. Vistar still had the real diamond. He slapped a battered felt hat on his head with the intention of putting the case in the hands of Lawyer Evans Chew. Then he realized that Chew, in common with all the other men of parts in darktown, disliked him and would take great pleasure in exploiting his discomfiture. He loved money passionately, but he knew that it was worth more than seventy-five dollars to conceal the story of his undoing. And he was wise enough to understand that he would have a very difficult time in proving that Vistar had substituted the imitation for the real. If he had her arrested and she should subsequently be acquitted — they'd certainly run him out of town.

He removed his hat and settled into the slough of despond. He was heartsick and weary. "Reckon I deserves it," he muttered bitterly, "for foolin' with wimmin." Semore Mashby's conversion to misogyny was complete.

There came a light tap on the door and it was flung open. Cass Driggers poked a grinning head into the room. "Hello, Ol' Spoht!" he greeted cheerily. "How you makin' it this mawnin'?"

Semore pulled himself together with a mighty

ALL THAT GLITTERS 37

effort. He tried to grin and met with sickly success. "Tol'able, Brother Driggers; soht of tol'able."

"So'm I, Brother Mashby. Jes' paused by to let you know bout'n that sevumty-five dollars you loant me yestiddy — you 'members it, don' you?"

"Yeh," choked Semore, "I 'members it tho'ough."

"I done finish a deal what tu'n it into th'ee hund'ed dollars," exulted Cass. "I is comin' 'roun' this evenin' to redeem that they ring back ag'in."

Worse and more of it. Ossa piled on Pelion. This new aspect to a phantasmagoria of misery smote Semore where it hurt worst. He temporized. "Ain't no hurry, Brother Driggers: you is got thutty days."

"I is got th'ee hund'ed dollars," chuckled Cass. "An' t'night I pays you eighty an' gits the ring."

Semore was face to face with the necessity for immediate and decisive action. His brain was sadly addled but not to such an extent that he failed to realize the urgency of saving the present situation at any cost. He knew that if he should be suspected of evil-doing, Cass Driggers would cheerfully railroad him to the chaingang.

And he couldn't return the diamond to Cass because he didn't have the diamond. He knew that Cass had placed in pawn with him a genuine diamond and that he had nothing to return save a cheap imitation. Sooner or later Cass would discover the substitution and he — Semore Mashby — would make the acquaintance of the city jail. He didn't fool himself. He realized that he had as much chance for mercy as a Brunswick stew at a nigger barbecue.

"Tha's a pow'ful nice ring, Cass."

"Reckon so. Cost a hund'ed an' fifty dollars."

"'Tain't wuth all of that."

"We ain't scussin' what i's wuth, Brother Mashby. I is gwine git it back for eighty dollars. That lets you out."

It did let him out — hard. "I is soht of growed fon' of that ring," murmured Semore.

"I an' you both."

"Sposin' you sell it to me?"

"That ring ain't for sale."

"How 'bout a hund'ed an' twen'y-five dollars cash: fifty more'n what I loant you on it yestiddy?"

"You is the humourestes' feller, Semore. That ring ain't for sale."

"Hund'ed an' fifty?"

"Nothin' stirrin'. If'n you want a di'min' ring for yo' ownse'f, whyn't you go downtown an' buy you one?"

For a wild instant Semore thought of doing that and attempting to substitute the new ring for that of Cass which had passed into the avid clutches of a heartless woman. But that would not entirely negative the danger of discovery. Cass must never know.

"Hund'ed an' sevumty-five? All what you is got an' a hund'ed mo'?"

"I wants my own ring back," snapped Cass impatiently.

Semore was on the rack. He knew that he was

ALL THAT GLITTERS 39

up against it good and proper. "T-t-t-two hund'ed?" he faltered.

Flat rejection trembled on Cass's lips but he choked it back. Here was a chance— "You is off'rin' all what we is borried an' a hund'ed an' twen'y-five mo' for that ring, Semore?"

"Uh-huh."

"Put it in writin'," commanded the budding financier.

Semore did so, every scratch of the pen making a furrow in his heart. Cass inspected the document and grinned. "Let you know this evenin', Brother Mashby. Way I figgers it out, I ain't gwine lose nothin' no way."

Semore knew that Cass was speaking fact. It seemed that for once in his life he was on the short end of everything. His opinion of women in general and of Vistar in particular at that moment dwarfed Schopenhauer's famous essay into a flaccid compliment by comparison. Cass paused at the door.

"If'n you ain't look shahp, Semore," he flung over his shoulder, "you is gwine begin' spen' some money pretty soon an' then you gwine die of a busted heart."

Cass ran down the stairway, turned the corner at top speed and accelerated all the way to the Nesbit homestead. He laid the proposition glowingly before the astounded Urias and backed it up by an exhibition of the documentary evidence. "So you see, 'Rias," he concluded triumphantly, "we is gwine take this extray hund'ed an' twen'y-five an' buy a new an' ginuwine di'min' for Elzevir an' the sevumty-five what we owes Semore will be extry profit for us."

Urias shook his head doubtfully. "Cain't be did, Cass. Elzevir'd know it, sho'."

"Huh!" negatived the optimistic Cass. "She ain't able to tell her ril di'min' fum a fake, so how she gwine know if'n we give her a ril, hones'-to-Gawd di'min' which we is gwine spen' a hund'ed an' twen'y-five dollars for?"

"They is some things, Cass, which is too much. . . ."

"A di'min' is a di'min', 'Rias, an' a woman is a woman. Even Elzevir."

Cass won. Two hours later he left the office of the prostrated Semore Mashby clutching in his hand the informal pawn ticket for eighty dollars and one hundred and twenty-five dollars in cash. Semore had fought a valiant but losing battle for the five dollars interest money.

Cass and Urias met on the corner and together selected a glittering diamond for which they paid one hundred and twenty-five dollars. Cass was all in favor of a seventy-five dollar stone with a pronounced flaw but Urias had been too terrified by the experiences of the immediate past to run further risks.

Luck was with them. They reached the Nesbit manse, reconnoitred, and saw Elzevir in the back yard putting the finishing touches to an extra washing. Urias sneaked into the house and slid open the bureau drawer.

The ring was not there! Then he knew that his wife had at this fatal eleventh hour heeded his nagging advice. The ring was locked in the trunk and his wife had the key. The irony of the thing struck him: Elzevir securely locking away an imitation diamond after having for years left a real stone open to any enterprising crook!

He lighted a cigarette and lounged through the back door. He noticed that the ring was not on her finger. " 'Lo, Elzevir."

" Howdye."

" You sho' does wuk hahd, Elzevir."

" Lot you knows 'bout wuk!"

Urias speculated briefly. " Is you got the key to yo' trunk, Elzevir?"

" Sho' is."

" Loand it to me a minute, will you, Hon?"

He did not detect the gleam of suspicion which leaped into Elzevir's eyes, nor did he take warning from the alacrity with which she handed him the desired key. He chatted with her for a few moments and sidled into the house.

It required only a few seconds to throw back the lid of the trunk and to locate the ring. He lifted it happily from the tray and fished the new and genuine diamond from his vest pocket.

He gazed at the two stones. They seemed twins. He couldn't tell which from t'other.

" What you is doin', 'Rias?"

Urias whirled. He experienced a sudden sinking sensation at the pit of his stomach. He gazed into the level eyes of his militant wife. She held his gaze for awhile, then dropped her eyes to the glittering, glowing diamonds.

Discretion and circumstance prompted a lie, but intimate knowledge of the woman before him warned that such a course would be troublesome and fruitless. And so Urias Nesbit for once in his life told the whole, unadorned, perfect and complete truth.

He pleaded passionately. He offered to escort her to every jeweller in town for appraisement of the ring. And as he talked Elzevir's lips lost their stern rigidity and expanded into a sunny smile. The sun was shining very brightly for Elzevir. And when he finished she merely said: "Call in that wuthless, no-'count Cass Driggers."

Cass entered sheepishly and stood twirling his hat. Elzevir's voice whipped out like the crack o' doom. "Is you done sol' that autymobile yet, Cass?"

"Uh-huh. Yas'm."

"How much?"

"Th'ee hund'ed dollars. I owes the gyrage twen'y-five dollars for mate'ial."

"An' you owes me sevumty-five dollars for the use of my ring."

"But Mis' Nesbit —"

"You owes me sevumty-five dollars for the use of my ring," she grated. "Lis'en at me an' perduce!"

Cass looked at Urias and Urias stared miserably back at Cass. Cass did the expedient thing: he handed the seventy-five dollars to Elzevir. "That leaves you two hund'ed," continued Elzevir mercilessly. "Give me the hund'ed what belongs to 'Rias."

"But, Honey. . . ."

"'Rias! You keep yo' mouth out of this heah settlin'ment. Han' it over, Cass."

Cass obeyed dumbly.

"Ise gwine keep this for you, 'Rias," smiled Elzevir. "Reckon you nev' will know nothin' much bout'n handlin' money. If'n you want five dollars—"

"Thanks, sweetness," murmured Urias humbly, as he took the crumpled bill which his wife generously tendered. Then an idea struck him. "What you is gwine do with that fake ring?"

His wife smiled enigmatically and gazed affectionately at her two genuine diamonds. "I reckon I'll wear 'em both."

"But if'n any one should ast. . . ."

"Tell 'em they is both ril di'min's."

"They might want a jooler to look at 'em."

"Reckon I c'n stan' that, 'Rias. Anyways, you lemme worry 'bout that side of it. All you got to do is jes' like what I says."

Urias shook his head in bewilderment. "I— I—ain't on'erstan', Honey."

"They's a heap of things you ain't never gwine on'erstan', 'Rias. They's some things a wife ain't got no time tellin' her husban'. This heah is one of 'em. Too much infermation is li'ble to go to yo' haid. By the way, Cass, who was fool nuff to buy that busted car?"

"That autymobile was better'n new," defended Cass stoutly. "Them flivvers ain't no good ontil they is been wrecked a few times."

"Who bought it?" repeated Elzevir firmly.

Cass grinned. "Cap'n Zacharias Foster," he chuckled, "the man what owned it fust off!"

POOL AND GINUWINE

POOL AND GINUWINE

THE melancholia of the ages shone in the eyes of the dandified young negro who leaned disconsolately against the lamp-post before the ornate portals of Champion Moving Picture Theatre No. 2 — Coloured Only. Even the frankly envious hail: " 'Lo, Bo Brumm'l!" of a one-time rival failed to rouse him from his lethargy.

For Florian Slappey had a grudge against the world. Society had done him dirt. The ponies persisted in running true to form when he played the long shots, his creditors exhibited an alarming, and ever-increasing, distrust of well-phrased promises, his favourite lottery gigs remained in the big glass wheel instead of appearing in the lucky dozen which was drawn twice daily.

It was all wrong. Not that Florian Slappey cared for himself: he was well content with a little money, an absence of the necessity for work, the glory of his social dictatorship and three square meals a day. But continued ill luck was tending to thwart the greatest desire of Florian Slappey's happy-go-lucky young life; — it was veering his bark of romance toward a surfy shoal, and —

" 'Lo, Florian!"

The lithe figure of the young darkey straightened so swiftly that the angle of the pearl grey hat was disturbed by three degrees. Then a hand — the fingers of which were tipped by well manicured, highly polished fingernails — flew to the top piece and it came off. The body bent gracefully at the waist and as Florian raised his eyes to the superlative pulchritude of Blossom Prioleau he flushed beneath his coat of racial brunette and gave vent to some of his surcharged emotion by the universal device of sighing.

For if Florian was a fashion-plate which the men of darktown's uppermost social stratum copied, Blossom was of a magnificence of feature, physique and raiment which defied emulation.

The blood of Jamaica had blended with the rich, red life stream of imported Africa through many American generations to make of Blossom a personal perfection. She was educated through the sixth grade, lacked none of the social graces, a good spender when she had money to spend, and various white ladies for whom she had toiled in a domestic capacity testified to the fact that she was a marvel of efficiency when she cared to be.

Blossom was not opposed to work, as such. In fact she rather favoured it — for the other fellow. For herself, she looked down upon domestic labor as menial and ill befitting her high social status. Besides, white folks were inconsiderate and lacking a sense of appreciation. They refused to make allowances for her undoubted attractiveness when garbed in nurse's cap and apron. They actually demanded the services which they expected to receive from girls less prominent socially. She craved a life of luxury, so when she and Florian —

Therein Florian Slappey was in a fair way to be hoist by his own petard, for Florian was a past master of the gentle art of fooling most of the pub-

POOL AND GINUWINE

lic all of the time and he had fooled it into the belief that he was perenially workless because pecuniarily insured against labour. The occasional appearance of the correct three numbers chosen from those between 1 and 78 in the lottery wheel had enabled him to keep up appearances since his advent from Montgomery more than a year previously; and it was in the flush of enthusiasm which followed the winning of the Blood Gig — numbers 5, 10 and 40, paying him four hundred dollars for the two he invested, that he proposed to Blossom Prioleau and was promptly accepted.

Their engagement, although nominally a secret, had been bruited about among the socially elect and was more or less of a gossip sensation. Florian and Blossom had denied it flatly — at Florian's insistence — for the simple reason that Florian could not afford a diamond engagement ring, dared not attempt to fool either Blossom or her friends with an imitation stone, and refused to sacrifice his position as male social dictator by an admission of his inability to supply his lady fair with the glittering, conventional badge of voluntary lifelong servitude.

Of late Florian had found reason for rejoicing over this canny foresight. And only Jackson Ramsay, the portly white man who operated the policy game, guessed that Florian was in financial straits.

Jackson Ramsay was familiar with the symptoms, but fortunately for Florian he was tight-lipped. But he saw the dawn of worry in Florian's eyes with the ill luck which followed the daily morning drawing — known as "Pool"— and the afternoon lottery — arbitrarily yclept "Genuine." Florian's bets were becoming more and more reckless. Not content with saddling his bets and winning modestly he played three, four — and even five — numbers straight. And he had won just as often as men who play that system usually win, which is not at all. The odds to the prospective winner were alluring; the odds against him well-nigh impossible.

For Florian, in common with many thousands of his fellow-negroes in the South, fondly believed that when 78 numbers are put into a wheel and twelve drawn therefrom there was a very good chance of guessing three of the numbers destined to be included in the dozen. So sure was Jackson Ramsay that the bettor could not perform this feat of clairvoyance that to the guesser of three of the twelve numbers he promptly paid 200 for 1, to the lucky chooser of four 500 for 1; and to the selector of five, 2,500 for 1.

But no one, and Blossom least of all, among Florian's friends, had suspected his pecuniary travail . . . which accounted for their failure to understand the sudden friendship between Florian and Sally Crouch — the latter a stout female of thirty-five years who owned and operated the Cozy Home Hotel for Coloured and was reputed to have on deposit in the First National Bank a sum in excess of three thousand dollars. And it was the look of frank disbelief in the lustrous black eyes of the adored Blossom Prioleau which brought a surge of apprehension over Florian Slappey as he gingerly squeezed her unresponsive hand. Florian was unpleasantly aware that he faced an emotional Armageddon.

POOL AND GINUWINE

"'Lo, Blossom."

"What you doin', Florian?"

"Nothin'. What you doin'?"

"Jes' walkin' 'round."

"Thought you was workin'."

"I is."

"Mis' Clarkson give you the day off?"

"She don't give no days off. Tell you how come, Florian: I'se sick."

"S'posin' she finds out?"

"She ain't goin' to. I tol' Ma to stay 'round the house till she comes down in her automobile. Ma'll meet her outside an' tell her I is sick in bed. That'll make it easier tomorrow."

"I see." He cleared his throat awkwardly. "You ain't lookin' fo' nobody, is you, Blossom?"

"No." And then, with quick suspicion: "You?"

"Me? Co'se not. Who'd I be lookin' fo'?"

"Reckon you ought to know that well as me."

"Blossom, you's the 'sinuatinest woman. . . ."

"I ain't 'sinuatin' nothin' I'se scared to say in plain English."

"How come you says—"

"I reckon you an' me is 'bout due to do some plain an' honest talkin', Florian."

"I ain't like no rucus, Blossom."

She sniffed disdainfully. "You ain't the on'y one. But they's things. . . ."

Florian cast a wild, hunted glance about the congested avenue with its battered taxicabs, its rows of stores operated by negroes for negroes, its pretentious nine-story office building owned and occupied by members of his race; the Penny Prudential Savings Bank on the ground floor . . . and finally his eye lighted on the inviting portals of Broughton's Drug Store. Unpleasantnesses annoyed him. He wanted peace and plenty of it.

"How 'bout a soda, Blossom?"

"I ain't keen 'bout no soda. What I want is to make talk with you."

There was no help for it: "Let's talk in there."

The sight of a frothy, creamy strawberry ice cream soda then in the process of being dispensed to an ebony urchin dispelled Blossom's opposition. "If you wanna —"

They seated themselves at a shiny-topped table in the farthest and most secluded corner. Florian gave the order with the nonchalance of a millionaire. Inwardly he was fidgety. He tried his best to avert the catastrophe: "Pink Broughton sure is got a swell place here."

"Is he?"

"He was tellin' me t'other day. . . ."

The ice cream sodas were served and Blossom's long spoon probed tentatively into the foam. "We ain't interest' in what he was tellin' you t'other day, Florian. What we's interest' in is what I is tellin' you now."

"You is actin' so strange, hon."

Blossom's lips compressed tightly. "Reckon I'll be actin' stranger befo' long. Why ain't you been to the house this last two nights?"

"Business," evaded Florian.

"Huh! Fust time I ever knew her name was Business."

"Who's name?" Innocently.

"That big, fat Sally Crouch."

POOL AND GINUWINE 53

Florian experienced a sinky sensation near the solar plexus. "Who said somethin' 'bout Sally?"

"I did."

"What for you mention her?"

"'Cause she's what I got to talk about. Fust off I want to ask you, Florian — is we engaged or ain't we engaged?"

"Why, honey . . ."

"Is we or ain't we?"

"Ain't you know —?"

"I'se tryin' to find out."

"I done tol' you. . . ."

"Yeh — you tol' me a lot of things. But there's other folks been tellin' me contrariwise. An' you ain't been 'round much lately an' I sort of been thinkin'—"

"You're the thinkenest woman, Blossom. You ain't got no call to be thinkin' all the time that-away."

"I reckon I got a right. Ain't it so I got a right when my fiansay goes traipsin' 'round with a woman who ain't got no education an' who runs a hotel which there ain't the best things in the world said about it? Ain't I — huh?"

"Ain't *been* runnin' 'round with her."

"Pff! Reckon that ol' sofa in her parlour ain't had a chancst to get cool these last few nights."

"You're the 'sinuatinest woman. . . ."

Her eyes compelled his and held them levelly. "I asks you this, Florian — is you in love with me or is you in love with Sally Crouch?"

"Honest t' Gawd, Hon — I ain't care a snap of my fingers for that woman. I ain't never loved no woman but you, an'—"

"When you gwine marry me?"

Florian flushed. "This ain't no time to make marriage talk, Blossom. Things is too 'carious."

"This is the time *you* gwine make marriage talk, Florian. I ain't calc'latin' to stand no fumadiddle from you nor no other man. You ain't never tol' no one we was engage' an' folks is sayin' that I is runnin' after you fo' your money. . . ."

"Folks don't know what they's talkin' 'bout," he retorted earnestly, thinking fearfully of his total worldly assets: an extensive wardrobe and about eight dollars in cash.

"Reckon you ain't the marryin' kind, huh?"

"Reckon I is."

"Then whyn't you marry me right off?"

"I sort of ain't ready, Blossom. They's business reasons. . . ."

"Hm! What you know 'bout business? You got 'nough money so's you ain't got to work."

"I does work."

"Playin' the lott'ry."

"I'se secretary of The Sons & Daughters of I Will Arise."

"That don't pay nothin' much."

He hesitated. . . . "'Tain't much, I reckon, Blossom; but I reckon I might's well tell you now as later,— I need that money."

"What. . . ?" She leaned across the table, the strawberry soda temporarily forgotten: "You means to tell me you need the money you git from The Sons & Daughters of I Will Arise?"

He hung his head in shame. "Uh-huh."

"How come? I thought you was rich."

"That's what they all think," he answered mis-

POOL AND GINUWINE

erably . . . for greater shame hath no man than to admit his wealth is a chimera. "But that ain't makin' it so."

"You useter have. . . ."

"*Useter* ain't *is*. I done had business reverses."

"Playin' th' lott'ry, I reckon."

"Sort of. An' other things. An' that's the truth."

Silence fell between them. Florian Slappey fingered the few crumpled bills in his trousers pocket. The girl tried to readjust in a second her preconceived ideas of the man and his worldly status.

"Broke?" she questioned directly. He was disconcerted.

"Not ontirely."

"Almost?"

"Uh-huh! I woul'n't be tellin' no one only you, Hon. . . ."

"Whyn't you git you a job?"

He shook his head. "My health ain't so good, Blossom. I got the misery. . . ."

"An' you —" And then a light came to her. Florian Slappey, wealthy, courted the perfect Blossom Prioleau. Florian Slappey, bereft of lucre, cast mercenary eyes upon the portly — and affluent — Sally Crouch: Sally of the ample figure, the big heart, the level head: Sally the uncourted, the hard-working, the unbeautiful, the none-too-young. Blossom half rose in her sudden accession of violent anger, and then dropped back to her seat. Florian missed none of the business and knew that his fowl was hung high. "So — so *that's* it?" breathed Blossom.

"What's it?"

"You go lose yo' money an' make a set f'r Sally Crouch 'cause she's got a heap."

The hour for evasion had passed and Florian knew it. He bent forward earnestly, his slender fingers with their polished nails clasping and unclasping. "That ain't the way to look at it a tall, Blossom. You knows well enough that I love you: you're the lovinest woman I ever been with. But gittin' married is something different. Honest, I love you too much to marry you an' then make you work fo' me. . . ."

"Pff! I see myself workin' for any man!"

"Sure — that's it!" He brightened perceptibly. "It woul'n't nowise be fair fo' you to have to work for me an' I ain't able to work fo' myself. White folks asks too much these days an' they don't pay nothin'. I been tryin' to make back my money. Mister Ramsay c'n tell you: I been playin' th' Pool ev'y mornin' an' saddlin' over to th' Ginuwine in the afternoon, but the gigs ain't been comin' right. I ain't call 'em right no mo'. Wunst I been win a few dollars . . . but I ain't aimin' to marry you on no few dollars, Hon. You is meant for fine clothes an' such like. I knows you woul'n't want to marry me if —"

"Listen here, Florian: you ain't tootin' a tall. I got a single mind, I is. I ain't fickle. I ain't never love' no man but you an' if you is willin' they ain't no reason why we cain't git married today."

He shook his head in sad negation. "'Twoul'n't be fair to you, Hon."

"Reckon I c'n jedge that."

"I cares too much to let you. 'Cause ef my

strength give out. . . . You ain't got no money save' up, is you?"

"No," suspiciously, "I ain't."

"Y'see —"

"You gwine marry me?"

"'Twoul'n't be right."

"You mean you *won't?*"

"I'm tellin' you —"

"S'posin' you jes' answer my question."

"Marriage ain't like credit, Blossom. Folks is got to have money or they'll be mis'able. I ain't got the heart to ask no good-lookin' woman like you to t'row herse'f away on ol' trash like me. I ain't aimin'—"

"You *is* aimin'," she flashed with sudden heat. "You is aimin' to marry fat ol' Sally Crouch an' make her s'port you all yo' nachel life. Tha's all the heart you got: jes' to make a woman work fo' you —"

"Hol' on, Blossom; hol' on. That ain't nowise fair. I ain't the kind of a man to take adwantage of no woman. Love is a fine t'ing, I says, but it's espensive — like a Ford. I ain't got no money an' I ain't able to work. Doc Simmons says I ain't. Last white gen'lman I work fo' said the same indentical t'ing. I sort of guess that poet what said 'bout bein' better to have love' an' lost than to have marry' the girl wasn't no liar at that."

"An' so," bitterly, "you is plumb sot on marryin' Sally fo' her money?"

"I ain't never goin' to stop lovin' you, Blossom."

"Hmph! Lot of good that's goin' to do either of us. Ain't you got no sense, Florian? Is you saw a picture of Sally Crouch as Missis Florian

Slappey? Why — why — she even talks like po' white trash. You is a disumpointment to me, Florian — that you is."

"Reckon you'd do the same thing —"

"You ain't know what you is talkin' 'bout. I se had chancsts, I is. I got a friend up home in Nashville name 'Zekiel Rothwell. He runs a jitney line an' he's got plenty money. I'se tellin' you, Florian, 'tain't his fault none a tall I ain't been Missis 'Zekiel Rothwell long time ago. Tha's what. But I ain't b'lieve in marryin' fo' money —"

"Tha's whar you makin' a mistake," he told her earnestly. "A honeymoon ain't last but a week or so, Blossom. Tha's whar its diff'rent from a bank account. We always c'n love each other, Hon. Guess we is just got to try an' be happy. . . ."

Blossom rose abruptly, a victim of unrequited love and hurt pride. Florian trailed her to the door. A few men seated at the soda fountain turned to stare with glittering eyes at her Junoesque figure. Florian swelled with self-pity and affection. There was a pleasant glow imparted by the knowledge that he was rejecting the hand of this regal creature; doing it, he told himself, for her own good — a Don Quixote. There was a hint of moisture in his eyes as he extended his hand to her in farewell. "Ef on'y I had the money like what folks t'ink I is got. . . ."

"I — I — woul'n't marry no — such — man as you," she choked.

"Don't you go hurtin' my feelin's, Blossom. An' don't you never fo'get I ain't never love' no woman on'y you."

"Ise goin' to remember ev'ything, Florian; 'specially that a man what'll sell hisself to a big, fat, wuthless wench ain't worth cryin' 'bout."

She turned suddenly and walked swiftly down the street. Florian stared after her thoughtfully. He sighed. Then he smiled. So much for that. The job, deliciously unpleasant as it had been, was finished. The Rubicon had been safely crossed, and he flattered himself that it had been rather adroitly handled. He was a bit sorry, of course, that he had been forced to break the heart of the most glorious woman in darktown's 400 . . . but there was an aftermath of quiet pleasure in the knowledge that it had been within his power to do so. There was no doubt that he had pursued the sensible course. He had too long worshipped at the shrine of the money god to underestimate by a farthing the social value of spot cash. He knew that he would always love Blossom, just as he knew she would always care for him. There was a tragic joy in the feeling. And there was always the chance that in the near future the lottery would solve his problems. He fancied himself — in that event — laying his fortune at Blossom's large and shapely feet . . . offering her that and himself in marriage.

But that day his gigs failed to materialize in either Pool or Genuine and the following morning he made his way downtown to be greeted by the news that Blossom Prioleau had departed the city.

"Whar she gone?"

"Dunno 'zactly, Florian."

"Y'ain't heard nobody say?"

"Not 'zactly, though I kinder t'ink like mebbe somebody says 'twas to Nashville whar she was bohn at. Funny you ain't know 'bout it, Florian."

"Me? Hmph! How come I should know whar she is at?"

The fact remained that Blossom had gone. Florian was pleased. He appreciated the fine display of tact which had prompted her to temporarily remove herself from the scene of his proposed commercial courtship. Thus his carefully planned campaign for the ample hand of Sally Crouch would not be injured by frequent distracting glimpses of the might-have-been Mrs. Slappey. Blossom had gone to visit Nashville. . . . Florian was mournfully happy. The martyr rôle secretly pleased him.

Theretofore Florian's attentions to the portly, good-natured Sally had been discreet. Immediately they became flagrant. Society gossipped, marvelled, then disgustedly washed its hands of the affair. Matrons ground their teeth as it became more and more apparent that Sally Crouch was destined to become Mrs. Florian Slappey. There would then be no denial of social eminence.

Florian held social leadership by virtue of brain, education, and — from the standpoint of the blind populace — wealth. He was a brunette Chesterfield and a born leader. Sally Crouch was the very antithesis. During the past four years she had worked too hard with her Cozy Home Hotel to bother much about society, and her social activities began and ended with lodge gatherings where she assumed a back seat. At the evening functions she played the dual rôle of wall-flower and chaperone. Being fat, and therefore good-natured, she cheerfully recognized the fact that she was not

POOL AND GINUWINE

meant to be a butterfly and did not bother her level head about it.

But after Florian Slappey had paid ardent and unmistakable court to her for a period of three consecutive weeks immediately on the footsteps of Blossom Prioleau's departure for Nashville — life assumed a fresh perspective. Sally's cosmic scheme was wrecked and rebuilt. For the first time in a neglected life Sally Crouch had reason to dream of social recognition and a husband.

And what a husband! Sally worshipped him blindly. He was all which she was not and which she suddenly found herself possessed of a desire to be. She was too happy and trustful to seek a sinister motivating impulse to his sudden passion. That he was marrying her for money never occurred to her for she, in common with others of the circle, fancied that he was more than comfortably supplied with the goods of this world.

So she accepted her good fortune with delirious blindness. Florian became a welcome nightly guest at the hotel dinner table and she heaped his plate with countless delicacies prepared as only Sally could prepare them: steaks expertly charred on the outside and rare and juicy within; crisp, crumbly toast; rich brown gravies; thin, tender bacon; oysters fried to a succulence beyond compare; puddings and pies and cakes warranted to melt at 98 degrees Fahrenheit. She couldn't understand the phenomenon brought about by the little blind God and she didn't try. Sufficient unto the day she found the pleasure thereof.

She plunged into an orgy of trousseau-buying. She assumed ill-fitting airs of elegance. She timorously allowed herself the exquisite luxury of patronizing a few hangers-on who had been wont to look down upon her from their higher rungs of the social ladder. And through it all she lavished upon Florian an intransigent adoration such as falls to the lot of few mere mortals.

As for Florian, he proved himself possessed of no mean histrionic ability. And at that it wasn't so hard after the initial sting of Blossom's departure had been soothed by time. He almost wished that she might be there to witness the cheerful fortitude which was his in the face of sacrifice. As for his nightly banquets — well, the future might be loveless but there wasn't any doubt that Sally was assaulting the famous road to a man's heart.

The Cozy Home Hotel was prosperous. He could see that with half an eye. Report credited Sally with a fortune of three thousand dollars. He fancied gossip had underestimated. It was hard indeed to forego the delights of the glorious Blossom, but he derived satisfaction in the vista of luxurious years.

And so he proposed. There may have been some of the passion and fire of his Blossom courtship lacking but to Sally Crouch his declaration of love was an epic. It was her first. She accepted him voluminously. Stunned darktown learned the news and congratulated dazedly.

It wasn't understandable, but Florian admitted the truth and as such it was accepted. The Sons & Daughters of I Will Arise elected Sally the following week to the post of Grand Exalted Princess which, while by no means a high office, was higher than any to which Sally had ever aspired. And Sally planned for a wedding which was destined to live for ever in social history. It was to be a thing stupendous, an artistic triumph calculated to place her incontrovertibly on the very pinnacle of the social heap. Sally was grimly determined that nothing she might do was to fail to bring credit to the proud name of Slappey.

As for Florian, he was alternately divinely happy and hopelessly miserable. Being human, he had never quite succeeded in ridding himself of the vision of Blossom's physical attributes. On the other hand he could not deny the appeal of Sally's affluence and her skill in catering to his gustatory senses. Too, he basked benignly in her worship of himself.

He played the lottery daily in sums ranging from a nickel to a dollar. His credit had improved since the announcement of the engagement. Jackson Ramsay, operator of Pool and Genuine, cautioned the young negro against too reckless play but Florian was in no mood to listen to reason.

"Winnin' a few dollars ain't goin' to help me, Mistuh Ramsay. I'm plumb sot on winnin' big or not a tall."

So he played from day to day: desperately — the size of his bets limited only by the state of his finances. He essayed every combination, or gig, known to professional policy players. The morning drawing — Pool — found him laying several small bets with instructions to carry any winnings over to the afternoon drawing — the Genuine. Once in a great while he won a few dollars.

Usually what small winnings were netted in the Pool were swept away in the Genuine. And the wedding day approached.

It was to be an epoch-making wedding with Sally footing the bills. The hotel on Eighteenth street was to be decorated with azaleas, dogwood and magnolias with a final marvellous touch of art in the shape of a monstrous pink and white tissue paper wedding bell. Reverend Plato Tubb, pastor of the First African M. E. Church, had been selected from six eager clergymen who bid down to a minimum of profit for the honour of tying the hymeneal knot. Flower girls were drilled daily. A pump organ was installed. Officers of The Sons & Daughters of I Will Arise were to be present in full regalia and the uniformed drill team had promised an exhibition in the street immediately preceding the ceremony. Every detail had been arranged with meticulous care. Even Florian found himself thrilling to the spotlight position. Matters, he felt, might be worse.

The wedding day arrived. Florian rose early. The sky was cloudless, the city droned with the activities of an early June day. Two buzzards circled lazily overhead but if Florian noticed the omen he gave no sign. At eleven o'clock he entered the lottery room and extended a dollar to Jackson Ramsay. "All that on the Green Back gig, Cap'n Ramsay."

"Straight?"

"Four full."

"All or nothing, eh?"

"Uh-huh!"

"Pool or Genuine?"

POOL AND GINUWINE

"Mawnin'— Pool. T'night'll be too late."

"Aren't you getting reckless, Slappey?"

"You spoke a mouffuf that time, Cap'n. If that four should win I gets five hundred fo' my dollar. An' nothin'— nary cent — less'n that'll help."

Ramsay shrugged his pudgy shoulders and wrote the ticket:

FLORIAN SLAPPEY
Pool ——————— No. 384
18-44-45-61 (Straight)
$1.00

The door swung back and a wizened negro woman entered. To Ramsay she handed a dime: "Train gig," she ordered. "I done hab a dream las' night."

"15–45–63," he checked off as he wrote the ticket: "Straight?"

"No — all."

"That's how *you* ought to play," said Ramsay to the disdainful Slappey.

"Huh? Me? If all th'ee comes out she on'y gets sixty for one."

"Yes," reminded the policy writer, "but if two come out she gets twenty-five for one, and if one of them come out she gets four for one."

"That ain't my game," commented Florian loftily. "I ain't no piker."

The little old woman gazed admiringly upon Florian. "Yo' shuah ain't, Mistuh Slappey. On'y I cain't 'ford to play it yo' way. You — you feelin' well today?"

"What you got to do with that, woman?"

"Ain't yo' know me?"

"Huh? How come I ought to know you?"

"I wuks wiv Mis' Sally down t' th' hotel. Mis' Sally, she kinder 'lowed maybe come I might see you down yeah an' she say tell you please to come by an' make talk wif her fo' a minute."

Florian waved a grandiloquent hand, left the dilapidated building, and strolled idly toward the Cozy Home Hotel. He wondered whether Blossom knew that this was his wedding day, he even speculated a bit on the ethical aspect of this mercenary marriage. He was selling himself and his social prestige for many a mess of pottage and a succession of breakfasts of crispy waffles.

Sally received him in the private parlour. Her greeting was effusive: she threw plump arms about his neck and implanted a fervent and resounding kiss upon his unwilling lips. She was radiant and palpitant as a schoolgirl. And finally when the amorous preliminaries were concluded she seated him beside her on the couch, placed his arm almost all the way around the place where nature had planned a waistline, and —

"Reckon you's wonderin' how come I wanted to see you, darlin'?"

"I'm always glad to answer yo' biddin'," he answered with forced, dignified gallantry, his mind busy with the terror that hereafter this woman was to be his daily companion. Of course, after the honeymoon he would no longer be forced to simulate affection. . . . He speculated briefly and bitterly on the fate which made Blossom poor and this creature rich.

"It's about disyer hotel," she started. Florian pricked up his ears. "Bein' as we'se most married I thought I might 'swell talk t'ings over wid you."

"That's right — honey."

POOL AND GINUWINE 67

She snuggled closer. "You is sech a brainy man, Florian, I jes' sorter wanted yo' adwice —"

"Yes?"

"Y'see, Florian — I ain't never had nothin' but hahd wuk sence I got hol' of dis hotel. Fust off w'en I took hol' I done de cookin' an' de laundry an' de maid wuk — an' I ain't had so much money, either. You ain't neber gwine know how hahd I wuk."

"That's right, honey; that's right. You is the magnificentest woman I ever did see. You ain't got to tell me that."

"I'se so happy, sweetness, I is got to talk wif you. I sort of got to t'inkin' dat Missis Florian Slappey cain't do all what Sally Crouch would do — ain't dat right?"

"You is always right, Sally."

"Yo' g'wan! I wuk so hahd wid dis hotel an' I got sort of wond'rin' ef you'd want yo' wife to keep on wukin' like what I been doin'. . . ."

"You mean you want to know is I — er — willin' you should keep on runnin' this hotel?"

"Da's it. Da's it. Yo' done said it dat time."

He crossed his legs and clasped slender, callousless hands over one knee. "Hon, I got awful lib'ral views; 'bout the lib'ralist what is, I reckon. I says a woman is got jes' as much right to work as what a man is got. 'Course things'll be different when we is married t'night, but I always says that a woman is got her rights an' no man ain't got no call takin' 'em from her."

"Da's right, Florian; da's jes' right. But I ain't want to take no 'portant step 'thout constultin' you, an' today was de last day."

"How come that?"

"It's de lease. Is disaway, sweetness: I done had a fo' yeah lease what says I got to gib dem agents t'ree months' notice ef I want it fo' another two yeahs. I 'most fohgot dat ontil I happen to look at de lease yestiddy. What I asks yo' adwice about is should I sign it up ag'in or should I let it drap?"

"I got them lib'ral views like what I done said," he repeated earnestly, "an' I got a fine admiration fo' a business woman — specially when her business is lucertive."

"It ain't de money, Florian; it's de sediment. I been a-wukin' dis hotel fo' yeahs. . . ."

"Tha's it, Sally; but the money counts too. I ain't never been no man to sneer with money. An', b'sides, ain't no matter what I thought I ain't got no call to make you give up a business what's makin' money like this hotel —"

She nudged him kittenishly. "G'wan, Florian. How come you t'ink dis hotel makin' money?"

"Huh?" He was momentarily nonplussed, then chose his words carefully. "It is, ain't it?"

"No! Ef 'twas makin' money I woul'n't of ast yo' adwice. 'Tis disaway: de fust-off yeah I run it I jes' 'bout break even; den de nex' yeah I make 'bout five hunderd dollars. Come de yeah after I jes' 'bout bust' even, but dis yeah — Lawdy! wid prices gone so high an' me jes' a-wukin' my fingers to de bone an' detrenchin' sumpin' terrible de bestest I could do was lose all what I is had saved up an' some mo' besides."

"Not — not really?"

"Sho' nuff. I ain't got no cause lyin' to you, is

I? An' I woul'n't go fo' to take de hotel fo' another two yeahs ef you was apposed to it, sence mebbe you might hab to put up de money to keep it goin'."

Florian sat up very straight. Something was radically wrong. He scrutinized the face of the woman at his side and found nothing there but guileless simplicity. He saw truth — and a truth which he did not want to believe. He *couldn't* believe it. "You — mean — you's *broke?*"

She nodded.

"Plumb *ontirely* broke?"

"Might' nigh."

"An'— an' you sort of wanted to find out would I stan' good fo' any *losin's?*"

"Not perzac'ly dat, sweetness. 'Course I ain't gwine lose more'n two or t'ree hundred dollar dis yeah, an' I knows dat ain't nothin' to you; but I sorter t'ought mebbe you should want me to sell de furniture an' gib up de hotel . . . anyways, dat would jes' 'bout clear up my debts."

"An'— an'— leave you how much in the bank?"

"I got 'bout sebenty dollars now. Ef I sold out an' paid all my debts I don't hahdly reckon I'd have nothin'. 'Course I'll have you, Hon, an' we'll be pow'ful happy, an' sence you ain't got no o'jections against wuk, mebbe I'd git a job cookin' up to de Claremont 'partments . . . less'n ob co'se you changes yo' mind an' decides you don't want yo' wife to wuk a tall."

He passed a shaking hand across a perspiring forehead. "I — I — ain't got no 'jections to you workin'," he said in a slow, dazed manner. "It ain't that —"

"Den yo' t'ink I better should keep de hotel?"

"I — I — guess so. . . . Y'see, I cain't think so awful good, Hon. I ain't feelin' jest so well. I always thought this here hotel was the payin'est thing. . . ."

She chuckled with good-natured amusement. "Ev'ybody t'ought dat. But what dey t'inks ain't bringin' in no dollars. 'Course I takes in plenty money, but money ain't always profit, an' I wasn't hankerin' to make my husband stan' fo' no debts —"

"That's right, Sally — that's right."

"So I done been hones' wif you. Tonight I becomes Missis Florian Slappey — an' I t'ought mebbe you ain't want yo' wife to wuk like what Sally Crouch done. It was right I should ask you 'bout disyer t'ing, ain't it, sweetness?"

"Yeh — it was right, Sally. On'y I got to 'fess it was a kind of s'prise. I thought this hotel was the *payin'est* thing."

She rose: "You set dere a minute, sweetheart, an' I'll show yo' my books."

One hour later Florian Slappey staggered blindly into the street and clung helplessly to a lamppost. The last scintilla of doubt had been dispelled. He had seen cold, stark figures: black on white. He shuddered at the prospect . . . he trembled at what he had done — Blossom gone and himself pledged to marry this fat creature who not only had no money but calmly proposed to saddle his insolvent self with her indebtedness. An old crony swaggered along the pavement and flashed a roll of bills under Florian's nose: "They's others that's in soft," he boasted.

"How come?" asked Florian, only mildly interested.

"Lott'ry."

"What yo' play?"

"Green Back gig."

"Huh!" Florian experienced a thrill of excitement: he had played the three numbers of the Green Back gig with a fourth one added. "Yo' play t'ree or fo'?"

"Three: 18-44-45."

"Sixty-one ain't happen to come out, too, is it?"

"You play them fo' straight?"

"Uh-huh."

The other inspected the printed list distributed by Ramsay to his patrons. "Tough luck. Ain't no 61 on it."

"Guess I might've knowed that," snorted Florian disgustedly. "'Cause if they had been I'd of won five hundred dollars. All the luck's ag'n me today."

The other laughed light-heartedly: "You always was a li'l joker, Florian."

Slappey glared balefully at his affluent friend, half inclined to quarrel. One more number — just one more right one included in the dozen drawn from the wheel that morning — would have made him temporarily wealthy. Discretion prompted —

"Lemme five dollars."

"Cain't."

"How come?"

"I — I'm owin' this."

"Fo'?"

"Honest, Florian. . . ."

"Th'ee-fifty?"

"You don't onderstan'—"

"Th'ee?"

"I c'n len' you a dollar," hedged the other desperately.

Florian took the dollar ungraciously and made his way down the street musing bitterly on the miserliness of his friends. Luck was certainly not running his way.

At that he retained enough of his sense of humour to chuckle at the irony of it. Blossom, at worst, would merely not have been an asset: Sally promised to be a heavy liability. There was still hope for him. He was not yet married to Sally. Suppose . . .

Florian became poignantly aware of the fact that he faced a vital strategic problem. Already the corps of amateur decorators were busy disfiguring the parlour of Sally's white elephant hotel. His feet led him past the hall of The Sons & Daughters of I Will Arise. They hailed him jovially and through a window he glimpsed certain present and past-grand potentates in the gilt and finery of their drill uniforms and gilt swords. He mooned silently through City Park, retraced his steps to the congested centre where he had met Blossom the fateful day which marked the termination of their dream of love and subconsciously his feet carried him into the ornate lobby of the Penny Prudential Bank Building. And as he crossed to the bank of elevators his lips expanded slowly to a broad, triumphant grin.

Florian Slappey had evolved another scheme.

The ceremony was scheduled for eight-thirty. At seven the last of the dinner guests finished the evening repast, and Sally's assistants cleared away the debris. Then they entered Sally's room and became French maids.

Sally was desperately fastening an expensive corset about her expansive figure. One female friend was assisting valiantly. Another struggled nobly to lace the white kid boots which did fairly well at the feet but were totally inadequate to the difficulties presented by the elephantine ankles. A foam of lace and lingerie was scattered about on the bed, and atop it all a creamy satin wedding gown.

Before the hotel the fife and drum corps of The Sons & Daughters of I Will Arise blared nobly and the drill squad executed its evolutions soberly — cheered on by a batallion of wide-eyed urchins of the Ethiopian persuasion. A carriage containing the Reverend Plato Tubb of the First African M. E. Church drove up to the door and the drill team from the lodge furnished him a guard of honour up the narrow stairway to the parlour.

The guests arrived bearing their wedding gifts: pink electroliers, boxes of plated ware, clothes for the bride. . . . These were spread on a camouflaged kitchen table in the centre of the parlour beside the donations from former employers of Sally.

As for the bride she was fluttery as though her age was twenty instead of thirty-five; and her figure thirty-six instead of ten inches more than that. For the first time in her life Sally Crouch held the centre of the social stage, and she had every cause to exult in her achievement.

Hitherto Sally had been regarded more as a person than as a woman. The sudden shift of Florian's affections from the magnificent Blossom to the more girthy negress was patently a tactical victory on her part. No one in the community suspected that Florian might be marrying her for money . . . for there was no one in the community who guessed that Florian was anything but flushed with worldly goods.

The Reverend Plato Tubb sent word of his readiness. Sally gave a fair imitation of a pirouette before the mirror. "Y'ain't t'ink I is look so bad, is you, Eva?"

"Lawsy, Mis' Sally — I ain't never saw a prettier bride."

"'Course I ain't got no figure. . . ."

"Ain' no man gwine look fo' no figure when you got them swell clothes."

"Ev'ybody here?"

"Ev'ybody. Drill team f'um the Lodge an' ev'ything."

"Where's Mister Slappey?"

"Dunno. . . . Livonia, yo' know whar is Mr. Slappey at?"

"Uh-uh! Ain't saw him."

"Go fin' him an' tell him we's ready."

Ten minutes later Livonia returned, her forehead puckered. "Cain't find Mister Slappey, Mis' Sally."

"'Cain't find. . . . Whaffo' you mean by dat?"

"He ain't yeah, da's all."

"You ast them Lodge members?"

"Yup. Dey ain't saw him."

"You mean dey ain't nobody saw him yeah a tall t'night?"

"Uh-huh."

Sally Crouch's thick lips came together firmly.

Gathering her bridal train in one large, white-gloved hand, and followed by her retinue, she sailed into the parlour. She faced the audience belligerently. " Looka yeah, coloured folks: I ain't keer how much jokes you play after dis ceremony done been over, but I ain't gwine stan' fo' no fumadiddles now. Whar Mister Slappey? "

" Really, Mis' Sally —" Reverend Plato Tubb bustled forward. " They all done said . . ."

" I ain't keer whut dey done said, Reverend Tubb —" A small boy entered the door, fought his way to Sally, and forced a crumpled envelope into her hand. " Letter for you, Mis' Sally."

" Ain' gwine be bothered with no letter."

" It's fum Mister Slappey."

Sally opened the letter with trembling fingers: then, without a word, she perused its contents and handed it over to the Reverend Plato Tubb —

℞
DR. VIVIAN SIMMONS, M.D.
Surgeon & Physician

Rates: Office Visit $1.   Office Hours:
House Visit $2.   9-10 A. M. 1-2 P. M.
All Accounts Cash.

TO WHOM IT MAY CONCERN (and especially Miss Sally Crouch)

This is to certify that I have on this day examined the patient, Mr. Florian Slappey, Esquire, and find that he seems to have acute articular rheumatism; indigestion; a slight fever and simptoms of neuritus, on account of which this is to certify that he is unable to attend his wedding tonight and should be excused. Also I certify that he isn't in no physical condition to get married shortly.

Given under my hand and seal this fifteenth day of June.
DR. VIVIAN SIMMONS, M.D.

Witness:
Doll White.

That night Florian Slappey had a dream. He

dreamed that he was on a railroad train bound for Nashville and the delights of Blossom Prioleau. The train reached Decatur, Alabama — there was a crash, a rending of timbers and Florian felt himself pitched through a window to land easily and hurtlessly on the turf.

He sat up in bed, eyes wide and slender figure trembling. The dream had been fearfully vivid. He rose and turned on the light to make quite sure that it was a dream. Down the hall he heard the voice of an irate woman: " Yo'-all better be keerful how you goes a-slammin' doors thisyer time o' night! "

Pretty girl — train — wreck! The main facts of his dream remained distinct even now that sleep had been banished. Florian had an idea. He hustled across the room, opened the lid of a battered trunk and extracted from the tray a much thumbed volume which bore the title:

> PROF. HANNIFER'S PERFECT DREAM BOOK
> With Translations into Lottery Numbers

He consulted the index, and finally turned to page 79.

Should you dream of a handsome woman in conjunction with a train wreck you will have enormous luck. Borrow one dollar from a friend without telling him your reasons. Play a quarter on each of the following in the morning lottery with instructions to carry winnings over to the afternoon lottery:

Train Gig 15–45–63
Little Louse Gig.............. 1– 2– 3
Baby Gig 1–12–40
Blood Gig 5–10–21

Play these for a single number to win. With your winnings play the following five numbers straight in the afternoon lottery:

9–17–39–46–78

At eight o'clock the following morning Florian Slappey approached Phillip Simpson and requested the loan of a dollar.

"Huh? Whut you want wid a dollar, Florian?"

"Cain't say. But I wants it, an' I got to borry it."

"Ain't you got a dollar?"

"Yeh."

Simpson's eyes brightened: "Tell you what I'll do: I'll lend you a dollar ef you gib me a dollar as 'scurity."

Florian speculated. The dream book ordered him to borrow a dollar. . . . "That's all right," said he, and the exchange of money was solemnly made. Phillip winked portentously. "Hope dat gig draws out de lott'ry, Florian."

"I ain't said nothin' 'bout no gig, Phillip."

"You ain't need to. I had dem dreams my own self."

Jackson Ramsay, the policy king, welcomed Florian warmly. "Renegged on the marriage game, Florian?"

Florian cocked one eye. "I is a sick man, Mister Ramsay: too sick to git married."

"Sure — I know. What can I do for you this morning?"

"Quarter each on train row, baby row, little louse row an' blood row: one, two, three numbers out — winnin's to be carry over from Pool to Ginuwine — ef they is any winnin's — an' played straight on 9-17-39-46-78."

"Straight on five numbers? You certainly aren't very anxious to win."

"Yassuh, Boss, I am. But I ain't no piker, Cap'n. It's big or nothin'. . . ."

"I've never known of a man winning five straight on my lottery."

"They's a fust time to ev'ything, Cap'n."

Ramsay nodded, took the borrowed dollar and wrote the tickets. "Hanging around, Slappey?"

"Nossuh. Got business to home. 'Fraid that almost wife of mine might come 'round to see how I'm gittin' 'long."

Florian proved himself an excellent prognosticator. At half past ten o'clock the stairway of his boarding house creaked ominously under the enormous weight of Sally Crouch.

Florian had set his stage with a keen eye to Sally's sense of the proprieties. On the dresser stood a half-empty bottle of suspicious shape and odour. A few pictures which never could have been sent through the Comstock'd mails adorned the walls. Her entrance found him propped in a chair immersed in the pictorial section of the latest *Police Gazette*. He spoke without turning his head. "'Lo, Sally."

"Honey!" Her arms went about his neck and she implanted a moist kiss on his neck. He abruptly brought the other two legs of his chair to the floor. "Careful, Sally. You might' nigh upsot me an' Doc Simmons says I ain't in no condition to stan' no sudden shock."

"I wanted to come 'round' las' night, Florian. . . ."

"I was pow'ful sick, Sally. Might' sorry, of course, that I couldn't git to come to my weddin'—"

Something suspiciously like a sob expanded her bosom. "I was pow'ful dis'pointed, sweetness. An' de guesses et up all de supper I done had fix'. When you gits well we'll jes' hab a private cerymony wid' de Rev'end Tubb."

Florian's heart sank. He was afraid that she was still determined. "I been thinkin', Sally —"

"Yeh, sweetness?"

"— That after what th' Doc done tol' me mebbe it ain't fair to no woman to make marriage with her right now, sick like I am."

Sally's eyes narrowed slightly. "You needs a woman's care'n tenshun, Florian. An' you talks like you was tryin' to hitch out."

"'Tain't that a tall, Hon. Ef 'twasn't fo' the booze —"

She sniffed. "I smelled it."

"Sure. That's the trouble. Doc says I needs to drink it to keep my heart a-goin' an' it makes me pow'ful wil'."

"Hmph!" she retorted coldly: "Reck'n Sally Crouch c'n handle de *wildest* man!"

He shook his head solemnly. "That's right, Sally — but I guess I ain't go no right askin' no woman to work fo' me —"

"How come you make talk 'bout wukin' fo' you?"

"*I* cain't work," he pleaded desperately, a bit alarmed by a rising inflection in her voice. "Doc Simmons done say so. An' sence I lost all my money spec'latin'. . . ."

Sally rose suddenly, and placed her hands on hips. Her lips came together tightly and she surveyed her might-have-been spouse witheringly:

"Mister Florian Slappey, is you mean to sit dey an' tell me you is broke?"

"Uh-huh! I is."

"An'— an' you was aimin' to marry me an' lemme s'port you?"

He was thoroughly alarmed by her manner. The bosom was heaving and the flood-gates were perilously near to opening. "You got me all wrong, Hon. I ain't aimin' to let you s'port me. I sort of got a pride 'bout that. I jes' tellin' you that my health ain't so good. . . ."

For perhaps fifteen consecutive seconds Sally stared at the thoroughly cowed Florian. Then suddenly she crumpled into a chair, buried her face in her palms and large, voluble sobs caused the room to tremble: "Oh! my Gawd! all men is alike! Dey ain' none ob dem don't try'n take adwantage ob a girl. I might've knowed he ain't wan' nothin' but de money he t'ought I had! I might've knowed dat ef I wa'n't so blind. Oh! Lawdy! An' he goes'n makes me redikerlous! He goes an' does dat —"

Florian crossed the room and patted her fearfully on a shaking shoulder. "Here now, Sally, Hon — that ain't no way to carry on! That ain't no way a tall. . . ."

"You lemme go, you wuthless no-'count. Take yo' hands offen me. I got a good min' . . ." She rose and faced him, fury and thwarted love flashing from her eyes. He retreated precipitately to a far corner and held a warding hand before him.

"Here now, Sally — that ain't no kind of way for no lady to ac'. . . ."

"I'se finish' wid bein' a lady," she flamed. "I'se

finish' wid dat! Huh! yo' t'ink I gwine s'poht you! Ain't de bestest man ever live' Sally Crouch would wuk fo'."

"That's right, Sally; that's right. I ain't wuth it."

"No, you ain't, you li'l low-down cheap spoht. I glad I foun' you out in time. I ain' gwine lay hand on you, Florian — not till yet. On'y I warn you dis, don't you make de mistake ob comin' widin' smellin' distance ob my hotel. You heah me?"

He nodded energetically. "Is you got to be goin'?"

She put her hand on the knob. "I ain't *got* to is, but Ise gwine, Florian — jes' 'cause ain't *no* girl safe wid you fo' long!"

Sally's departure effected a quick cure for Florian's malady. Less than half an hour after she left the house he was garbed in cream flannels with a straw hat perched jauntily on the side of his head and a once-broken but cleverly-spliced malacca cane on his arm. Quite as a matter of habit he made his way to the room where Jackson Ramsay held forth as policy king. The bets of the morning lottery — Pool — had been paid off and Florian casually inspected the dozen numbers which had been drawn from the seventy-eight in the wheel and posted on the board. Number 63 of the Train Gig was on the list.

"That paid you a dollar," greeted Ramsay cheerily. "Gives you an even break on the morning bets. I carried it over to five straight on the Genuine this afternoon."

Florian nodded happily. Matrimonial troubles seemed far behind. "'Twas on the Train Gig, too,

Cap'n. I reckon Florian Slappey's 'bout due to come in fo' a good-luck break."

"Not with five straight," gloomed the policy king. "It has never yet been done."

"Hmph! They's other things been done today ain't never been done befo'. I got a hunch this my lucky day."

The hunch persisted despite Florian's veteran knowledge of lottery wheels. He had played five numbers straight: which meant that from seventy-eight numbers in the wheel his five must all be included in the dozen to be drawn. Should four of them appear he would get nothing — but should all five come out he would be paid two thousand five hundred dollars for the dollar carried over by Ramsay from Pool to Genuine.

Had Florian been a piker he would have saddled his bet, in which event the success of his chosen quintet would pay 200 for 1 instead of 2,500 for 1. But, on the other hand, the appearance of four of his five would pay 80 for 1 instead of nothing, and three of the five would net 20 for 1. The negroes of the city had played policy six days a week since carpet-bagger times and the winning of a five straight had never been known. But it was innate gamblers of the Florian Slappey breed which made Jackson Ramsay — with his elaborate central office and twenty-odd branches and agents through the city — certain of a sizeable daily profit.

Florian shambled about the negro section during the long, sultry afternoon elaborating upon the symptoms which Dr. Vivian Simmons had outlined in his alibi letter. In response to repeated statements that he never looked better in his life, Flo-

POOL AND GINUWINE 83

rian said that his questioners were not physicians and therefore could not understand a man's innards. He tried to appear ill and failed miserably. He was too exalted by his hunch.

The Genuine was to be drawn at six o'clock. At five-thirty Florian Slappey was on hand, teetering a battered old chair on its hind legs. He puffed tensely on a cheroot and muttered to himself over and over again that he would not win. But the hunch would not down.

It was a dingy room lacking all the tawdry finery which the central offices had boasted in the palmy days of police tolerance. In one corner was the printing machine on which the lucky numbers were stamped out and in the foreground on a platform a huge glass wheel. Spread out on a table were little squares of paper on which numbers from 1 to 78 had been printed. Behind the table was the desk of Jackson Ramsay and a small steel safe. Beside the policy king sat his ebony secretary.

Within five minutes of Florian's advent the agents began to arrive from the various sub-offices scattered about the city and the bets were transferred from their books to the central office books. Interested bettors drifted in silently and seated themselves tensely. Most of them were regulars, men who played the lottery morning and afternoon, winning enough here and there to supply them with the money to lose later on. At three minutes before six the clerical work had been completed, the numbers from one to seventy-eight were folded under the eyes of the two-score spectators and dropped through a panel into the glass wheel. When the last one had disappeared the panel was shut and the wheel spun to mix the numbers. A little boy was brought in from the street and carefully blindfolded.

Silence settled over the gathering. The negroes, ranging in age from sixteen to sixty; in colour from a creamy chocolate to blackest ebony; leaned forward in their chairs and stared fascinatedly at the transparent wheel. Jackson Ramsay nodded and the thing spun violently, the seventy-eight numbers within tossing about in sight of all.

And then the wheel stopped and the panel was opened. The blindfolded boy reached in a skinny arm and extracted a bit of paper. The quiet was oppressive. Slowly Ramsay unfolded the paper, and held it up to the gaze of the bettors.

"Seventy-eight!"

The secretary wrote the number on a huge blackboard. The printer at his little machine slipped in two pieces of type and printed the figure which was displayed to the spectators and placed in a little rack.

Florian Slappey drew in his breath sharply. Seventy-eight was one of his five. Of course. . . .

"Thirty-nine!"

Another one! Ten more numbers to be drawn and two of his had already appeared!

"Forty-six!"

Another! Three out of three! Already if he had saddled his bet he would be twenty dollars to the good. He was on his feet now, heart pounding and temples throbbing; muttering to himself all the incantations taught by Professor Hannifer's Dream Book. Three out of three! Nine more numbers to be drawn and only two more needed.

POOL AND GINUWINE 85

Nine and seventeen! Nine and seventeen! If only. . . . Nine and seventeen . . . and two thousand five hundred dollars!

"Seventy-one!"

Slappey sighed and settled back in his chair, paying no heed to the wild shrieks of a woman who had bet twenty cents on 46–71–78 and had won forty dollars thereby. For ten minutes her pæns of joy continued until Jackson Ramsay paid her off in five-dollar bills and sent her from the place.

But seventy-one was not on Florian's list. Still, there were eight more numbers to be drawn and only two were needed. If only they'd come . . . the needed nine and seventeen:

"*Nine!*"

"Oo-o-o-oh!" came the wail from Florian Slappey's chair. He rose and crossed to the wheel, great beads of perspiration on his forehead. The word went round that he had played five-straight and that four of them had already appeared. "What you need?" wheezed one old woman. "Which un you need, Florian?"

"Seventeen . . . seventeen! Pray fo' that seventeen, niggers. Pray fo' it, all of you."

Seven more to come. Seven more numbers and only one needed to make Florian wealthy. Seven numbers out of seventy-two left in the wheel!

"Three!"

Florian's breathing was audible. Six more chances. Six more. . . .

"Sixty-three!"

Five chances left. And number seventeen needed. "Come, you number seventeen! Come t' yo' daddy, ol' darlin'!"

"Twenty!"

Four more chances. Four more chances for seventeen to come. Florian's fists were clenched. His excitement had spread about the room. Even the man who had won a paltry ten dollars with a five cent bet centered his attention on Florian's fight for the needed seventeen. "Ol' Daddy's a-lookin' fo' you, seventeen! Come out, you beauty! Ol' seventeen's a-comin' to his Daddy...."

"Eighteen!"

"Oh! you seventeen! T'ree mo' chancsts. Jes' come out one in that three, ol' seventeen, an' I'll never ast you to come out no mo'."

"Thirty-two!"

Two more to be drawn. Two more . . . sixty-eight numbers left in the wheel. . . .

"Seventy-seven!"

"A-a-a-a-ah! Ol' seventeen. . . . Come out, darlin'! Come t' yo' Daddy, ol' seventeen. Ain' never ast you no mo' ef you'll come this time. . . ."

Florian's face was pathetic. The perspiration streamed from it. The darkies who crowded the room had forgotten everything save Florian and his bet. One more number to be drawn: sixty-seven in the wheel. His fingers closed spasmodically. Veteran professional gambler though he was Jackson Ramsay felt the strain . . . he was shaking from head to foot . . . shaking and fidgety. . . . One more chance. . . .

The skinny arm of the blindfolded negro boy stretched timidly into the wheel. His fingers closed about a folded slip of paper. "Come, ol' da'lin' seventeen. . . ." The paper dropped from the trembling fingers. The sigh that went up could

POOL AND GINUWINE 87

have been heard a half-block away. Perhaps that was seventeen which had been dropped. The boy fished for another slip of paper . . . his fingers closed about it. . . .

Jackson Ramsay took it from his grasp. The fat fingers of the policy king trembled visibly. He opened it face outward so that the audience could read the figure. . . . It opened! A roar split the roof. . . .

"*Seventeen!*"

At five minutes before midnight the northbound Louisville & Nashville train puffed out of the shed. In the negro coach was a dandified young man who lounged comfortably in his seat and seemed ineffably at peace with the world. The fingers of his right hand never left his trousers pocket where they caressingly fingered a roll of bills containing something under two thousand five hundred dollars in United States currency.

Florian Slappey was in the grip of a radiant happiness which comes to but few men. After blackest darkness rosiest dawn had come. He was emancipated from money trouble, he had engraved his name in policy history, he was well rid of the too ardent and too stout Sally Crouch, and, above all, he was speeding northward to lay his fortune and his heart at the feet of the glorious Blossom Prioleau.

Never had she seemed as desirable as at this moment. Blossom and money! A honeymoon to New York or St. Louis! An epoch-making wedding! A handsomely furnished home! **A phonograph!** Perhaps, even, a Ford!

Florian Slappey did not sleep that night. He was too drunk with unalloyed joy. His dreams were waking ones . . . and all of Blossom.

At seven o'clock he left the train, climbed a long flight of steps, passed through the coloured waiting-room and stepped into the street. Nashville was rousing itself sleepily from a cool, pleasant night. Street cars clanged impatiently before the Union Station, jitneys scudded up and down the avenue — to the left he could see the beckoning gates of Parthenon Park.

Florian turned to his right and a block down the street stopped at a restaurant where he ate heartily of bacon and eggs and pancakes and coffee. At eight-fifteen he entered a negro barber shop and was shaved and shined and shampoo'd.

Then he resumed his march down the street until a cross street gave him a glimpse of the Tennessee State Capitol to the left. He followed this street leisurely until he reached the imposing grey-stone edifice, where he paused to admire impartially.

His watch told him that the hour of nine-thirty had been reached. He resumed his walk — passing the Capitol and descending a very steep hill toward a section where the coloured royalty resides. He took a short cut through an alley. On the corner of the alley and the next avenue was the Prioleau family home.

He walked slowly, wishing to surprise Blossom. He approached the cottage from the rear. His heart bounded!

There was Blossom on the veranda: Blossom, radiant, alluring, irresistible, delicious in a waist of yellow georgette crepe, a skirt of red serge, lace boots of grey. He started toward her. . . .

A handsome limousine rolled down the street and stopped before the Prioleau house. The negro chauffeur leaped to the ground and opened the door for his mistress: a regal example of the best of Nashville's white folks. The lady spoke to Blossom in dulcet, soothing tones. " I'm looking for Blossom Prioleau," she said.

" Well? " answered Blossom noncommittally.

" Are you Blossom Prioleau? "

" I *was*," came the soft answer. " I'm Missis 'Zekiel Rothwell now! "

" Oh! " The lady was taken back a bit, and then, just because she felt that it was up to her to explain: " I'm looking for a washwoman. . . ."

" So am I," returned Blossom conversationally. " Servants is pow'ful hahd to get these days, ain't they? "

Florian Slappey turned abruptly and retraced his steps up the alley. Blossom married — married commercially. He was surprised and infinitely pained. He had thought better of her than that.

His fingers pressed against the huge roll of bills. Two thousand five hundred dollars! A warm glow of satisfaction stole over him.

" Well, anyway," he murmured philosophically, " reckon I ain't got no call 'specting *ev'ything* to break my way! "

THE AMATEUR HERO

THE AMATEUR HERO

ELIAS RUSH waked to find himself a hero. His eyes flickered open upon a sea of anxious faces ranging in colour from uncompromising black to a rich, creamy yellow. Babel beat upon his water-soaked eardrums: "Stan' back, coloured folks. Ain't yo'-all see he's comin' too?" "Giv'm air!" "You, Florian Slappey, quit that there trespassin' on my toes — you want to t'row me over on him?" "Stan' back — stan' back — yonder comes Doc Simmons!"

Dr. Vivian Simmons, slender, immaculate, pompous; his rich chocolate complexion framed behind horn-rimmed spectacles, shouldered through the crowd, dropped to one knee beside the waterlogged sufferer and produced a stethoscope. He fitted the tubes into his ears, opened Elias's near-silk shirt, palmed his watch and frowned portentously. Then he rose, shook his head gravely and summoned to his aid the dandified Florian Slappey.

Of what occurred immediately thereafter Elias Rush has an indistinct but decidedly painful recollection. Somebody magically produced a barrel and some one else placed Mr. Rush, face down, across it. Strong hands seized his feet and under the direction of Dr. Simmons, and without heed to the patient's wild yells, proceeded to knead his tummy.

The treatment was heroic, — the results more

than satisfactory. Eventually Elias Rush stood on his own feet; very weak and infernally trembly. Water cascaded from his Sunday clothes, which were shrinking alarmingly despite their all-wool guarantee. His eyes roved above the heads of the coloured human mass to rest upon the amusement devices of Blue Lake Park: the Shoot the Chutes, the Roller Coaster, the blatant Carousel and the dozen or more eating concessions. He was no longer even mildly interested — until his gaze lighted upon a crowd nearby absorbedly engaged in a task which reminded him nauseatingly of the barrel experience he had just survived. Then remembrance of the wherefores returned.

There had been a hiring of a rowboat and a tentative poking about in the middle of the lake. He remembered watching with impersonal interest the bobbing head of a Venus-like young coloured lady who dared the deepest part of the lake — then a sudden facial twisting of terror, a plunge . . . and a long-drawn whooshy howl.

He had leaped to the bow of his skiff in the attempt to seize the arm of the drowning girl. But she sank before he got there. His boat drifted away. Tough luck. . . . But as he drew back his foot slipped and he found himself in the water. Thereupon he grabbed for whatever was nearest and it proved to be Imogene. He clung to her frantically and both went down.

Once, many years before, Elias Rush had been able to swim. His little knowledge came to his aid, terror-spurred. He struggled like a madman to free himself from the girl's desperate clutch. He managed to remain above the surface long enough

THE AMATEUR HERO

to grab the side of his boat. There he clung . . . and Fate itself couldn't have broken his clutch. He was pale green with terror. He was scarcely conscious of the woman whose plump, rounded arms clasped his thin neck. It was fortunate for Imogene that her head happened to be above water.

In the first place he was not intended to be a hero. He was not of the stuff of which heroes are made. All his life he had been shy, wistful, retiring; keeping always in the rear ranks of a crowd, shunning leather-voiced, coarsed-mouthed men and finding himself excessively timid in the presence of women . . . and especially beautiful ones.

The head of Dr. Vivian Simmons rose commandingly above the crowd ganged about the prostrate Imogene. He beckoned authoritatively to Elias and Elias sloshed uncertainly to the centre of the circle.

He gazed down at the girl and for the first time experienced a warm glow of satisfaction in the knowledge that he had saved her life. Truly she was a regal creature: a woman he had known only in his love-studded dreams. She was large and rounded and amply curved and — well, he was not too ill to notice that the bathing suit she wore concealed none of her feminine charms.

Her dusky face was a bit paler than normal, but the look she bestowed upon Elias Rush's bedraggled figure was not hard to interpret. She questioned him direct:

"Is you him?"

"Is — is I *who?*"

"Is you the man what saved my life?"

Shy — bashful . . . Elias fidgeted. "That warn't nothin'."

" 'Twas too."

Elias was not an argumentative chap which was why his disclaimer of intention never passed the tip of his tongue where it momentarily hung trembling. Besides, he was beginning to take stock of himself. . . .

All about him was a buzz of conversation. Each person of the thousands who had gathered at Blue Lake for their regular Sunday outing had been there for the special purpose of being an eye-witness to Elias's rescue of the radiant Imogene. And each eye-witness insisted on telling his story — feeling it incumbent upon him to supply some vital detail which the last story-teller had overlooked. Elias Rush listened pop-eyed to Florian Slappey, who at that moment held the centre of the stage —

"You folks ain't know what you is talkin' 'bout. I was sittin' by the boat-house a-lookin' at that Imogene 'cause I had a hunch they was somethin' wrong the way she was strokin' 'bout. I says to myself, I says: 'Florian, that they woman is feelin' bad. Florian,' I says, 'she's gwine git in trouble.' An' sho' 'nough, jes' 'bout that time she gives a wiggle an' a twist an' down she goes.

"That there — what yo'-all say his name is?"

"'Lias Rush. He come up here from Dothan."

"I know all 'bout whar he come from. Anyway, 'Lias Rush was rowing right by there an' he give one look an' seen her go down. He jes' a-leaped fo' the front of the boat an' grabbed at her. But he missed an' then he stood up jes' as ca'm an' cool an' put his hands above his haid an' dove over.

THE AMATEUR HERO 97

Purties' dive I ever did see. W'en he come up he had her but she was a-fightin' sumthin' terrible. Any other man would of let go — but he didn't. Nossuh: not him. B'lieve me, folks, that was the terriblest fight I ev' did see. Fin'ly they come up ag'in an' he jus' plumb grabbed her by the neck an' swum fo' that boat. How he got there is a puzzle to me an' I'm tellin' yo' I was watchin' close. 'Twas a even break they was both gwine git drown', but he nev' let loose,— not fo' one minute. I'm tellin' yo', coloured folks, that there 'Lias Rush from Dothan is a hero right!"

Elias moved off meditatively in the direction of the carousel. He felt a battery of approving eyes upon him. The hum of enthusiastic: "Thar he goes!" "Da's de man what rescued Imogene Carter: da's him." "Ain't he de modestest man?" "Reckon dey ain't no *real* heroes goes *boastin'* 'bout what dey done!"

Elias Rush ceased to bemoan his soaked garments. They had become the habiliments of a hero. The discourse of Florian Slappey had converted him. Florian, in the first place, was darktown's social mentor; a wealthy young negro — magnificent in self-importance. In the second place Florian had convinced him of facts that he had not before realized. Of course he could have let go of Imogene had he cared to do so. But he wasn't that kind of a man: not him. 'Magine 'Lias Rush leavin' a woman to drowned jes' to save heself. Why, he'd risk his life any day to save somebody else. It come jes' as easy.

A clerical looking gentleman fell into step beside him. "They tell me yo' name is 'Lias Rush."

"Yassuh — da's me."

"Stranger here?"

"Been heah 'bout a month. Up from Dothan."

"Living here?"

"Yassuh. Shuah is. Bought a half int'rest in Pinetop Roller's pressin' club."

An ebony hand came out to clutch Elias's skinny fingers. "I'm the Rev'end Plato Tubb of the Fust African M. E. Chu'ch. It done me proud to see how come you to save that gal. I wisht you would come to services t'night at eight o'clock so's I c'n offer up a prayer of thanks fo' the d'liverance of you both."

Elias promised. He would have promised anything about then. He left the Reverend Tubb and found himself hedged in by a crowd which demanded a personal recital of his heroism: "'Twarn't nothin'," disclaimed the hero. "Over she go, an' over I go. Git in de water an' grab her. Hol' on. Swim in. Da's all. Ain't nothin' to make no fusses over."

"I 'clare to goodness: heah dat man. Saves a 'ooman an' mos' dies an' says 'tain't nothin'."

Elias expanded to the occasion. "Co'se 'twarn't nothin'. Jes' savin' a woman from drowndin'? Sho'— dat ain't nothin' *tall!*"

"Y'ain't never saved no others befo' this, is you?"

"Save folks from drowndin'?" Elias's skinny chest protruded with indignation. "Woman, you talks foolish. Co'se I is save folks befo'. You reckon I acted like I wasn't use' to it?"

A deep basso boomed across the lot: "*Mi-i-isto' Rush!* Misto' *Rush!*"

THE AMATEUR HERO 99

"Heah yis," shrilled a youngster in the group about Elias.

A large, bullet-headed, well-dressed negro strode across and towered above the diminutive hero. "Is you 'Lias Rush?"

"I is."

"I'm Cla'nce Carter — brother of the gal what you done save her life. Lemme thank you. . . ."

"Da's a'right — a'right. Jes' li'l excercise," answered the exalted Elias, striving not to grimace under the bone-crushing grip of the grateful brother.

"Huh! Reckon any man what'll save a gal casyal like an' 'most drownd hisself doin' it ain't goin' to boast 'bout it. But what I want to ast you is what is yo' doin' this evenin'?"

"Nothin'. Why?"

"I got a cyar out heah — I was thinkin' mebbe you'd drive home with Imigene an' me, an'—" with an owlish wink, "take a bit of a nip to keep you from catchin' col'."

Elias agreed readily, more than a little dazed at the nonchalance with which the brother of the girl he had saved spoke of his car. The car proved to be a very presentable, six-cylinder, seven-passenger affair, and Elias later learned that Clarence made an extremely good living with that car in his capacity of free lance taxicabber.

With Clarence at the wheel, Elias settled shiveringly in the tonneau beside the still weak but openly adoring Imogene. As they rolled out of the gates of Blue Lake Park the crowd huzza'd a farewell.

If Imogene had appeared bewitching in her one-piece bathing suit, she was bewildering now. A large red and white straw hat flopped tantalizingly about her well-shaped head; she wore a V-cut, yellow crepe-de-chine waist and a white duck skirt. Her face had assumed an appealing pallor, and her lustrous black eyes shone into his with a frank avowal of adoration. And scarcely had Clarence let his gears in and sent the car rolling down the smooth, white road toward the city than Imogene nestled unashamedly against her damp hero and snuggled a warm hand into his.

It was a new experience for Elias Rush. Of course there had been women in his life . . . but this regal product of the city, this radiant creature of education and of culture, this — this — his skinny fingers closed tightly about hers and he sighed deeply.

"I ain't had no chancst to thank you, Mistuh Rush. . . ."

Elias was a-tremble from head to foot: his capitulation to this first grande passion was as thorough as it was nerve-wracking. "'Twarn't nothin'," he mumbled thickly, "'twarn't nothin' tall."

"Reckon *I* think different," she returned coyly. "Ef you ha'n't risked yo' life I'd of been dead."

"Hmph! Reckon I ain't lettin' no wimmin drownd 'round whar I is at."

She spoke very softly: "I owes you my life — 'Lias."

"G'wan wid you. . . ." His eyes met hers: "Aw, sa-a-ay. . . ."

"I does."

"I ain't done nothin' tall. . . ."

"I owes you my life. But," wistfully, "I reckon they ain't no way I c'n pay. . . ."

"Yes, dey is."

"How so?"

"You — you —" The years of chronic self-effacement asserted themselves and Elias found himself tongue-tied on the verge of an avowal of love. "'Twarn't nothin' I done — not nothin' tall."

"I owes you my life," she repeated doggedly. "They ain't nothin' you could ast me I woul'n't say yes to."

He flushed redly beneath his natural brunette. "Y-y-yes, dey is."

"Not *nothin'!*"

"S-s-s-sposin' I ast you to — to —"

"To — what?" she cooed softly.

"To — to — S'posin' I ast you to kiss me?"

Imogene flashed a quick glance around. The discreet Clarence was gazing straight ahead. They were speeding through a brief stretch of country — not a house within half a mile.

A pair of warm, plump arms wound suddenly about the thin neck of the delirious Elias, a pair of luscious lips came close — closer — and were pressed against his in a long, clinging kiss of surrender. He sighed mightily and shivered deliciously. Then the lips withdrew and the arms unwound. . . .

"Reckon *that* ain't nothin' to do fo' the man what you owes yo' life to," defended the lady.

"I — I ain't want no kiss ob gratitude," dared Elias.

"What is it you wants?"

"It — it's — Reckon you woul'n't b'lieve me ef I was to say — ef I was to say —"

"Ye-e-es?"

"I — I'se pow'ful stuck on you, Imigene. Co'se you is on'y jus' met me. . . ."

"Huh —'Lias! Reckon they ain't *no* woman could help fallin' in love wid a man like you!"

During the three days which followed Elias Rush became aware of the fact that he had grossly underrated himself. All his life he had been shy and bashful and retiring. At social affairs in Dothan he had been a congenital wall-flower. The elderly women and the old men liked him, and children found him congenial. But among those of his age he had been supine — avoiding turmoil and strife and argument as one shuns the plague.

In fact, when the opportunity of buying a half-partnership in Pinetop Roller's Pressing Club for two hundred and fifty dollars, which amount included fees for Hon. Evans Chew, coloured attorney and counsellor at law, presented itself, Elias held back for some time because he was secretly afraid of the big city in which the business was located. That he had accepted eventually had been principally due to the professional efforts of the aforementioned Chew, whose fees from the parties of the first and second parts hung in the balance.

His unwilling rescue of the divine Imogene taught Elias many hitherto unsuspected things regarding himself. He had experienced, for one thing, the exquisite agony of requited love. He learned that he was a hero. He learned, furthermore, that since he had proved his prowess in public, that same public was eager to believe anything which he might say in private. And whatever Elias may have lacked in bulk of body he more than made up in flexibility of imagination. His tales of derring-do became wilder and more improbable with every telling, but his audiences had seen for themselves and were in no mood to doubt. He was, figuratively speaking, handed around on a silver platter and the girls of the society set were frankly envious of Imogene.

There was little secret to the fact that Imogene had engaged herself to Elias for better or worse, richer or poorer. Whereupon hero-worshipping Society adopted him. He joined the exclusive First African M. E. Church and became a member of The Sons & Daughters of I Will Arise. He was wined copiously and dined frequently. It was a unique experience and he was not one to shun the spotlight at this late date of his hitherto backstage life.

The business of The Pinetop Roller Pressing Club picked up overnight, and Elias, who handled the administrative end, was kept busy. His evenings were spent in the clinging arms of the delectable Imogene, who, by day, was nurse for three very young scions of a leading white folks family. They planned rosily for the future: Imogene was to interest the quality folks in The Pinetop Roller Pressing Club, the business was to expand, move into larger quarters, have a red and white sign painted, install a De Haven steam presser and. . . .

It was after dinner at the Carter homestead on the night of the Fourth day after the rescue that something came up casually to disturb Elias Rush's blissful serenity. Clarence was puffing away at a rank pipe, Elias dry-smoking a two-fer cheroot and Imogene nestling at his side. Elias had completed a vivid recital of a fictitious experience in the course of which he had valiantly saved the life of a certain Colonel Ransome of Dothan. Imogene pressed the hand of her hero and Clarence nodded his bullet head approvingly.

"That's fine, 'Lias; that's fine. An' how 'bout them young bucks down to Dothan: did you ever have any trouble with them?"

"Meanin' de *men*, Cla'nce?"

"Meanin' that."

Elias laughed lightly. "Sho' nuff, now, Cla'nce: you ain't s'posin' I'd go 'round fightin' wid no men, is you?"

"You is little —"

"Li'l an' loud; da's me, Cla'nce. Li'l *an'* loud! They ain't none of them niggers down to Dothan ast fo' none of my game sencst de day me an' Scipio Barrow mixed it up."

"How come 'bout that?"

"Me an' Scipio was a-shootin' high dice an' they was plenty niggers 'round watchin'. Come Scipio shoot a 'leven an' I tickle a twelve. Den he mouth somthin' 'bout I ain't roll 'em honest. After *dat* . . ." he paused dramatically.

"Yeh, Honey; yeh? What happen then?" breathed Imogene.

"Well, I'se heah, ain't I? An' after Scipio git out de horspital he ain't bother wid me much."

"Was he bigger'n you?"

"Bigger? Cla'nce, jes' as sho' as hell's a mousetrap dat nigger was so big I had to jump plumb offen de groun' to hit him. I jes' ain't fool wid nobody ain't twice my size. I skeered I might kill 'em by hittin' too hard. I'se small, Cla'nce, but I'se wiry — I'se pow'ful wiry."

"I'm plumb glad to hear you is a fighter, 'Lias, 'cause me an' Imigene was discussin' 'bout tomorrow bein' payday out to the Madoc mines."

"How come I interest' in dat?"

"They's a man out there by the name Cunjer Bill Johnson, an' me an' Imigene was kinder scared that when Cunjer Bill foun' out 'bout you an' Imigene lovin' each other. . . ."

Elias Rush experienced a sudden sickening sinking sensation in the region of the midriff. "Whut disyer Cunjer Bill pusson got to do wid Imigene?"

"Nothin'!" she negatived tartly: "Big ol' brute!"

"Big man?"

"More'n six feet," confided Clarence cheerfully, "an' a pow'ful bad man. He's plumb jealous of Imigene."

"You been 'gage' to him, Imigene?" questioned her fiancee pointedly.

"Me? Him? I ain't *never* have nothin' tall to do with no such trash."

"Den how come him to git sore wid me?"

"'Cause since he's been lovin' Imigene they ain't no other man hereabouts dared fool with her. They's all scared of Cunjer Bill."

"He's dat bad?"

"Worser." Clarence gazed at his prospective brother-in-law sharply. "You ain't scared of him, is you, 'Lias?"

Elias Rush laughed a white, sickly laugh. "Skeered? Me? I ain't skeered of but one t'ing, Cla'nce, an' dat is ef dat nigger monkeys wid me I'll be 'rested fo' manslaughter. Da's all what *I* is skeered of."

"He's a pow'ful big man, 'Lias."

"De bigger dey is de better de meat. An' 'sides — mebbe he won't come to town."

"He always comes to town paydays," was the cheerful response. "Jus' to see if any other man been fool 'nough to been co'tin' Imigene."

Night brought little sleep to Elias Rush. For the first time in his delirious four days he regretted that he had allowed his tongue to keep step with his imagination. By dint of much high class lying he had builded for himself a reputation of champion all-'round hero and untamed bad man. Clarence and Imogene and Lawyer Evans Chew and Dr. Vivian Simmons and Florian Slappey and Rev'end Plato Tubb and all of the other men of parts in the community knew perfectly well that the elimination of the formidable Cunjer Bill Johnson would be a mere incident in the day's work of Elias Rush.

The trouble was that Cunjer Bill Johnson didn't know it!

Chances were Cunjer Bill would come to town, seek Imogene, and learn from her disdainful and vitriolic lips the tale of the newly arisen Man of the Hour. Whereupon Cunjer Bill Johnson, ignorant of his danger, would camp on the trail of the aforesaid hero, seeking to quaff of his heart's blood. Elias was sickeningly fearful of the prospect.

He spent a weary, floor-walking night. The following morning Pinetop Roller, his pal and partner, commented upon his haggardness. Then Pinetop went out to collect suits in need of pressing and Elias was left alone in the little office. He wondered at what time they paid off out at Madoc and how long it would take Cunjer Bill to reach town, and —

"Mornin', Mister Rush."

At the cool suavity of the voice Elias jumped as though he had been shot. Then, as he recognized his visitor, he smiled a weak smile. "Mawnin', Mistuh Chew."

"How's the pressing business this morning?"

"Tol'able. How's de law business?"

"De trop. Very de trop, I might say. I wanted you to send around to Mrs. Chew for a suit of mine. Have it pressed before night, will you, Mistuh Rush?"

"Sho' will. I — I — say, Mistuh Chew; what you know 'bout disyer Cunjer Bill Johnson nigger?"

Lawyer Chew *chk-chk'd* and shook his head hopelessly. "Bad egg, Mister Rush; a real *bad* egg."

"I mean —'bout —'bout him an' Imigene?"

"He's pow'ful jealous of Imigene, Mistuh Rush. I hope you and Mister Johnson ain't calc'lating on fightin' over her?"

"*We* ain't," answered Elias miserably. "Mebbe so *he* is, but *we* ain't — sho' nuff."

"He's a bad customer, Mistuh Rush; a very bad customer."

Elias Rush produced a ten-cent cigar and stuck it in the face of Lawyer Evans Chew: "Set down an' tell me somthin' 'bout disyer Cunjer Bill Johnson, Mistuh Chew — set down an' tell me somthin' 'bout him. F'rinstance: do he skeer easy?"

Lawyer Evans Chew sat down.

Insofar as Cunjer Bill Johnson was concerned, things happened according to schedule.

He checked out at the tipple-house at noon, made his way to the marble showers which the Madoc Mining Company provides for its negro employés, and his Herculean physique glistened under the chilly spray.

He was a massive man: broad and brawny, a clear generation behind the girl of his heart's choice in the matter of evolution. He smiled cheerily with his fellow-workers, but once he stepped on a bit of wire and the expression which momentarily disfigured his face wasn't at all pleasant. Fortunately for his own peace of mind, Elias Rush was not there to see.

Cunjer Bill left the shower-room, dried off with a fresh Turkish towel — also furnished gratis by the company — dressed in the Sunday-go-to-meetin's which had been hanging in his locker for a fortnight, presented his tag at the pay window, and was handed fifty-eight dollars for two weeks' work. Cunjer Bill was an excellent ore mucker.

At three o'clock he boarded the Accommodation for the city and at five he was at Sally Crouch's Cozy Home Hotel for Coloured and comfortably installed in one of her best rooms. An hour later he had purchased an almost-silver comb-brush-and-mirror set in a plush case, secured a shoe shine and was on his way to the domicile of his lady love.

Reverend Plato Tubb stopped him en route and

THE AMATEUR HERO 109

gossiped fussily about things in general, and when Cunjer Bill would have unceremoniously pulled away, the Rev'end Plato compelled his interest by mention of Imogene. Then he tactfully and gleefully proceeded to tell Cunjer Bill of Imogene's near-drowning and of her subsequent engagement to one, Elias Rush. Cunjer Bill jerked away.

"Where you going?" inquired the Rev'end Tubb.

"Gwine see Imigene an' heah dis fumadiddles f'um her own lips."

Which is exactly what he did. He heard it not once or twice, but several times; and Elias did not lose in the telling. She elaborated on his heroism and painted him a fire-eater and a man-killer, thereby sowing the seeds of doubt in the breast of Cunjer Bill. She supplied details of the rescue which had been manufactured by much repetition since the previous Sunday afternoon.

Reverend Plato Tubb happened by; his sensation-loving soul impelling him to the scene of impending drama. Later, Clarence came in. With him were Lawyer Chew and a friend.

And it was into the midst of this gathering that the unsuspecting and terrified Elias Rush, seeking sanctuary from the hobgoblin Cunjer Bill, stepped.

"Mister Rush," said Imogene sweetly, "I want you to meet my frien', Mister Johnson. Mister Johnson, meet my fiansay."

Elias's face was pathetic. He stood in his tracks, back against the door, eyes rolling wildly and showing white. Cunjer Bill loomed like a mountain with a thundercloud crest. And his voice rumbled:

"So dis de man whut done me dirt, huh?"

"Mister Johnson," broke in Imogene sharply, "remember where you is at!"

"I 'members whar dis li'l shrimp is at," came the menacing roar. Then he turned his attention to the terrified Rush. "You know what I is got a good min' to do?"

No answer from the petrified Elias, whose wide-open eyes were now fastened blankly on the other's face. He hoped vaguely that Cunjer Bill was not a fast runner.

"Y'ain' answer me, huh? Well, whut I is got a good min' to do to you is to sqush you like dat — see?" and he pressed thumb and forefinger together. "I got a good min'. . . ."

Lawyer Chew bustled forward officiously. "Now, now, Brother Johnson — this ain't neither the time nor the place. . ."

"Y'all lay off of dis, Lawyer Chew. It ain' healthy fo' no man to combat wiv me w'en I'se mad — an' I'se plumb mad now. Ef 'twas a he-man cut me out. . . . But a shrimp like dis! Huh!"

"I woul'n't go foolin' with him, Cunjer Bill," warned Clarence. "He's a powerful bad nigger."

Cunjer Bill looked at Elias and then at Clarence. There was truth reflected in Clarence's face, his words were saturated with the nuance of conviction. Cunjer Bill wondered whether he might not be mistaken. Maybe Elias was a real killer: and he knew that all the brawn in creation is not proof against a bullet. Still — Elias didn't look bad, and — doubtful as he had become — Cunjer Bill was not ready to capitulate.

"Him?" he muttered doubtfully. "Dat li'l speck o' nothin' *bad?* I got half a min'. . . ."

"Elias' face was pathetic. He stood in his tracks, back against the door, eyes rolling wildly and showing white."

THE AMATEUR HERO   111

Cold, clammy terror gripped Elias Rush. For the first time in his life he knew physical fear. And also, for the first time in his sequestered life, he experienced the courage of a cornered rat. He opened parched lips — closed them again — then croaked a warning:

"Keep yo' hands offen me!"

"I reckon." Cunjer Bill took a tentative step forward: "I'll jes' sqush you!"

"Careful, Brother Johnson," warned the Rev'end Plato, "Brother Rush's gittin' mad."

Cunjer Bill paused. He sensed that the fear of the spectators was fear *for,* and not *of,* him. He advanced another step in the direction of his quivering rival.

Elias's voice rose high with hysteria: "Folks, yo'-all better keep him offen me! I — I — gwine *kill* him!"

He was startled by his own words. The others were not. Even Cunjer Bill was not startled. He began to fear that he had undertaken a job which common-sense demanded that he abandon. He got the idea that Elias was fighting to restrain himself. Rush, nerves raw, rattled on hysterically —

"I ain' got nothin' ag'in you, Cunjer Bill. But sho's you come nigh me I'll kill you. . . . Keep 'im offen me, folks. I ain't askin' fo' no rucus! Keep 'im offen me!"

Evans Chew took the arm of Cunjer Bill. And this time his peace proposals met with no opposition. "Better come away, Bill. He's awful bad, that Rush feller. You is li'ble to get him angry an' he's a killer, he is. Got a bad record down to Dothan. Packs a gun an' a knife, both."

"Ef I had a gun," temporized the rapidly subsiding Cunjer Bill.

"But you ain't. Better come with me befo' there's bloodshed."

Thoroughly cowed, grumbling defiance to camouflage the fear which had been born in his heart, Cunjer Bill Johnson gladly allowed Evans Chew to convoy him into the alley. Once there the lawyer breathed a sigh of infinite relief.

"Brother Johnson," he proclaimed convincingly, "you sure done had one terrible narrow escape."

"Dat — dat li'l shrimp don't look lak no killer."

"You mean to tell me, Brother Johnson, that nobody warned you he was bad medicine?"

"Yeh, dey warn me. But he ain' *look* bad."

"Ain't you see it in his eye? He wasn't more'n ten seconds from killin' you. An' I ain't so sure he ain't countin' on it yet. Take my adwice an' git out of town befo' he gets a good chancst at you in the open."

"Whut c'an he do to me, huh?"

"He ain't never missed a man yet. He's plumb bad. They re'lly ain't but two things you can do."

"An' dem is?"

"Get out of town or put him under a peace bond."

"Whut dat peace bon' business?"

"Make a afterdavit that he threatened to kill you an' then swear out a warrant. They'll 'rest him an' put him under bond to keep the peace ipso facto."

"How dat ipso facto t'ing 'fect me?"

"When he's under a peace bond," explained the

THE AMATEUR HERO 113

attorney and counsellor, "the law don't allow him to kill nobody!"

"Dat so? How much it cost me to git dat peace bond ag'in him?"

"My fee in the matter will be twenty-five dollars."

"An' you t'ink ef I don't git it he'll plug me?"

"I do. He's an awful bad nigger."

"A'right," and Cunjer Bill drew a deep breath. "I reckon it's cheap at dat, ain't it?"

"It is," agreed Lawyer Evans Chew. "It's pow'-ful lucky you didn't temp' him no further, 'cause if you had you'd of been around a heap of flowers an' soft music an' you woul'n't of knowed nothin' about it."

The following morning Elias Rush found an athletic-appearing white man waiting for him at the door of The Pinetop Roller Pressing Club.

"Are you Elias Rush?"

"Yassuh."

"Come with me."

"Whar to?"

"I have a warrant for your arrest on peace bond proceedings."

"Fo' me?"

"Yes, for you. Come along."

"Jes' a minnit, Cap'n. Who swear out dat warrant?"

"William Johnson, also known as Cunjer Bill Johnson."

Elias Rush went. At the magistrate's office he found Cunjer Bill Johnson under the wing of

Lawyer Evans Chew. Under Chew's questioning Cunjer Bill made out an excellent bill of causes why Elias Rush should be placed under a cash bond of two hundred dollars to keep the peace. And finally the magistrate turned to Rush.

"Elias Rush?"

"Yassuh, Jedge; da's me."

"What have you to say for yourself?"

"Nothin', Jedge; nothin' tall."

"Did you threaten this man?"

"Reckon I did, Jedge." Out of the corner of his eye Rush glimpsed the adored Imogene in a corner of the tiny courtroom. "Reckon I kinder mentioned I might hu't 'im ef he gallivanted 'round wid me."

"You threatened him with bodily injury?"

"Reckon da's de onlies' kin' ob injury he'd onderstan', ain't it?"

"Can you state any good and sufficient reasons why you should not be placed under bond to maintain the peace and dignity of the State, and especially against the person of William Johnson, also known as Cunjer Bill Johnson?"

"Guess dey ain' no reason tall, Jedge; 'cause if I ain't put under dat bon' I'se li'ble to *sqush* dat big lummix an' I ain't anxious to do no time fo' no sech wuthless, no-'count —"

"That'll do, Rush." The magistrate scribbled swiftly on a legal form. "When can you raise a cash bond of two hundred dollars?"

With easy nonchalance Elias Rush produced from his battered wallet ten twenty-dollar bills. "Ef I don't beat dat feller up, Jedge, will I git dis money back ag'in?"

THE AMATEUR HERO

The magistrate smiled. "At the end of six months — *if* you keep the peace."

With Imogene on his arm — Imogene atremble with pride and love — Elias Rush swaggered from the courtroom. He waited on the corner and intercepted Cunjer Bill.

"Mistuh Cunjer Bill," orated the little negro: "You is wiser'n you look. Whut you is jes' done saves yo' life. Ef you hadn't of stopped me by law from killin' you, you would of been a daid nigger befo' night. Now git outen my path: I'se walkin' wid my lady frien' an' I don't wanna be bothered wid no trash!"

The following morning Lawyer Evans Chew again dropped into The Pinetop Roller Pressing Club. Elias Rush was behind the counter whistling happily.

"Mornin', Brother Rush."

"Mawnin', Lawyer Chew."

"It certainly worked, didn't it?"

"It done dat, sho' nuff."

"Cunjer Bill's done left town: scared stiff. Ain't any chance of his bothering you again."

Rush chuckled. "An' I'se boun' by law not to hu't him. Dat was a swell scheme, Brother Chew."

"I got some pretty good ideas, Brother Rush. 'Course, I had to talk mighty convincin' to make him believe you meant to kill him. An' now there's a little matter . . ." He hesitated delicately.

Elias Rush reached into a drawer from which he extracted twenty-five dollars. This he handed to Lawyer Evans Chew: "Da's yo' fee fo' makin'

Cunjer Bill git out dat peace bon' ag'inst me, an'," he grinned broadly, " I reckon you c'n put some ob dat into a weddin' present. Me an' Imigene is gwine git married nex' Sunday!"

TEMPUS FUGITS

TEMPUS FUGITS

"YONDER he comes!"

The crowd pressed close against the gates of the coloured exit of the Terminal Station, straining eyes into the gloom of the passageway.

"Tha's him: tha's Spider!"

"Yeh — tha's him; sho' nuff!"

"Hey! Yo' Spider!"

The dapper little negro grinned and waved his be-jewelled hands to the reception committee. He tried to appear unconscious of the fact that his sartorial appearance was creating a furore — and failed miserably. He was glad now that he had bedecked himself in his very newest suit: a pearl grey serge of ultra English cut. His vest was a rich cream exquisitely flowered in crimson. His tie was scarlet, his sox vermilion. The long-visored cap, insignia of his profession, perched jauntily on the side of his head. His long-toed tan shoes glowed in the light of the electric bulbs.

He mounted the steps two at a time, every move a symphony. Behind him clambered two red-capped station porters, each lugging a heavy suit-case. The exit gates rolled back and Spider Hawkins, jockey, found himself smothered in the ample maternal bosom.

"Spider — honey! Is yo' come home to yo' ol' Mammy? Is yo' r'illy, truly heah, Spider?"

The little negro laughed gaily and implanted a fervid smack on his mother's lips. He held her at arm's length with hands in which there was a surprising strength and allowed his mouth to expand into a happy, prideful grin.

"Golly! Mom, yo' shuah is growed. An' dressed up!" He faced the welcoming crowd: "On the level, folks, ain't she the bestest lookin' 'ooman heah? Ain't she, now?"

"Aw, Spider, yo' quit. Yo' allers was teasin' with yo' ol' Mammy. Law', boy, *yo'* is the dressinest man!"

Spider shrugged. "Jes' some ol' clothes I happen' to dig up ontray noo. It ain't pay wearin' no r'il good clothes on the train." He dug into the pocket of the peacock vest and extracted two quarters which he placed in the eagerly outstretched hands of his attending porters. He did it grandly, with the air of one to the manner born. "Yo' boys run buy yo'selfs some ice cream sodas." Then, to the crowd: "Thisyer shuah gives me the homecominest feelin'. . . ."

They pressed closer about him, these representatives of the city's very selectest coloured social circle. Society was doing him proud. There was the Rev'end Plato Tubb of the First African M. E. Church and Lawyer Evans Chew and Dr. Vivian Simmons and the immaculate Florian Slappey, his own tailored pre-eminence unselfishly displayed against the greater perfections of his friend. And there was Simeon Broughton, and Pearl, his radiant wife; and Tempus Attucks and Charity Chism and — teetering forlornly on the outskirts of the crowd, glum of expression and diffident of manner

— Pliny Driver, boyhood chum of the returning Spider.

Spider spied him and hurled his ninety-three pounds through the crowd. He seized the gloomy Pliny by the shoulders and shook him delightedly.

"Yo' Pliny! I'm dawg'd ef this don't seem like ol' times shuah nuff. Sa-a-ay! ain't yo' got nothin' tall to reemark?"

"Glad to see yo'," mumbled Pliny dolefully.

"Huh! Yo' look glad, yo' does — not. Looks like yo' jes' been put out the Lodge 'cause they's skeered yo' benumficiary gwine c'lect yo' insurance."

"They ain't nothin' the matter with me, Spider."

"Then yo' face needs a operation fo' the removal of su'plus expression. That mug of you'rn'd make a stake hawss fall down in the homestretch."

"Hmph! Spider — yo' don' know *nothin'!* That's all — yo' don' know nothin' tall."

Spider poked his friend playfully in the ribs. "Mebbe not, son; but I'se shuah gwine fin' out."

Mother Hawkins had stifled the loud protests of a thrifty soul and chartered a seven-passenger car for the child of her bosom. She and Spider and Pliny occupied the big tonneau seat: Lawyer Chew and the Rev'end Tubb balanced precariously on the folding chairs designed for the daring sixth and seventh passengers. Charity Chism, her eyes everywhere save on the mournful face of the dolorous Pliny, climbed in beside Clarence Carter, the chauffeur whose generous cutrates had made the chartering possible.

As the car rolled down the smooth paving of the avenue toward the glaring lights and early evening bustle of the big, prosperous southern city, Spider Hawkins leaned luxuriously back against the cushions and gave himself over to a thorough enjoyment of the moment.

For the first time in two years, Spider was at home. He envisioned himself as he had been: a spirited, mischievous kid — a youngster whose stature he had never outgrown. Every street-corner, every building, was chock-full of joyful memory. The soft, balmy breeze floated in through the tilted windshield and fanned his happy face.

Spider was glad to be home: glad to be away — even for so short a time as a month — from the odour of the stables, the reek of the tack rooms, the sight of quivering thoroughbreds, the clang of the bell in the judges' stand, the raucous yodle of the exquisitely profane starter. Latonia, Havre de Grace, Sheepshead, Saratoga — they were wine in the head of Spider Hawkins, jockey. But just now he was suffering from a surfeit and wanted a rest. And home he had come — home with a roll of money which would have caused serious inconvenience to an elephant's esophagus, a wardrobe destined to be vainly imitated by the young bloods for two years, a perennial good nature and a general warmness of the heart toward the community which so obviously adored him.

The four-room manse of his childhood had been fittingly decorated for the occasion. A picture of himself in riding silks had been garnished with goldenrod. Prohibition punch filled a large, near-cut-glass bowl; tasty crackers were piled high. There were huge dishes of persimmons and chinquapins. Parlour, dining-room, veranda and tiny front yard were crowded with the quality of the city's coloured folks, vieing with one another in homage to Jockey Spider Hawkins.

The air was permeated with infectious hilarity. Spider, fairly bubbling over with happiness, alternately teased his portly, good-natured mother and regaled the crowd with new and funny stories, inimitably told. Within ten minutes he had them all in paroxysms of laughter.

All save Pliny Driver. Pliny gloomed alone in a corner of the parlour, his eyes focussed tirelessly on the radiant Charity Chism and the ingratiating, oily-smiling Tempus Attucks who hovered about her — now serving a clinking punch, now a toothsome cracker: whispering softly into her dainty ear. . . . Murder was in Pliny's heart.

But if Pliny dripped sadness, Spider more than evened things up. The little jockey fairly sizzled with good nature. He effervesced all over the room, the roving centre of an admiring crowd. And finally he was cornered by a group of men under the leadership of Lawyer Evans Chew and the talk turned to shop — Spider's shop.

"Guess yo' is makin' a heap of money, eh, Spider?"

"Guess I is."

"Not all of it ridin', either."

"Meanin' which?" snapped Spider quickly, as he singled out his interrogator as Tempus Attucks. The big, blatantly over-dressed Tempus hastened to take cover.

"Nothin'."

"Yeh — yo' sho' nuff meant sumpin', Mistuh Attucks."

"Er — a-playin' the hawses: that's what I meant."

"I see."

"You does make a li'l sumpin' on the side thataway, ain't it so?"

"I reckon," murmured Lawyer Chew enviously, "that y'all jockeys git a heap of inside info'mation."

"Reckon we do, ol' spoht. 'Tain't so onnat'ral fo' us to be on the inside."

"An' when yo' gets a tip thataway," persisted Attucks, "yo' most gin'rally plays it?"

"Most gin'rally. Ef it looks good."

"Ain't got nothin' up yo' sleeve, have yo', Spider?" questioned Chew.

"Pair of good ridin' arms."

"Meanin' tips like. You just come down from Sarytoga —"

"I'se bettin' he knows more'n a thing or two," insinuated Tempus.

"Yo' win, Mistuh Attucks." Spider turned his attention again to Evans Chew: "Yeh! I sort of reckon I know of a r'il good thing gwine be pulled no later'n Sat'dy."

"G'wan, Spider. . . ." The crowd ganged closer. "Reckon y'd oughter tell us, Spider. We is all frien's of yourn. . . ."

Spider laughed. "Yeh — an' ef I was to spill y'all'd be jes' fools enough to go bettin'. Then come th' ol' dawg to trail the fiel' an' I'd git the blame."

"Nossuh, Spider; that ain't so a tall. Not a tall it ain't."

"Well. . . ." Spider drew a deep breath:

"Bet y'all'd even be fools enough to b'lieve me ef I was to say a r'il long shot was gwine win the fo'th race up to Saratoga Sat'dy."

"Reckon we would, Spider."

"Yassuh, we would that. Is yo' sayin' it, Spider?"

"Ise warnin' yo' folks they ain't no long shot that's a safe bet."

"We'll take the chance, Spider, ef y'all jes' say yo' think they's a chancst. Is it a chancst?"

"Ise sayin' they is. Co'se, I ain't 'sinuatin' the race is crooked. Don' hahdly reckon that kin' of stuff goes no mo' on fust class tracks lak whut I ride on. But they ain't no tellin' but what the owners of a suttin hawss by the name Laddie Buck is been primin' 'im fo' a killin'. He been comin' in ev'y race jes' in time to clutter up the barrier fo' the next one. Slower'n Jinuwary m'lasses. Five yeah ol' an' still a maiden. Fo'th race Sat'day is fo' three-yeah-ol's an' upperds, an' they's some class showin'. Laddie Buck'll go to the post anywhar f'um thutty- to fifty-to-one."

Lawyer Chew leaned forward earnestly. "That from headquarters, Spider?"

"Might' nigh."

"Yo' reckon it's a good bet?"

"It's a good bet," quoth the trackwise Spider, "even ef yo' lose."

Mother Hawkins appeared in the offing and swooped down upon the executive session, dispersing it by mass tactics. A string-and-reed orchestra arrived and dancing started. At one o'clock in the morning the tired, happy crowd disintegrated. But when the disconsolate Pliny

Driver would have oozed out of the front door, Spider held him.

"Hol' on a minnit, Pliny. I wanna make talk with yo'."

"Yo' ain't wanna talk with me, Spider. I ain't no fittin' comp'ny these days."

"Reckon I is took a chancst befo', Pliny. Le's walk."

Arm in arm the chums stepped out into the clear, bracing September night,— Pliny, himself by no means a large man, looming like an ebony giant beside the diminutive Spider.

For half an hour they walked silently southward. They climbed and reached the crest of the mountain on which the city's fashionable residential colony is built: reached it and seated themselves on a boulder they had known of old and from which they could gaze down upon the fire and smoke of the factories which justified Birmingham's existence. Spider heaved a deep sigh.

"Golly! It's good to be home."

"Is it, now?"

"Yeh. . . . Say, Pliny, I ain't saw yo' so happy sencst yo' ol' man tanned yo' britches fo' stealin' doughnuts fum Sally Crouch."

"Reason is 'cause I ain't so happy, Spider."

"How come?"

"Nev' mind. On'y I wisht I was li'l like what yo' is."

"Hmph. . . ."

"I'd leave heah an' be a jockey. Anythin' to git away fum thisyer town."

"What's wrong with th' town?"

"Nothin'. 'Tis jes' folks."

" Coloured folks? "

" Niggers! "

" Name which? "

" Name Tempus Attucks, tha's which."

" That long, tall, shiny-colla'd, greasy-smilin' ol' sellin'-plater what was hangin' 'round Charity Chism all evenin'? "

" Yo' said it."

" G'wan, Pliny. He ain't went an' cut yo' out with Charity, is he? "

" Not no surer than I'se a nigger he ain't."

" *Chk!* How come that? "

" He's one of these heah slipp'y talkers. Says to a gal: ' Nice day t'day!' an' makes it soun' like po'try an' a perposal of marriage all in one. He's jes' a nat'ral-bohn lover. Swell chancst I got ag'in him: me wukin' on a ice-wagon an' him a broker."

" Broker? Him? "

" Tha's what he calls hisse'f. Brokes his cli'nts: tha's all what kin' of a broker he is."

" How he make his livin'? "

" Gamblin'."

" Yo' wrong sommares," declared the jockey seriously. " Onless Charity Chism is change a whole heap she woul'n't stan' fo' no fo'-flushin' crap shooter."

" He ain't no bone-tickler," came the gloomy response. " Him's agent fo' Jackson Ramsay's gamblin' house."

" The lott'ry man? "

" Him's which. On'y they's mo' to it than jes' bein' a agent. The p'lice ain't so lib'ral like what they use' to be. They kinder down on Cap'n Ramsay. He's op'ratin' awful close to the chist these days. Y'see, they is got a new nimisipal 'ministration."

"An' they's down on him?"

"On account they is got some crusaders 'mongst the coloured folks. Rev'end Arlandas Sipsey what pastorizes the Primitive Baptis' Chu'ch stahted the refawm movement."

"To refawm all the coloured folks or jes' Tempus?"

"Mostly Tempus."

"'Bout him, then: is he hones'?"

"Yeh! He's always hones'— sometimes. Fur as I c'n see, Spider, that they Tempus Attucks is so crooked ef he swallied a nail he'd spit up a corkscrew. 'Co'se it ain't always good business fo' Tempus to be crooked an' them times he's straight."

"Jackson Ramsay useter be on the level."

"He is yit. An' he woul'n't stan' for' no fumadiddles fum Tempus ef he knowed it. But he don't an' they ain't no way of provin' up on him."

"How come the coloured folks cain't deal d'rec' with Cap'n Ramsay?"

"Skeered. Sencst the p'lice got such a conscience, Spider, they an' him been pow'ful skeered. Ain't hahdly nobody riskin' goin' to the Pool an' Ginuwine drawin's 'count ef the place git raided it's a long term in the Big Rock. So in ev'y coloured section Cap'n Ramsay is got a agent an' all the bettin' is done th'oo him."

"Cap'n Ramsay runs a hawss-racin' pool, too?"

"Shuah's yo' bohn, he do. Reg'lar two drawin's a day fo' the lott'ry an' his hawss-pool an' sometimes w'en he's pretty shuah they ain't gwine be no p'lice intumfe'ence, he totes out his crap table. But times ain't lak what they was, Spider. Seems like white folks ain't want niggers gamblin' a tall. 'Mostly all the bettin' what is goes th'oo Tempus: tha's how come him to call hisself a broker. Got a office an' all that. 'Tain't nothin' but camelflage."

"An' thisyer Tempus feller done took yo' gal away?"

"Most onti'ly. Me'n my stiddy job with the icewagon ain't look so good longside a broker with offices in the Penny Prudential Bank b'ildin'."

Spider Hawkins gave himself over to several minutes of concentrated thought. He was worried by his friend's abject misery. "One trouble with yo', Pliny, is the face what yo' wears when Tempus an' Charity is in sight."

"It's the on'y face what I got, Spider."

"Yeh . . . but that ain't no call to make yo'se'f look like a long shot with a broken laig."

"Cain't he'p it."

"C'n, too."

"Hmph! Guess yo' don' know nothin' 'bout love, Spider —'bout havin' yo' gal lovin' another feller. Come thataway it's like the stummick-ache — yo' jes' nat'rally cain't he'p it fum showin'."

"An' Charity — was she lovin' yo' pretty strong an' stiddy befo' thisyer Tempus pusson stold her?"

"Tol'able strong."

"An' ef he was to git removed away fum thisyer city sort of sudden like —?"

Pliny perked up with the ray of hope inspired by his friend's words. "Ef 'twas to rain gol' dolla's, Spider. . . ."

"Ef he was to be r'moved away?" repeated Spider firmly.

"— Then I reckon I'd have a pow'ful good chancst. But they ain't no man gwine git removed away f'um a town where he's makin' money. An' no matter what faults Tempus Attucks is got, he shuah has a itch fo' the dollar, an' it's a itch whut gits scratched frequent."

Spider Hawkins rose to the full of his five feet of height. He placed an affectionate hand on his friend's arm. "Pliny, me an' yo' is been frien's fo' a might' long time. I reckon it's soht of up to me to git Charity Chism clinchin' 'round yo' neck pretty pronto."

"Yo' cain't do nothin', Spider."

"Mebbe so an' mebbe not. But I got a hunch wunst I git ol' Tempus Attucks runnin' free in the homestretch I c'n kick a li'l bit of dust in his eyes an' romp home under wraps."

"Yo' mos' prob'ly knows hawses, Spider," gloomed Pliny, "but thisyer Tempus ain't no hawss. He's a mule an' he cain't be driv'."

"Hmph! But mules c'n be pushed!" proclaimed Spider, and thereupon put an end to the subject, his beam of hope seeping through the Stygian blackness of despair to dimly light the soul of the doleful Pliny.

But that night Spider did little planning. Five minutes after he deposited his tiny but well-knit frame on the home couch he was off into a deep and dreamless sleep from which he was waked at ten o'clock by his voluminous mother, who proudly bore aloft a tin waiter containing a breakfast such as Spider had almost forgotten. As he munched he beamed gloriously from his background of pink silk pajamas and brought delight to the maternal ears:

"Hones', Mom, thisyer shuah is the bestest grub done pas'd my lips sencst I been No'th. Ain't nobody makes no waffles an' coffee like what yo' does. Tha's how come li'l Spider aint never got him no gal. Swell gals up where I been at — plenty of 'em — but, shucks! ef I was to marry one of 'em I'd git d'vohced pow'ful quick on account of tellin' her how Mom useter cook. Yassum: Jes' shuah's a jinny ain't no race-hawss. Gimme s'mo' that they jelly, Mom. I 'clare, yo' is the bestest jelly maker what is. Yo' jelly an' waffles is the fondest thing I'm of, an' tha's a fac'. B'lieve me, Mom, my ol' man was lucky fo' to ever marry a gal like what yo' is."

When he left the house a half hour later his mother was contentedly chanting an old and almost-forgotten plantation melody as she busied herself with the luncheon preliminaries. Mamma Hawkins was happier than she had been in two long years. She found herself gazing after the tiny, swaggering figure of her elegant son and marvelling that she had been blessed of the Gods.

At the ornate lodge rooms of the exclusive Sons & Daughters of I Will Arise, Spider found several indolent brothers who were equalizing a sudden raise in wages by laying off for the day. From there he dropped into Broughton's drug store where he quaffed an ice cream soda and jollied the grinning soda-jerker. He wandered forth and passed the time o' day with the portly ticket taker of Champion Moving Picture Theatre No. 2; and later dropped into the editorial sanctum of *The Weekly Epoch* where he furnished sufficient data for a two-column sketch of himself.

Meanwhile there was much deep thinking disturbing the mental processes of coloured professional circles. In the veins of Lawyer Evans Chew, for example, there coursed the hot blood of a speculating race and flaming in his mind was remembrance of the tip dropped so casually and good-naturedly by Jockey Spider Hawkins the previous night.

A maiden five-year-old by the name of Laddie Buck, Spider had prognosticated, was a sure thing for the fourth race at Saratoga the coming Saturday. Laddie Buck was going to the post a long shot. Anywhere from thirty- to fifty-to-one. Five dollars bet on Laddie Buck at thirty — minimum odds — stood to net the successful bettor one hundred and fifty dollars. The risk was small; the potential reaping, large. Lawyer Evans Chew nodded, wrote a check for five dollars, cashed it at the bank downstairs and made his way forthwith to the office of Tempus Attucks, broker and general agent for Jackson Ramsay, arch operator. He met Dr. Vivian Simmons emerging.

"Howdye, Doctor Simmons."

"Mornin', Lawyer Chew."

"Been transacting some business with Brother Attucks?"

"Most likely."

Evans Chew grinned. "Business named Laddie Buck, ain't it, Doctor?"

"Jus' about. You on the same mission?"

"Five dollars' worth. How about you?"

"Five for myself and one for Sally Crouch."

"It's a good chance, Doctor."

"Fine chance, Lawyer Chew. There's heaps of others believing that Spider Hawkins gave us an accurate tip. They're all goin' to lay wagers: Simeon Broughton and Florian Slappey — of course Florian would — and while I ain't sayin' it's so, mind you, Sister Callie Flukers was hintin' that she heard that Rev'end Plato Tubb of the Fust African M. E. Chu'ch was considerin' risking two dollars."

The attorney chuckled. "Rev'end Tubb has a lib'ral conscience, Doctor Simmons. Reckon he'd argue he wasn't betting on account he's so sure he's goin' to win."

For Tempus Attucks, business maintained a terrific pace throughout the day. By some magic, the news of Spider Hawkins' sure-thing for the fourth race Saturday had spread through darktown. To the office of Tempus Attucks came the élite and the humble, laying wagers ranging from twenty-five cents to five dollars on Laddie Buck at the best odds obtainable at the opening of the books Saturday. There was an indefinable something in the calm confidence of the bettors which seeped into Tempus's blood and set it a-simmering.

He had known Spider Hawkins only by reputation, but the day's business indicated that the community had implicit confidence in Spider's judgment. Folks believed that Laddie Buck was destined to romp home ahead of the field as Spider had forecasted. If that were the case. . . .

Tempus Attucks was sufficiently affluent to covet real wealth. At no time in his soft life had he ever been down to his last dollar. Conversely, he had at no time possessed more than eight hundred. At present he was seized and possessed of just about three hundred and fifty. And he calculated rapidly that if Laddie Buck should win and he had happened to bet at long odds. . . .

The community was confident. When Tempus closed his books that night his friends and fellow citizens had entrusted him with no less than seventy-two dollars, every cent of which was to be laid on Laddie Buck. It went to Tempus Attucks' head like wine. He determined to get in on the game himself. But Tempus was canny. Taking a chance had no place in his cosmic scheme. He sought the fount of knowledge: he insinuated himself upon Jockey Spider Hawkins, whom he found puffing a black, gold-banded cigar in the doorway of Sally Crouch's Cozy Home Hotel.

"Evenin' Brother Hawkins."

"Howdye, Mistuh Attucks."

"Have another cigar?"

Spider sniffed it delicately. "Good terbaccer, Brother Attucks." He slipped it into a silver cigar holder. "How yo' makin' it, Brother Attucks?"

"Slow — pow'ful slow. Things don't seem to pick up none whatever."

"Sorry. Might' sorry. Folks been prospectin' to me yo' been gittin' on tol'able well."

"Gittin' on?" Tempus laughed a short, bitter laugh. "Gittin' on means a diff'ent language to these heah niggers an' to you an' me, Brother Hawkins."

Spider nodded. "Ain't it the truth now, Brother Attucks? Ain't it the truth?"

"Shuah is. These heah niggers, ef they got a hund'ed dollars they think they got all the money what is. Me an' you: us knows that ain't nothin' on'y a baggytell."

"Ain't it so? Hund'ed ain't nothin' tall. Not nothin' tall — it ain't."

"Co'se I got a good business. Makes a trifle ev'y li'l heah an' there. Always 'members my frien's: always do. Anybody'll tell yo' that 'bout Tempus Attucks. Yassuh: they shuah will. But times is slow. What I wants is r'il money. Sho' nuff lots of it."

"Mos' all of us is 'flicted thataway, ain't it?"

Attucks nudged Spider playfully. "Yo' is shuah the humourestest feller. . . ."

"Aw, sa-a-ay. . . ."

"Yo' is, shuah nuff. Reckon yo' knows a heap of things."

"Reckon I does."

"'Bout hawses an' sech."

"Soht of."

"What I likes 'bout yo', Brother Hawkins — what I likes the very mostest 'bout yo', is yo' ain't no tight-lipped feller 'mongst yo' frien's."

"Me?" Spider's brows arched with surprise. "Reckon yo' ain't knowed me ve'y long, Brother Attucks. I'se the tight-liptest man what is."

"Not 'mongst yo' frien's."

"Shuah is."

"Ain't yo' say right out in public last night 'bout that hawss Laddie Buck winnin' the fo'th race Sat'dy up to Sarahtoga?"

"Laddie Buck? Lad —" Spider swung suddenly and his eyes bored into those of his interrogator: "Law', Brother Attucks, yo' ain't gone an' bet no r'il money on that they dawg, is yo'?"

"Why — I — I — thought. . . ."

"Oh! Golly, Brother Attucks; tell me yo' ain't took serious what I said las' night 'bout that they ol' jack," pleaded Spider. "Tell me the truth — yo' ain't bet on him, is yo'?"

"Yo'— yo' said —"

"I wasn't on'y foolin'. Tha's all. Ev'y man c'n have his li'l joke sometimes. But I woul'n't go spillin' no live tips thataway. Law', no."

"Yo'— yo' means to stan' up they, Brother Hawkins, an' tell me Laddie Buck ain't got no chancst to win thisyer fo'th race Sat'dy?"

"Win it? *Win?*" Spider threw back his head and laughed ringingly. "Say, Brother Attucks, ef yo' was ever to see that they she-cow yo'd die laughin'. On'y way that dawg could win, Brother Attucks, would be ef ev'y other hawss in the race done fell down at the barrier — an' on'y then pervidin' Laddie Buck could travel th' distance a tall. Hones' a th'ee-legged nannygoat c'd give that nag a six-fu'long staht in a seben-fu'long race an' breeze under the wire a length to th' good. Laddie Buck's jes' one of them hawses wasn't nev' meant to win. W'en he's down to staht the jedges write his name in the also-ran colyum an' fohgit he's alive. En all the time I been spohtin' silk, Brother Attucks, I ain't saw nothin' slower'n that Laddie Buck 'ceptin' a lame snail I knowed oncet."

"But — but yo' said —"

"Listen heah at what I'se tellin' yo', Brother

Attucks: is yo' done gone an' bet yo' money on Laddie Buck, or isn't yo'?"

"I ain't bet none yit."

"Then don't! An' tha's the bestest adwice I ev' gave anybody. Ef yo' wanna git some r'il fun out of that they money yo' was gwine bet on Laddie Buck, change it into si'ver dollars an' climb to the top of the mount'in an' see how far yo' c'n scale 'em. B'lieve me, w'en the hawss stawk brought Laddie Buck, Brother Attucks, she made a mistake. He should of been drapped in a liver' stable."

"Yo' said —" floundered Tempus weakly.

"Tha's what comes of yo' not knowin' me, Brother Attucks. Ef yo' had of knowed me long yo'd of knowed I was on'y jokin'."

"Hmph!" remarked the disgruntled Tempus cryptically, "I reckon they ain't many folks in thisyer town what knows yo' r'il well, Brother Hawkins. Not many."

And with that Tempus Attucks walked away, shaking his head slowly. He was thinking earnestly of the seventy-two dollars in his pocket; money left with him by those friends of Spider Hawkins who had believed in him and the decrepit Laddie Buck.

On Saturday evening Tempus Attucks eased into the odorous, dingy sanctum of Jackson Ramsay, the white and portly professional gambler who made a more than merely excellent living from the contributions of the coloured community.

Tempus responded absently to Ramsay's cheery greeting and retired behind a cloud of fragrant cigar smoke. Ramsay busied himself with arrangements for the drawing of Genuine — the afternoon lottery — and paid small heed to the visiting agents.

There came a tap at the door, it swung back and a small boy darted in. Tempus Attucks sat up stiffly in his chair, the cigar gripped between his teeth. He watched Jackson Ramsay rip open the telegram and impassively peruse its contents.

"From Sarahtoga?" queried Tempus thickly.

"Yes," answered Ramsay, and then turned to his assistant: "Put these results down." The assistant stationed himself before the blackboard, chalk in hand.

"Ready, Cap'n Ramsay."

"Saratoga: First race — Baboon Baby, Mother Hubbard, Terrapin. Second race — Farrallon, Carl K., Little Sister. Third race — Venita Strome, Grosvenor, Carlisle. Fourth race —" Jackson Ramsay paused in his dictation and whistled softly. Tempus Attucks felt every muscle in his body grow tense. Tiny beads of perspiration stood out on his forehead.

"Fo'th race, Cap'n —?"

"I'll be horn-swoggled!"

"Boss-man . . . please . . . 'bout that they fo'th race?"

"Forty-to-one shot romps home!"

The room swam before the eyes of Tempus Attucks: "Fohty to one shot, Cap'n?"

"Forty-to-one. I'll be —"

"Cap'n Ramsay — *please,* suh — what the name of that they fohty-to-one shot?"

"Laddie Buck! Hey, what's the matter?" for,

with a groan of agony, Tempus Attucks had risen.

"Ain' feel so well, Boss-man." He staggered toward the door.

"But Tempus —"

"Ain' got no feelin's fo' no convuhsation, Cap'n. Be back d'rec'ly." Tempus opened the door. "Fohty-to-one! Oh! my Law'!" The door closed gently behind him.

Haste was slow in comparison with the method of transit employed by Tempus Attucks in getting to the Terminal Station. Pop-eyed and trembling, he bought a ticket for Washington — that train being the only one scheduled to start within the next fifteen minutes. And when the train pulled out, a limp and lachrymose Tempus Attucks was huddled in an inconspicuous corner.

Meanwhile the news of Laddie Buck's victory spread through darktown like wildfire. Jubilant bettors sought Tempus Attucks, agent. Tempus was nowhere in evidence.

One hour later the truth was suspected. Another hour and the truth was known. Tempus Attucks had departed the city: when or whither no one knew. But the thoroughly aroused populace was poignantly aware of the fact that Tempus owed it something in the neighbourhood of three thousand dollars. The sentiment against the departed gentleman was thoroughly crystallized, supremely unanimous and utterly murderous.

The only ray of light came to the doleful Pliny Driver from the lips of his friend, Jockey Spider Hawkins. Spider slapped his pal on the back with a jovial: "He's done flew!"

"Hmph!" sceptically, "tha's what they say."

"They is sayin' the truth."

"How come yo' to know that?"

"Pliny Driver, ain't I done tol' yo' no longer ago than las' Toosday I'd git rid of ol' Tempus Attucks so's yo'd have a cl'ar road to Charity Chism?"

"Yeh. Yo' *tol'* me. . . ."

"I done it!"

"Done what?"

"Got rid of Brother Tempus so's he'll nev' come within a hund'ed miles of thisyer town ag'in."

"How come that?"

"N'r two hund'ed. N'r th'ee hund'ed."

"Yo' is makin' foolishments with me."

"I'se serious."

"Splain it to me, Spider," begged Pliny hopefully. "An' for Gawd's sake, Spider, splain it *tho'ough!*"

"Come this way, Pliny. Ol' Tempus plays 'em safe. An' day after I got heah an' drapped that they tip 'bout Laddie Buck shuah gwine win the fo'th race this afternoon, ev'ybody stahted layin' they money with Tempus to place with Cap'n Ramsay. That's too much fo' Tempus an' he 'lows he'll git in on the killin'. So he braces me is my tip straight.

"An' Pliny, I tell him Laddie Buck ain't got no mo' chancst of winnin' that race than what you is got of not marryin' Charity Chism. An' 'member thisyer, Pliny: I nev' tol' my frien's nothin' but the straight truth. What I tol' a ol' crook like Tempus don't matter to nobody ef I was a li'l bit lib'ral in my guesses."

"But," groped Pliny dazedly: "Why'd yo' tell

Tempus Laddie Buck didn't have no chancst to win?"

" 'Cause I had ol' Tempus' number, Pliny. Come him to b'lieve Laddie Buck ain't got no chancst he thinks how foolish to waste all them seventy dollars he's got when they's gwine be lost. So he c'ludes better fo' them seventy to stay in Tempus's pocket than to go to them race-track men.

"Tha's how come, Pliny. Tempus never laid them bets a tall! Nary dollar! Come Laddie Buck romps home like what I knowed he was gwine do — Tempus Attucks finds hisse'f owin' theseyer niggers nigh onto th'ee thousan' dollars.

"They warn't but one thing he could do, Pliny; an' he run true to fohm. Mahk my word: foh about a hund'ed yeahs or so 'round this heah town Tempus Attucks is gwine be 'bout the scarcest thing what is!"

NOT WISELY BUT TOO WELL

NOT WISELY BUT TOO WELL

"REMEMBER, Gussie, I want the dining-room thorough-cleaned. The Browning Club meets here this afternoon and —"

"Yassum, Mis' C'ruthers, it'll be so clean you ain't gwine know it."

"And the flat silver must be polished."

"I'se gwine 'tend to all of that. You trot 'long downtown, Mis' C'ruthers, an' leave it to me."

Mrs. Franklin Carruthers heaved a sigh of ineffable contentment. "You are a very valuable servant, Gussie. Good-bye."

"G'-bye, Mis' C'ruthers. Be sho' an' have a good time."

The front door of the apartment slammed. Miss Gussie Muck, coloured maid-of-most-of-the-work, mopped the polished floor of the dining-room viciously for perhaps two minutes — until the thrum of Mrs. Carruthers' automobile came to her ears — then gently turned back the corner of the axminster art square. When she replaced the corner the dust had disappeared. Then Gussie leaned her mop against the door, strolled into Mrs. Carruthers' bedroom and seated herself at the dressing-table.

A coating of talcum, a touch of face powder, a dab of rouge and Gussie was well satisfied that she had enhanced the physical glories of feature with which she had been endowed by nature. She made her way to the living-room, selected a lurid novel from the bookcase and dropped languidly into an easy chair after having first helped herself to a quartet of particularly toothsome glacé fruits from the box on the library table.

She was interrupted by the strident ringing of the kitchen bell. Her face expressed complete disapproval of the interruption. But at sight of the man standing on the tiny back porch the expression underwent a decided change.

Aaron Segar was not unused to the phenomenon. Aaron had been born with a gift for making women smile and grow warm all over. He was handsome and tall and broad and divinely chocolate-creamy of skin. He unleashed his most fetching laugh for Gussie.

"Howdye, Miss Muck."

"Mawnin', Mistuh Segar."

"Wukin' hahd?"

Gussie sighed. "Reckon I is. Ain't nobody livin' these days what ain't wuk hahd, Misto' Segar."

"You shuah said sumpin' then, Miss Gussie. Wuk, wuk, wuk all the time. Me more'n you."

"Huh!"

"That's the truth. Ain't no gittin' off fo' me. Bein' a janitor is a pow'ful hahd perfession, Miss Gussie."

"Reckon you is strong enough to stan' it, Mistuh Segar."

"Reckon I is. But it's pow'ful ti'esome an' lonely, Gussie. It been diffe'ent down to S'vannah whar I come fum. They ain't 'spec a man to do no th'ee men's wuk down they."

"You was a 'pahtment-house janitor there same as heah?"

"Uh-huh!" He lowered his voice discreetly. "Ain't I saw Mis' C'ruthers go off in her car jes' now?"

"Yeh."

He opened the screen door. "Don't mind if'n I drap in, does you?"

"He'p yo'se'f, Mistuh Segar."

He waved his hand grandiosely. "You'n me is gwine be good frien's, ain't we, Gussie?"

"Guess you c'n answer that well as me."

"Then call me 'Aaron.'"

"Ain't knowed you but th'ee days."

"You gwine know me longer'n that. Boun' to."

"Well. . . ."

"All the gals what I likes, I asks them to call me Aaron. I nev' was no shakes fo' fo'mal'ty. Fust names atween frien's, I says. Tha's how come I to call you Gussie. You ain't got no 'jections, is you?"

"This town ain't S'vannah, Mistuh Segar."

He rose. "If'n you ain't gwine call me Aaron —"

"Aaron!"

He re-seated himself. "Tha's better. No — this heah town ain't like S'vannah, Gussie. Up heah, they ain't no tellin' who's quality folks an' who ain't — that is, 'mongst the white folks. An' I'se always been pow'ful p'tic'lar 'bout what soht of white folks I wuks fo'."

"I ain't blamin' you, Aaron. Us coloured people cain't be too 'ticalar. How you like it up heah?"

"Tol'able. On'y tol'able."

"How come?"

"I'se lonely, Gussie. Ain't know nobody in this heah town. On'y a few. Come night, they ain't nothin' fo' me to do but go down to the 'pahtment what they gives me in the basement an' set 'roun' an' wisht I was married so's I woul'n't be so lonely."

"Huh! Bet you *been* married!"

Aaron Segar laughed heartily. "Is I look it?"

"We-e-ell: not 'zactly."

"An' they's a reason, Gussie. I ain't nev' met the gal I wan'ed to marry. Not twell yet."

"Reckon you is might' hahd to please, Mistuh Segar."

"Aaron!"

"Aaron."

"Reckon I is hahd to please. Tha's how come I to watch ontil Mis' C'ruthers' gone off in her car, an' then come up heah."

"How that?"

"I ain't make much talk with you, Gussie — but you shuah looks pow'ful good to me."

"G'wan, Aaron. You is some loose flatt'rer."

"Reckon I is got the cou'age of my convictions."

"Reckon you think I is like them S'vannah gals — swally all that bull."

"Gals whut I is went with heahtofo' ain't got so many compliments fum me."

"How I know that?"

"B'lieve it or not. I cain't *make* you."

"Well. . . . Hongry?"

"Always, 'ceptin' when I c'n git to town. Does my own cookin' downstairs, Gussie. Man's got to, come he ain't got no wife. So I ain't git ve'y good food. Why you ask me?"

"They was a couple chops lef' over fum breakfas'. . . ."

"You cook 'em?"

"Uh-huh!"

"Trot 'em out. Bet they is some fine-cooked chops."

Gussie spurred herself to real activity for some five minutes whilst she basked in the light of Aaron Segar's unqualified approval. She heated two succulent lamb chops, made three slices of crisp toast which she buttered liberally, and poured the solid cream top from the quart of fresh milk. And Aaron exhibited his appreciation by a marvellous display of gustatory gymnastics. Finally he finished, sighed and regretfully shoved his plate aside.

"Golly! you shuah is *some* cook!"

"Reckon I is got to be if'n I hol' my job with Mis' C'ruthers. White folks is awful capshus, Aaron. They spec' they coloured he'p to wuk all the time."

"Aint you talkin' now?"

"Sometimes I is got a pow'ful good notion to cut loose an' git married."

Aaron delayed his departure with one hand on the door. All the wealth of a contagiously sunny nature went into the smile which he bestowed upon her. "When you makes up yo' mind to git married, Gussie, don't fohgit my telephone number cas'n you have any trouble findin' a husband."

As he stomped down the steps leading to the decorative back court of the Glen Ridge apartments, Gussie dropped into a kitchen chair and stared raptly into space. Aaron Segar! What a man! Of their own volition her thoughts veered dreamily to the little apartment which the proprietors of the Glen Ridge apartments furnished their janitor. Bedroom, dining-room, kitchen — gas, steam heat, hot and cold water. . . . Gussie sighed.

Meanwhile the magnificent Aaron paused at the back door of Mrs. Percival Connor's apartment. His hypercritical eyes rested with infinite appreciation on the trim little figure of one Mallissie Cheese, cook and nurse girl in the Connor menage.

"Mawnin', M'lissie."

The girl shrugged with simulated indifference: "Mawnin'."

"What's the matter: somebody been rub you the wrong way?"

"No."

"You seem 'bout as happy as a live pig at a barbecue."

"Reckon I is happy, Mistuh Segar."

"Mis' Connor been givin' you down-the-country?"

"Reckon they ain't no white folks try no sech fumadiddles on me, Mistuh Segar."

"How come you to fohgit my name Aaron?"

"Reckon I fo'gits so Gussie Muck up to Mis' C'ruthers' c'n remember it."

Aaron threw back his head and gave vent to a hearty laugh. "Shucks! You ain't gwine git jealous of a ol' frump like Gussie Muck, is you?"

Mallissie looked up. More — she smiled. "Gussie Muck is a pow'ful pretty gal, Aaron."

He shook his head in diplomatic negation. "Reckon you an' me is got diffe'ent tastes, Mallissie. I like 'em li'l — like what you is."

NOT WISELY BUT TOO WELL 151

When Aaron departed from the Connor kitchen about five minutes later he left Mallissie Cheese humming happily and dated-up to accompany him to Champion Moving Picture Theatre No. 2 that night to see the nineteenth episode of "The Fighting Fate" which they agreed upon as the high-water mark in motion picture production.

The new janitor reached the back court — and he met Fashion Wilson, a girl of the Gussie Muck type — only a trifle more so. She was seated on a bench under the big oak giving half an eye to the care of two children and the other one and a half to Aaron.

"Been paintin' Mis' Connor's kitchen, Aaron?"

"Naw."

"How come you in they so long?"

"Been tryin' to git down heah an' talk with you. Fashi'n, but that skinny li'l gal what wuks fo' Mis' Connor — whut her name is?"

"Mallissie Cheese."

"Tha's it — I plumb fo'got. It jes' seemed like she woul'n't lemme git away. Jes' settin' they an' makin' a whole passel of foolish talk. . . ."

"Mallissie's a might' nice gal."

"Guess they is some things you'n me won't nev' agree on, Fashi'n."

"An' pretty —"

"I likes mo' of them than what they is of M'lissie." He cast the eye of a connoisseur over Fashion's junoesque proportions. Then he eased himself to the bench beside her. "How 'bout goin' down to Champeen number Two with me tomorry night, huh?"

"Whyn't you ask Ella?"

"Ella which?"

"Ella Dungee."

"That funny-lookin' gal whut wuks fo' Mis' Hammond? Whut fo' I should ask her?"

"You is been hangin' 'roun' that 'partment right smaht lately."

"Huh! Reckon I is *had* to. Way that gal keeps Mis' Hammond's kitchen, Fashi'n — if'n I di'n't git that they place cleaned out they'd be roaches all over this heah 'pahtment in a week. Guess Ella Dungee ain't Aaron Segar's style a tall, a tall."

But twenty minutes later when he met Ella Dungee after having conducted a strategic retirement from the immediate presence of the buxom Fashion, he gave her a heart-warming smile. "'Clare to goodness, Ella — if'n you ain't the ve'y purties' gal I ev' did see!"

"Bet you is said that th'ee hund'ed times today, Aaron."

"Cain't be. Ain't seed you but this oncet."

"Nothin' pretty 'bout me."

"I gwine buy you a lookin' glass, Ella. By the way: got a date fo' Sat'dy night?"

"No-o."

"How 'bout gwine to Champeen Number Two with me?"

"Well. . . ."

He waved cheerily as he descended to his basement. "Man sho' is lucky when he c'n date up with a gal like you, Ella."

"You is a sof' talker, Aaron."

"Me? Shucks! I woul'n't know how to pay a complyment if'n I wan'ed to!"

NOT WISELY BUT TOO WELL 153

It really wasn't Aaron's fault. He had been created with a talent for women and was no believer in burying any talent. Women gravitated toward him. They clung to him. They pestered an otherwise equable existence.

His obliging nature was the petard upon which he was hoist. He hated to disappoint anybody — especially a lady friend. And he was frankly flattered by their unanimous and unconcealed adoration.

And these girls were different from his Savannah friends, just as the Glen Ridge apartments were better than the unpretentious things he had janitor'd on Savannah's Abercorn street. These girls had more *élan*, their ideas were metropolitan. They were women of fine discrimination and delicate appreciation — as different from the crude, provincial product of Tybee and Thunderbolt as high yaller is different from ebony.

More — standing in with the cooks was a material proposition. His own culinary labour and expenses were reduced. Aaron was an epicure and appreciated the fact that the Gray, Connor, Hammond and Carruthers families lived upon the fat of the land. The lagniappe from their pantries tickled his palate and brightened his philosophy.

He liked the city and the city liked him. Within two months he had become somewhat of a social lion. He was initiated into the exclusive Sons & Daughters of I Will Arise; he joined the ten-cents-a-week Over The River Burying Society and became a prominent and valued mourner at the obsequies of the dear departed brothers and sisters who were ushered from this mortal coil with full panoply of parade — and music. He sang a pleasing baritone and joined the choir of the Primitive Baptist Church — much to the delight of the Rev'end Arlandas Sipsey, pastor thereof. Reverends Plato Tubb and Wesley Luther Thigpen of the First African M. E. and the Shiloh congregations respectively, admitted that the Reverend Arlandas had outgeneralled them. Aaron Segar was an acquisition of which any church might well be proud.

He was decidedly a man of parts. His salary of eighty-five dollars per month was exclusive of perquisites such as a steam-heated, furnished apartment at the Glen Ridge and estovers provided by the admiring cooks over whom his spell had been cast.

But the swift flight of time brought a wrinkle to the normally placid forehead of Aaron Segar. He found himself facing a near-domestic problem to which there was no apparent answer, and he besought the professional services of Lawyer Evans Chew, leading light of darktown's legal fraternity.

The buxom stenographer warmed to Aaron's sweetest smile and carried his name into the private sanctum of Lawyer Chew. She returned promptly.

"Lawyer Chew will see you in a minute, Mistuh Segar. He's in confe'ence now."

Aaron waited patiently, amusing himself by flirting violently with the stenographer, whose hitherto impregnable heart pounded with wild hope. Finally the pompous conferees departed and Lawyer Chew — slender, immaculate, horn-rim-spectacled — personally ushered Aaron into the private office.

NOT WISELY BUT TOO WELL 155

"Mister Segar — I am delighted to meet you."

"Me, too, Lawyer Chew."

"You wish to consult me on a professional matter?"

"Yassuh — tha's it 'zactly, Lawyer Chew."

"Ahem. . . . Proceed, please."

"Yassuh —" Aaron groped blindly, then smiled wanly. "I ain't 'zactly know whar to begin at."

"What sort of a case is it?"

"Dunno — less'n you'd call it britch of promise."

"A-ha! You have become involved with *lay patect femme,* as they say in French."

"How that?"

"You are involved with a member of the — er — gentler sex."

"Yassuh! Involved is right — sho' nuff."

"How did it occur?"

"It ain't occur, Lawyer Chew — it jes' happen."

"What is the lady's name?"

"'Tain't no lady."

"What?"

"Nossuh; it's fo' wimmin."

"Four?"

"Tha's it: one, two, th'ee, fo'."

Lawyer Chew leaned forward incredulously. "Do you mean to tell me, Brother Segar, that you are faced by four britch of promise suits?"

"I c'n cut it down to th'ee, if'n that'll help any."

"How so?"

"Marry one of them wimmin an' let the other th'ee scratch."

"Ahem! Strawdinry! A case prob'ly without

parallel on the books. How does it happen that you have fallen into the error —"

" 'Twarn't no error, Lawyer Chew — 'twarn't nothin' but a mistake."

" I suppose it was. Who are the ladies in question? "

" They's M'lissie Cheese an' Ella Dungee an' Fashi'n Wilson an' Gussie Muck. They wuks out to the Glen Ridge 'pahtments whar I is janitor at. An'," his eyes twinkled irrepressibly, " they is mighty lovin'."

" I see: I see. Continue, please."

" I'se tellin' you this right heah an' now, Lawyer Chew — they ain't hahdly no man c'n handle *one* woman. But *fo'* wimmin, Lawyer Chew, is an unpossibility. I *knows!* "

" You are sure that they will all sue you? "

" I ain't know as any of them is because I sort of got 'em guessin'. But a woman ain't got but so much guessin' in her, Lawyer Chew — an' when that gits used up, she wants action. Y'see, right now they ain't nary one of them gals knows which one I is gwine pick out. They is jes' 'bout tearin' one-nuther's ha'r out by the roots — but they's all kinder skeered to light in on me 'cause they's the chancst that they is the lucky one.

" I been playin' both ends 'gainst the middle, Lawyer Chew — an' the middle is might' nigh reached. I ain't know whether I is comin' or goin'. Meanw'ile they is all tryin' to find out whar I stan' at."

" What have you told them? "

" I done swore to each of them gals she is the **one I gwine marry.** An' they is gittin' pow'ful impatient. I sort of wan'ed to fin' out what is the law on britches of promise — not jes' one britch, but a whole lot of 'em."

Lawyer Chew cleared his throat and thumbed portentously through the Alabama code. He next consulted his Southern Reporter and his Cyc. He shook his head discouragingly. "The dictas ain't ve'y clear about yo' sort of a case, Brother Segar. Seems like the men what wrote the law books never entertained no idea of a man gettin' engaged to four women at one time."

"Oh! Golly. . . . You mean to set they an' tell me, Lawyer Chew, that they ain't nothin' in all them books gwine show me how to git out of the pickle Ise in?"

"No," reflectively. "I don't see —

"Not no way?"

Lawyer Chew brightened with an idea. "If you were married to all four of them women, Brother Segar, I might help you, because the law is ve'y specific about bigamy."

"Huh! If'n I was married to them fo' wimmin, Lawyer Chew — they ain't *no* law could he'p me."

"I still don't understand how you got into this mess."

"I di'n't git in. Hones' I di'n't. I was jes' sort of pulled in like a feller listenin' at the bones click. Reckon you ain't nev' had the sperience of wimmin fallin' in love with you in job-lots, is you?"

"Not — er — precisely."

"Tha's the trouble with you lawyers. You ain't had no sperience. All what you know is what has been wrote in them they books. What you reckon them they men knowed 'bout M'lissie Cheese an' Ella Dungee an' them other nigger gals? Huh? Whut you reckon they knowed 'bout them? White folks wrote them books an' white folks don' know nothin' 'bout how a yaller gal c'n co't a man if'n he looks good to her. Ain't that so, Lawyer Chew — ain't it the truth, now?"

"And you have personally pledged yourself to each of the four girls?"

"Absotively an' ontirely. They woul'n't stan' fo' nothin' less."

The attorney and counsellor rubbed the palms of his hands unctiously. "As they isn't any statute or decision of a co't of las' resort covering the case under consideration," he proclaimed sententiously, "the best I can do is to consider the circumstances from the light of expediumcy."

"Tha's it, Lawyer Chew — you sho' is tootin' now."

"In that light, the best adwice I can give you, Brother Segar, is that you bring about a quarrel with each of the girls to which you is engaged and make them break off the engagement."

Aaron Segar rose abruptly. His face was wreathed in disgust. "Huh! Reckon you ain't no diffe'ent fum them foolish books, Lawyer Chew. Maybe you know the law — but you ain't know them gals!"

Mr. Segar left the office of Lawyer Chew more perturbed than he had ever been in his placid, happy-go-lucky life. He even forgot to flirt with the stenographer. For once he was up against a proposition from which his cheerful smile and sunny disposition could not extricate him: a di-

NOT WISELY BUT TOO WELL 159

lemma, in fact, where they were arrayed with the liabilities instead of with the assets.

"I reckon," he soliloquized miserably, "they ain't no nigger could ever git in no worse scrape than what I is in."

In which he was wrong. There was one darkey capable of getting in deeper. There was one dusky gentleman who promptly proceeded to do it.

The name of that negro was — Aaron Segar!

For — two nights after his interview with Lawyer Evans Chew — Aaron Segar met his affinity!

The epochal event occurred at Blue Lake Park, the negro amusement grounds some six miles from the heart of the big southern city in which the Glen Ridge apartments and Aaron's amorital troubles were located.

The time was night, the occasion a gala jubilee of the society season: The Eleventh Annual Barbecue and Picnic of the Primitive Baptist Church. Tickets, including Gent and Lady — Fifty Cents. Children, half price. Come one — come all. Rev. Arlandas Sipsey, Pastor.

It was a noble revelry: a glory of fires burning in shallow ditches — fires which reached the succulent pork quarters sizzling as they revolved on the iron skewers; fires which kept hot the iron vessels filled with luscious brown gravy. Barbecue specialists hovered over the gravy vessels, armed with long mops and small tree branches. These they soaked in the gravy and then spattered over the roasting meat. The ample Sally Crouch presided nearby in queenly fashion over the Brunswick Stew division — without which no barbecue is complete.

The double quartet from the Primitive Baptist

Church choir was harmoniously on hand and between songs the string and reed orchestra of Professor Alec Champagne rendered toe-tickling melodies which ranged from the classic Memphis Blues to an elegantly syncopated version of the Miserere which Professor Champagne claimed as an original composition. Children romped and shouted and got in every one's way. Church deacons clustered in groups: grim-visaged and ponderous whilst they argyfied about the heat of the hereafter and the spiritual benefits of total immersion.

Young couples took shape from the darkness and other young couples disappeared into the night. The other congregations were plentifully represented: Rev'end Plato Tubb was there and so was the Reverend Wesley Luther Thigpen. Then, too, there was Dr. Vivian Simmons, M.D.; and Amos Stump, the perpetually smiling undertaker; and Florian Slappey and Mr. and Mrs. Simeon Broughton, and Pliny Driver with his gaily-plumaged fiancé, Charity Chism; and Peter and Mrs. Sampson, and Elias Rush and his wife — née Imogene Carter; and Imogene's brother, Clarence; and Pinetop Roller and ponderous Mrs. Ella Hawkins and Sister Callie Flukers and the dynamic Crispus Breach, fiery-penned editor of *The Weekly Epoch* — Crispus glaring intensively into the black void for new adjectives with which to embellish his account of this social triumph.

And there, too, was Ione Drought!

Aaron Segar, harassed — overwrought and harried with the nerve-strain of placating each of his four fiancés and compromising himself with no one of them — Aaron Segar saw Ione Drought!

Aaron fell.

Gone on the instant were his fervent resolutions to eschew women. Gone was the misogyny inspired by the utter failure of his most fervid attempts to unleash himself from four pair of ardent, clinging, feminine arms. Gone for ever was the solemn pledge of celibacy.

He forgot Mallissie Cheese. He forgot Fashion Wilson. He forgot Ella Dungee and Gussie Muck. He forgot everything and everybody save Ione Drought; Ione the magnificent, Ione the unique, Ione the reserved, Ione the neglected, Ione the desirable.

"Who — who — that gal?" he inquired of Florian Slappey, mentor of the younger social set.

"Which gal?"

"Over yonder: that they gal with the green dress an' the yaller hat?"

Florian raised languid, bored eyes. "Oh! her? She ain't nobody but Ione Drought."

Aaron glared — but retained his tact. "Perduce me to her, will you?"

"Shuah! Anythin' to 'blige a frien'."

Ten minutes later the enslaved Aaron and a happiness-dazed Ione dislimned into the shadows of Blue Lake Park. Four pair of affianced eyes searched in vain for Aaron Segar. He had disappeared and for one glorious hour he forgot that love of woman had been his undoing — forgot everything save that he tightly clasped the warm, responsive hand of the woman who had been preordained as his.

Aaron Segar had fallen utterly, blindly, hopelessly, miserably in love!

Better men than Aaron Segar have fallen in love, but none more deeply. He told Ione all about it so often that he repeated himself. Finally he gave up in disgust the verbal attempts — declaring himself no orator — and took to verse:

> Ione your eys burn up my heart like fier
> and wen I say that I shure ant no lier
> Im fond of you so passinate and true
> I only wish you coud love me strong like I love you.
> yrs. respectfuly —
> AARON SEGAR.

Ione capitulated before the poetic shafts. Aaron wasn't any Robert Browning, but he, at least, was understandable. And from the outset Ione had been considerably dazed by Aaron's sudden passion and had been wary and sceptical. But a week proved to her beyond peradventure of doubt that his intentions were as honourable as they were obvious, and thereupon she brought into action the great fund of common sense with which she was endowed.

She gave in — with reserve. She let Aaron understand that he was being considered — seriously considered; that he might, in fact, presume to claim the perquisites of an engaged man. But she succeeded admirably in holding the deliriously happy man at sufficient distance to keep him in constant terror of losing her.

Ione was a new type to him. She was a girl whom the white folks instinctively and universally liked. She was quiet and not at all inclined to flamboyancy. The coloured folks kow-towed to her poise and ungrudgingly made a place for her on the topmost social stratum. She had never been deluged with masculine matrimonial attention, and it was her frank disbelief in her own colossal luck which kept her head on her shoulders until she had Aaron hooked and landed high and dry. And wiggling.

During the first week of his cyclonic courtship Aaron Segar struggled heroically to keep from her ears any morsel of gossip pertaining to his relations with the four amorous kitchen empresses at the Glen Ridge apartments. And then — because there was something about her that — Oh! well, you know, a feller jes' cain't help talkin'— he himself told her!

She listened attentively and with his final abjectly despairing words disengaged the hand he had been clutching.

" Now, honey . . ." he pleaded.

" How I to know I ain' jes' the fif', Aaron? "

" You is the fust."

" Bein' engage' is a kind of a habit what you is got, ain't it? "

" 'Tis now, sweetness. Befo', 'twas jes' a accident."

" Nev' heard of fo' things happenin' jes' so accidental."

" Did with me, hon! Them they wimmin jes' woul'n't lemme 'lone."

" Huh! They sho' Lawd must've been hahd up fo' a man."

" Tha's right, sweetness; that shuah is right. They must of been pow'ful hahd up fo' a man."

The completeness of his abnegation curbed her sarcasm. She was really sorry for Aaron and genuinely jealous on her own account for she admitted to herself what she was wise enough to keep from Aaron — she fairly worshipped him and above all else in the world she desired to become Mrs. Aaron Segar. She wanted Aaron, but she wanted him free of encumbrances or prior lien. Furthermore she had no intentions of 'lowin' no fo' brown hussies to make fumadiddles with the man what she was 'gage' to! All of which she confided in herself. To Aaron she merely presented a terse ultimatum.

"I ain't gwine live in the Glen Ridge pahtments, Aaron, twell them wimmin is went."

"You sho' ain't!" he echoed with vast sincerity.

"So what you is got to do befo' you make any mo' marriage talk with me is to git them away fum there."

"Huh! Whyn't you tell me to do sumpin' easy like to buy a limmysine or sumthin'?"

"Guess if'n you was much anxious to marry me, Aaron, you'd git rid of them wimmin pretty quick. Once they gits away fum there they ain't gwine bother you no mo'."

"I wants to git rid of them, hon. But how I is gwine do it?"

"Ain't they a old sayin', Aaron, 'bout true love knows how things is done?"

Aaron scratched his head. "Reckon they is, sweetness. An' I sho' is got the truest love. P'raps —" Suddenly he smiled. "If'n I was to git a good idee, Ione, reckon you'd help me out?"

She nodded. "Yep, Aaron: reckon I would."

"Then heah yo' chancst is, honey. Lis'en at what I got to seggest."

She listened.

NOT WISELY BUT TOO WELL 165

Ella Dungee descended from apartment 6 of the Glen Ridge to the back court where for five minutes she sought Aaron Segar. Failing to discover him she made her disgruntled way to the street. Once she had completely departed Aaron detached himself from the shadows of the section B stairway and mounted to apartment 6 where he presented himself, hat in hand, to Mrs. Jacob Hammond.

"Mawnin', Mis' Hammond."

"Good morning, Aaron."

"I brung up some of that roach powder. Beggin' yo' pahdon, Mis' Hammond —" as he cast a critical eye about the kitchen, "— but the tenints is all 'cusin' the roaches of stahtin' heah on 'count —'count —" he paused discreetly.

"On account of what?"

"On 'count Ella don't keep the kitchen so awful clean. Scusin' me sayin' that, Mis' Hammond — 'tain't meant fo' no 'flection on you, but —"

"What you say is all true, Aaron. For the past two or three weeks Ella has been a changed girl. I don't understand her at all. I'm not admitting it outside, but she has grown lazy and shiftless and indifferent and of recent weeks she has kept my kitchen looking like a pigpen."

"Yassum — she do that, sho' nuff, Mis' Hammond. I'se a clean man myse'f an' I loves cleanity, an' I says to myse'f Ella ain't the good cleaner what she useter be. Tha's what troubles all these heah se'vants, Mis' Hammond: they ain't know how to 'preciate a good job with quality folks like what you an' Mistuh Hammond is. Come they to git use' to it an' they c'mences stayin' home or else they gits lazy an' shif'less —"

"And Ella isn't the only one," said Mrs. Hammond wrathily. "Mrs. Gray's Fashion and Mrs. Connor's Mallissie —"

"Hmph!" disdainfully. "M'lissie is got the stayin' home fever, sho' nuff, Mis' Hammond. I kep' a-tellin' her an' a-tellin' her she di'n't 'preciate a nice place like what she had with Mis' Connor, but shucks! she ain't no dif'ent fum these other new-fangle' coloured gals — none of 'em ain't know when they is got sumthin' good."

"But what can we do about it?" exclaimed the good lady hopelessly. "We must have servants."

"Tha's so, Mis' Hammond: that shuah is so. Mis' Connor been make that ve'y indentital remark this mawnin' w'en I tell her that M'lissie warn't no mo' sick yestiddy than whut I is now. She say — jes' like what you said: 'I got to have a gal,' she say. Tha's how come I to git her Lily Belle."

"You obtained a new servant for Mrs. Connor?"

"Yassum, on 'count M'lissie was gittin' so wuthless."

Mrs. Hammond wrung her hands. "If you knew of a competent servant, Aaron, why didn't you tell me? If I could only get the right sort of a girl I wouldn't stand Ella another day."

Aaron's face brightened perceptibly. "They's Lily Belle's sister, now —"

"Lily Belle has a sister?"

"Yassum — an' seein' Lily Belle is mebbe gwine wuk fo' Mis' Connor, I been thinkin' Sarah might like to wuk heah. Co'se Sarah's a better gal'n what Lily Belle is —"

"What is she like, Aaron. Tell me all about her — please!"

"Huh! I been knowin' Lily Belle an' Sarah sencst they was knee-high to a pair of ducks, Mis' Hammond. They ain't nuthin' tall like the niggers what clutters up these heah kitchens. Ain't nuthin' fancy 'bout 'em an' they ain't got the haids all full up of sassiety. Both them gals is the best cooks whut is: waffles whut melts in yo' mouf an' broilin' steaks so's they's all charred on the youtside an' rare in the middle. An' they's the cleanest gals whut is. They even keeps they own rooms clean, Mis' Hammond, an' w'en a coloured gal keeps her own rooms clean, she is some cleanin' gal an' tha's the truth. Ain't neither of 'em no flossy dressers but they's pow'ful neat an' tidy, an'— nuther thing — they gits to wuk *early!*"

"There isn't a day of the past two weeks that Ella has gotten here before twenty minutes to eight."

"Law', Mis' Hammond — Sarah an' Lily Belle ain't know whut 'tis to git to no place of wuk later'n six-thutty. Las' lady Sarah wuk fo' useter tell me that when she'n her husband come out to breakfus' eight o'clock all the house'd be cleaned up an' breakfus' on table an' a fancy salid made fo' lunch. But I'se tellin' you right now, fair an' hones', Mis' Hammond — Sarah ain't gwine wuk fo' no th'ee-fifty a week less'n it's gwine be a pummanent place."

Mrs. Jacob Hammond sighed. A nonpareil — a quiet, efficient servant who wanted a *permanent* place! "I — I didn't know there were any servants like that any more, Aaron."

"They ain't, Mis' Hammond — on'y Lily Belle an' Sarah. Reckon you'd like to make talk with Sarah?"

"I certainly would. And you may tell her in advance, Aaron, that if I like her appearance I will start her in at four dollars a week with every Sunday afternoon off. When can I see her?"

"I'se gwine bring Lily Belle 'roun' heah at seven o'clock t'night, Mis' Hammond — so's she c'n make talk with Mis' Connor. I cou'd bring Sarah then."

"Please do."

Aaron grew cautious. "You sho' Ella's gwine be gone by that time? Bein' janitor heah I cain't 'ford to have these heah cooks knowin' I been buttin' on they business. Woul'n't do it nohow on'y I think so much of you an' Mistuh Hammond."

"I understand, Aaron — and I appreciate your interest tremendously. Here's fifty cents for you. I just simply can't tell you how grateful I am —"

"Tha's all right, Mis' Hammond. Nev' min' 'bout that fo' bits."

"But you must take it."

He fingered the coin affectionately. "No'm — I feel like it'd be an intrusion."

"You really must take that money, Aaron. This servant question is such a problem —"

"Yassum," rejoined Aaron fervently, as he dropped the coin into his pocket, "yo' sho' said sumthin' that time, Mis' Hammond."

He was whistling as he made his way downstairs. He was humming happily at eight-thirty that night as he sat in the street car with Ione Drought en route for Champion Moving Picture Theatre Number 2. And just about that time Mrs.

Jacob Hammond dropped in informally on Mrs. Percival Connor. Both good ladies were all of a flutter.

"My dear Mrs. Connor — I have just engaged a treasure: a veritable treasure!"

Mrs. Connor smiled. "Aaron was telling me all about it. I have engaged Lily Belle at four dollars a week. She offered to start in at three-fifty, but —"

"I'm starting Sarah at the same wages. I haven't felt so relieved and happy over the servant question in all my married life. I don't know if Lily Belle is anything like her sister, but if she is, she *looks* like a perfect gem."

"And she talks so intelligently. None of the society airs which irritate me so. She agreed to come Monday morning and Aaron vouched for her appearance promptly at six-thirty."

"Sarah starts in with me Monday morning, too. I'm going to discharge Ella Sunday afternoon when I pay her off."

"I shall do the same thing with Mallissie. I feel that we are very fortunate, my dear."

"We are. And we mustn't forget to be grateful to Aaron for our good luck."

The following morning Aaron Segar entered the kitchen of Mrs. Charles Gray. He was patently perturbed. "Mis' Gray — I b'lieves in a man doin' his duty."

"Yes, Aaron, so do I. What is the trouble now?"

"Ain't nothin' the trouble *now,* Mis' Gray. On'y if'n them chillun of your'n had of been killed by that truck they'd of been trouble a-plenty."

Mrs. Gray stiffened. She clutched weakly at the edge of the kitchen table. "What are you talking about, Aaron?"

"'Bout what happen jes' now down to Five Points. I been comin' 'crost the circle fum the grocer-shop an' a big ol' truck been takin' the curve at about thutty mile an hour. An' who should I see rompin' right 'crost the middle of that street but yo' two chillun!"

"My God! Aaron—"

"'Tain't nothin' to worry 'bout, Mis' Gray. I grab 'em an' pull 'em back befo' the truck done hit 'em. On'y it kind of made me mad, 'cause if'n that Fashi'n Wilson had of been watchin' them 'stead of makin' monkey eyes with ol' Florian Slappey who was loafin' 'roun' there, then mebbe you woul'n't of almos' had no chillun lef' a tall."

"Do you mean to tell me, Aaron, that Fashion allowed those two little darlings to walk alone into the middle of the street? Is that what you mean, Aaron?"

"'Tain't none of my business, Mis' Gray. . . ."

"It is your business, Aaron. Human life is everybody's business. I've suspected for some time that Fashion is very derelict in the way she looks after the children. Why, do you know, Aaron, that sometimes they come home actually bruised and scratched where they have fallen down?"

"*Tchk!* Sho' nuff, now, Mis' Gray!"

"That really is so. Fashion is hopeless."

"She ain't no wuss'n all the other city nu'ses, Mis' Gray," defended Aaron stoutly. "All of 'em lets the chillun run wild. It's a Gawd's mercy they ain't kilt ev'y day. 'Co'se maybe Fashi'n *is* a li'l mite mo' careless'n them other nu'ses, 'cause this ain't by no means the fust time I've saw —"

Mrs. Gray collapsed limply. "I simply cannot tell you how much I appreciate this, Aaron."

"Tha's all right, Mis' Gray. 'Co'se I'd be 'bliged if'n you woul'n't mention to Fashi'n was me that tol' you —"

"I won't, Aaron; I won't. But what am I to do? I'm not a strong woman, Aaron, and I can't run this apartment and take care of those two children alone."

"Guess they ain't nothin' you c'n do, Mis' Gray. Less'n you could git hol' of a gal like Pansy."

"Who is Pansy?"

"Gal I been knowin' fo' yeahs. She ain't highfalutin' like Fashi'n an' these other gals 'roun' the Glen Ridge. She's a Georgy nigger. Las' job she had was fo' a lady what had a 'pahtment one room bigger'n what you is got — an' th'ee chillun. Pansy useter do all the cookin' an' the housewuk an' take care of the two oldest chilluns fo' brawtus an' she useter say to me: 'Aaron, the wuk heah is so easy I kinder hates to take my week's wages.' Yassum, tha's 'zactly what she useter say, Mis' Gray."

"Where — where is Pansy now?"

"Right heah in town, Mis' Gray. She's kind of lookin' fo' a *pummanent* job.'

"Aaron!"

A few minutes later Aaron descended the steps, wealthier by a dollar. "Yassum," he called back cheerily, "I'll bring Pansy heah t'night shuah at seven-thutty — after Fashi'n is gone. An' if'n you like her I reckon she c'n come to wuk Monday mawnin'."

Before he reached the basement he was intercepted by Mrs. Franklin Carruthers, who summoned him to apartment 17. "Aaron, did you succeed in seeing Mary?"

"Yassum, I seen Mary, sho' nuff."

"Did she have a place?"

"No'm, she ain't had no place. Course'n she had offers, but Mary's right 'tic'lar an' she wants a pummanent place."

"Do you think she'll work for me, Aaron? Do you — really?"

"Sho' does, Mis' C'ruthers. I does, sho' nuff — an' that ain't no lie. Mary most'n always goes by my adwice. She says she'll be heah t'night at eight o'clock sha'p — soon's she's sho' Gussie Muck is gone. An' then if you likes her you c'n let Gussie go when you pays her off on Sunday an' Mary'll be heah Monday mawnin' sha'p at six-thutty."

"I'm so grateful to you, Aaron. I'll confess to you that Gussie was getting positively unbearable. I didn't see how I could continue to put up with her, but in these days of servant famine I couldn't see my way clear to letting her go. You, Aaron, have been my Aladdin."

"Yassum, I sho' have. You done said it that time. An' I understan's jes' how you feel. Gussie Muck is one mo' wuthless gal. But Mary! Hones', Mis' C'ruthers, that gal'd ruther cook an' clean house than eat, an' that sho' is the truth. Yassum — jes' sho's my name's Aaron Segar!"

On Sunday afternoon the Mesdames Carruthers, Connor, Gray and Hammond discharged the four fiancés of Aaron Segar. On Sunday night the four worthy ladies retired early that Monday morning might sooner arrive. They were bulwarked behind the happy thought that this glorious Monday morning was to bring to each of them a servant who desired nothing so much as hard and permanent work.

Early Monday morning the Mesdames Carruthers, Connor, Gray and Hammond opened their eyes upon a sky of gray overcast with low-hanging, swiftly-scudding clouds. Each became aware of a void. Mrs. Charles Gray was first in action. Her two children were yelling lustily for the dear departed Fashion.

Aaron Segar was summoned to the kitchen of each of the four ladies in turn. To each he made the same shocked speech —

"I 'clare to goodness gracious if'n that gal don't beat all creation. Spec' they ain't *no* gals you c'n trus'. Take my oaf I'd of swore she'd be heah this mawnin' fust crack of day. I'se mighty sorry 'cause tha's what makes white folks look down on us coloured people w'en we treats you-all like that. Downright shame — tha's what I calls it."

To each he gave a solemn promise to search for the delinquent treasure; to each he reported two hours later that she was not to be found. Whereupon four highly-nervous and thoroughly disgruntled ladies entered four automobiles and placatingly sought four discharged servants — only to discover that they had obtained overnight easier positions at greater wages.

That day and the next and the next there was a pall of gloom over apartments six, nine, fourteen and seventeen. They didn't blame Aaron. In fact, they were sorry for him, he was so evidently cut up over the defection of his four servants. He railed against the quartet in particular and the genus housegirl in general.

But in the privacy of his basement apartment there was no hint of gloom. By some miracle it had worked. Gussie and Mallissie and Fashion and Ella had departed for sections of the city unknown. Small likelihood that they would bother him further now that the dangerous element of propinquity had been removed. He was by nature sufficiently insouciant to worry over the troubles of the immediate present only. Once again life had taken unto itself a roseate hue: a hue which it retained until Thursday afternoon.

On Thursday afternoon Aaron Segar, elegantly groomed, paraded proudly up Highland Avenue with the beloved Ione on his arm. He had eyes for nothing save her radiance and her orbs were modestly downcast which is why neither of them had an opportunity to dodge Mrs. Jacob Hammond who veered around the corner of Arlington Avenue and clutched Ione by the arm.

"Sarah!" cried Mrs. Hammond.

"Y-y-yassum!" gasped Ione.

"Where in the world have you been? Why didn't you come to work Monday?"

"I — I been sick," faltered Ione. Aaron rallied loquaciously to her support.

NOT WISELY BUT TOO WELL 175

"Yassum — she been sick, sho' nuff. Jes' met her, I did, an' I was givin' her a talkin'-to on account she didn't show up fo' wuk like she says she was gwine do, an' she tell me she been sick. If'n you don' b'lieve it you c'n call Florian Slappey, sec'terry of The Sons & Daughters of I Will Arise, an' he'll tell you she's been gittin' her sick benyfit." It was a glorious bluff, but it worked. Mrs. Hammond did not know that coloured insurance fraternities pay no benefits for illnesses lasting less than one week.

"But you are well now, aren't you, Sarah?"

"Yassum, I'se well now," answered Ione eagerly. "Well's I ev' was."

"And you still want the place?"

"If it's pummanent, Mis' Hammond. I was gwine to see you 'bout it this evenin'. . . ."

"It's permanent," wheedled Mrs. Hammond pathetically. "The position is yours for ever if you want it. Please don't disappoint me again. May I count on you for tomorrow morning?"

"You sho' c'n. . . ."

Aaron gave a sudden gasp. He clutched Ione's wrist. His eyes opened until it seemed that they must pop from the sockets. Small beads of cold perspiration stood out on his brow. But he was too late. The little car pulled up at the curb and the Mesdames Franklin Carruthers and Percival Connor alighted. Each of them pounced upon the petrified Ione —

"Mary!" cried Mrs. Carruthers.

"Lily Belle!" exclaimed Mrs. Connor.

"Uh-huh . . . yassum . . ." trembled Ione weakly.

"Why didn't you come to work Monday morning?" chorused the newcomers. Ione said nothing. Aaron Segar said the same thing.

"There is some mistake," cut in Mrs. Hammond icily. "Isn't there, Sarah?"

"Y-y-yassum: they's a mistake."

"They sho' is!" muttered Aaron to himself.

"Why do you persist in addressing her as 'Sarah'?" interrogated Mrs. Connor frigidly. "Her name is Lily Belle and I hired her to come to work for me Monday morning."

"But — but —" groped Mrs. Carruthers blindly, "she agreed to come to work for *me* Monday morning and she said her name was Mary!"

Mrs. Hammond whirled on Aaron. "What is the meaning of this?" she snapped.

Aaron took one wild glance at the three faces. His knees quaked. His eyes rolled toward Ione, girl of his choice. His muscular fingers tightened around her arm and he gave her a violent jerk. Man and woman, they started up Arlington avenue at a pace which should have entitled them to the heel-and-toe championship of the world.

"S-s-s-see you-all ladies later," chattered Aaron over his shoulder. "We is got to be goin'!"

Two blocks farther on they paused and faced one another. Aaron mopped his face with a lavender handkerchief.

"Ione," he proclaimed solemnly, "I is been thinkin'."

"So is I, Aaron."

"I is been thinkin', Ione, that mebbe it might be po' business takin' you to the Glen Ridge 'pahtments to live."

"Reckon 'twould, Aaron."

"I — I so't of favour the idee, hon, that mebbe I'll git me a job out to the Ensley steel mill. They ain't no wimmin out there. I guess that'd be safer fo' a man like what I is."

"Yes," answered his bride-to-be significantly, "I reckon it would!"

BACKFIRE

BACKFIRE

"'TIS repeated myse'f over an' over again enough times a'ready," remarked the ebony gentleman at the head of the battered table, "an' seems like by this time yo'd see they ain't no use argifyin' no further."

"But I is the big loser," mournfully answered the dandified young negro two stacks of chips removed, "an' seems like yo'd ought to stake me some — jes' a li'l bit."

"You ain't in Atlanta, Mistuh Stiggars: this heah place is Anniston, Alabama."

"Jes' a few dollars —?"

"Reckon we-all ain't in the cha'ity business, Mistuh Stiggars. If'n you want to stay in this heah game jes' tickle the bank with a li'l coin."

"Huh! You know well's me that Ise broke. Ain't even one of you gen'lemen gwine len' me five dollars?"

He glanced appealingly around the crack-topped table. Five stony faces gave wordless answer of negation. "Jes' five dollars? Or fo'? Or th'ee? Ise been sweetenin' ev'y pot —"

"Lis'en heah to whut I is sayin', Mistuh Stiggars: if'n you ain't got no mo' money you is delayin' the game. I ain't aimin' to keep none of yo' glory fum you. You is contribbited 'bout a hund'ed an' fifty dollars —"

"Hund'ed an' sixty-th'ee, fifty."

"An' s'far's I know they ain't nobody in this

heah neighbourhood gwine len' you no money to follow where that is gone at. Yo' credick would be better, Brother Stiggars, if'n you wasn't sech a rotten poker player."

"I ain't askin' on'y. . . ."

The local spokesman caught sight of a languid young negro who leaned apathetically against a battered bureau; a young man of superlative elegance and conscious ego. From the top of his carefully brushed Velour hat to the tips of his scintillating russet shoes, he bespoke affluence and contemptuous ennui.

"Over yonder," said the Annistonian, indicating the sartorial triumph by the bureau, "is Mistuh Florian Slappey of Bummin'ham. Brother Slappey has mo' money'n he knows what to do with. If'n he is foolish 'nough to len' you some . . ." and the speaker shrugged his shoulders to signify that he washed his hands of the affair.

Selkirk Stiggars shoved his chair back from the table and rose to his six feet of height. In elegance of dress he ran Florian a close second. In physique he was an easy first. He towered menacingly above the patently bored gentleman from Birmingham but in his eyes glowed a light which was unmistakably composed of equal portions of worry and supplication.

The five other players meticulously piled their chips into stacks of red, white and blue. A stranger had knocked upon their gates and they had taken him in — good and proper. One hundred and sixty-three dollars and fifty cents of good Atlanta money had enriched the coffers of five Annistonians. It had been an epoch-making windfall.

An oil lamp on the washstand in the corner sent its weak, flickering light to all corners of the room, playing weirdly on the set faces of Anniston's premier poker players, and causing grotesque shadows to dance on the walls. As the stranger rose and approached Florian Slappey they allowed themselves to relax somewhat from the strain of inflated stakes and bloated pots.

"Mistuh Slappey?"

Florian's eyes were raised slowly without show of special interest. "Yeh?"

"My name's Stiggars — Selkirk Stiggars of Atlanta. Ise Past Gran' Royal Mona'ch of The To'ch Bearers of Glory, Council Number Thutteen. Is you a member of that lodge?"

"No," answered Florian wearily, "I ain't."

"Ise a K. P."

"I ain't."

"Sho'ly you an' me is feller Masons?"

"Nope."

"I b'longs to the Baptis' chu'ch."

"Ise a Methodis'."

The lack of fraternity was appalling. The stranger was forced to a new tack. "Is you the Flo'ian Slappey what won twen'y-five hund'ed dollars in the Pool an' Ginuwine lott'ry 'bout six weeks ago?"

"Ise him," answered Florian with a hint of pardonable hauteur.

Stiggars' hand caught that of Florian and crushed it. "I is sho' d'lighted to meet up with you, Mistuh Slappey. I sho' is. We is heard 'bout you over to Atlanta."

"That so?"

"Co'se! Sech a spoht as you is. . . ."

"We ain't nev' heard of you over to Bummin'ham."

Selkirk Stiggars was momentarily nonplussed. Nothing seemed to pique Florian's interest: not even the Open Sesame of flattery. Selkirk made a direct frontal attack. "Ise broke."

"You sho' ac' thataway."

"But luck's jes' beginnin' to break my way —"

"Yeh! I noticed them fo' nines you jes' held 'gainst that straight flush."

"— An' if'n I c'n borry five dollars —"

"My business is real 'state — not money lendin'."

With the dexterity of a master of legerdemain, Mr. Selkirk Stiggars detached from his cerise scarf a veritable headlight. "This heah di'mon', Misto' Slappey, is gua'anteed fo'teen carat."

"Hmph! Gua'anteed by which?"

"By the jooller which sol' it to me."

"I ain't even know his name."

"— An' if'n yo'll lemme have fifty dollars on it fo' jes' 'bout twen'y minutes —"

"Haw!" ejaculated Florian with ponderous irony. "Reckon you thinks I is a Anniston nigger sho' nuff."

"I'll add this to the s'curity," and Selkirk slipped a twin diamond from a finger of the left hand.

If Florian was impressed by the glittering brilliance he gave no sign. He produced a silver-plated cigarette case from his pocket, extracted therefrom a Turkish cigarette which he tapped reflectively on his fingernail and then lighted with exasperating lack of haste. He inhaled deeply and blew a puff of the fragrant smoke into the face of Mr. Selkirk Stiggars.

BACKFIRE

"Not a thing stirrin'," he responded briefly.

"Them di'mon's —"

"Nev' did like di'mon's."

"You ain't 'sinuatin'—?"

"I ain't 'sinuatin' nothin', 'ceptin' Flo'rian Slappey ain't never takes no chancsts."

Selkirk Stiggars gazed hopelessly about the dingy, dusty room with its battered furniture and its curtains discreetly drawn against the prying eyes of the police. The atmosphere was redolent of the odour of vile cigars, the room clouded with the rancid smoke. One of the fortunate poker players seized the moment to rattle a stack of blue chips. The clicking of what had recently been his money was too much for Selkirk.

He had driven into Anniston that evening from Atlanta behind the wheel of a handsome limousine; one hundred and sixty-four dollars in his pockets. Fifty cents had gone for dinner and the balance had been his admission ticket to a poker game. Selkirk had entered that poker game very confident that he would win a comfortable amount, lord it over the provincial darkies for a while and then seek new pastures. And now eleven o'clock had come and he was as clean of money as a fish of legs, his credit rating unknown, his scintillant collateral gazed upon with frank distrust. He was a stranger in a strange land.

Without money he was helpless. So too was the limousine which he had driven royally into Anniston, for money means gasoline for the tank and oil for the crank-case, and the automobile was sadly bereft of both.

The car! The car was worth money. So was

Florian. He clutched his unwilling benefactor by the shoulder with a grip which caused Florian to wince and shoved him toward the door. "If its jes' s'curity you is after, Mistuh Slappey. . . ."

"Reckon you ain't got no s'curity I is interest' in."

"Huh! Guess I is."

"Whar 'tis?"

"Outside."

Florian's eyes narrowed. "Outside?"

"My automobile!"

"Huh?"

"Heah's the how of it, Mistuh Slappey. I done 'scovered that these heah small-town niggers don' know nothing 'bout poker. Craps is they game. But poker — the reason they is won fum me is 'cause I was gittin' onto they system. If'n I gits me another stake I'll clean 'em flat. You c'n see that, sho'— it's plain as a nigger in a snowstorm. But I needs that other stake, Brother Slappey, an' I is willin' to take a chancst —"

"I ain't."

"— Nor neither I ain't askin' you to. Seein' as you won't 'cept my di'mon's as s'curity, how 'bout lendin' me five hund'ed on that car?"

Florian hesitated — and was lost. Ever since he had come into possession of twenty-five hundred dollars by a lucky lottery guess he had yearned passionately for an automobile of his very own. But automobiles come high and Florian was fair canny. He wanted the car. . . .

"Reckon you think I is a millionaire."

"Five hund'ed —"

"— Is five hund'ed. An' b'sides, I don't carry that much with me — usually."

"How much is you got?"

Florian shrugged. "Dunno . . . but I'm sho' 'tain't more'n two hund'ed."

The minds of the two men leaped to opposite conclusions from the one premise. Selkirk Stiggars was a poker egomaniac and was gripped by an overpowering hunch. He knew that with a stake of two hundred dollars he could win back all that he had lost — and a good deal more. He wasn't selling the car — it would merely become a bailment in the hands of Florian Slappey: a pawn for a few hours.

Florian figured contrariwise. A keen analyst of his fellow-beings he recognized in the egocentric Mr. Stiggars a fully developed individual of the genus sucker. And he knew that if he could secure the limousine — which he had previously examined very carefully and appraised as worth not a cent less than fifteen hundred dollars — for two hundred, it would become his property at that price.

"Two hund'ed ain't nothin'," sneered Stiggars.

"You 'spec' to git it back, don't you?"

"Sho'."

"You ain't sellin' it to me. What's it matter how much you gits on it if'n you gwine redeem it right back? I take the car an' give you two hund'ed. You c'n git that they car back fum me any time befo' seven 'clock tomorrow mawnin' by payin' me two hund'ed an' twen'y-five dollars — cash money."

They haggled. They argyfied. They finally

reached a decision — Florian's decision. He had been wise enough to discern that all of the aces were in his hand and he played them. He gave Mr. Selkirk Stiggars two hundred dollars and directed the attention of the assemblage to the terms of the transaction. The two hundred dollars represented a loan for which the limousine stood unprotestingly as security. The time limit for redeeming the pledge was seven o'clock the following morning. Failure to redeem within the time limit acted as an automatic conveyance in fee simple to Florian Slappey. But before turning back to the poker table, the disgruntled Stiggars, acutely aware of the fact that he was a victim of business acumen and adverse circumstance, transfixed Florian with a stare which caused that gentleman to tremble beneath his silk shirt.

" 'Member this in yo' haid, Mistuh Slappey — Ise a man of my word and you is got to be a man of your'n. If'n you sh'd be so unfortinate as to try any fumadiddles with me, jes' don' forgit that I warned you I was plumb bad — bad all the way th'ough."

The ensuing hours proved that he had spoken part truth at least. He was certainly a bad poker player — bad all the way through. At three minutes after seven o'clock in the morning the game disbanded after a heart-breaking hand which started at 6:56 in which Selkirk Stiggars held an ace-high flush against a pat full house — kings up. Better men than Stiggars have been fooled into believing a pat full meant a low flush or straight. But none have been fooled more thoroughly from a financial point of view.

Florian yawned. He oozed through the door and into the street. He approached the limousine — his limousine. He stepped within and tentatively poked the luxurious upholstery. It was the crowning touch of affluence. He touched the starter button and the rythmic hum of the motor wafted back to his ears in pleasing symphony.

On the sidewalk stood Selkirk Stiggars, completely surrounded by the gentlemen who had relieved him of his money. Selkirk's cerise necktie was awry, his hat was crushed and shoved back upon his bullet head, there was blood in his eye. The strong breeze of early morning whipped back his coat and Florian caught a disquieting bulge in the right hip pocket. Florian had a constitutional aversion to hip pockets which bulged, nor did he relish the glare which Selkirk Stiggars furnished gratis. Florian reached a decision. He decided to place a maximum of distance between himself and Mr. Stiggars in a minimum of time.

He waved an insouciant farewell and wisely restrained a gay little pleasantry having to do with Mr. Stiggars' poker-playing abilities. He let in the gears and the car rolled ahead. Something prompted Florian to keep his eyes straight to the front. He mounted a gentle acclivity at high speed and not until he hit the descent on the other side of the ridge was he able to shake himself free from the menace of the Stiggars' stare.

At a filling station on the outskirts of Anniston he replenished his gas tank and filled his crank case. Then he headed for the open country and let the car out, reclining luxuriously against the cushions and revelling in an intoxicating feeling of proprietorship.

He made the journey from Anniston to Birmingham in record time. He parked his car at darktown's civic centre: Eighteenth street, north, between Third and Fourth avenues. He stretched his legs, cut off the ignition and stepped to the sidewalk where he bumped into Pliny Driver — melancholy and trusted employé of the City Ice Company. Pliny inquired quite naturally about the car and Florian answered nonchalantly: " Bought it."

" Whar at? "

" Anniston. Off'n a feller name of Stiggars."

" How much? "

Florian did not mean to tell an untruth. But sometimes naked truth is entirely too naked. And a few hundred dollars more or less — anyway, the words slipped out before he was conscious of them. " Eight hund'ed dollars."

Pliny's whooshy whistle of undisguised admiration amply repaid Florian for the slight exaggeration. " You sho' is became one of these heah bloated democrats, Flo'ian."

" Well," airily, " I ain't nev' yet met myse'f when I was broke."

Pliny reported Florian's financial flyer to Lawyer Evans Chew and Lawyer Evans Chew told it to Dr. Vivian Simmons, M.D., who maintained a suite of offices on the same floor of the Penny Prudential Bank Building. Dr. Simmons told Clarence Carter and Clarence passed the story on to Mr. and Mrs. Elias Rush. By six o'clock that evening all of the members in coloured social circles were in possession of the facts, some of which facts were actually accurate. With a single exception they expressed a unanimity of admiration.

The exception was Sally Crouch, the voluminous proprietress of the Cozy Home Hotel for Coloured. She shrugged her ample shoulders with sceptical disdain: "Sho', that nigger ain't nev' seed no eight hund'ed dollars!"

"You is disremember, Sally, that 'tain't so long 'go he won twen'y-five hund'ed dollars in the Pool an' Ginuwine lott'ry."

Sally had not forgotten the episode. She had cause to recall every humiliating detail. Those were the days when Florian had been penniless and had courted Sally Crouch for her money. Luck had broken his way at the eleventh hour and he had turned up missing at his wedding. Sally was the forsaken bride and forsaken brides neither forget nor forgive easily. Said she: "I ain't nev' seed no money 'roun' that they Flo'ian Slappey! Maybe so it's all right but it sho' soun's fishy to me. Seems like somebody had ought to fin' out the pertickerlers."

The story of Sally's plain-spoken doubt was also passed from lip to lip. With embellishments.

For eight months Florian had held undisputed sway as masculine mentor of the younger social set. His acquisition of the limousine bade fair to make the tenure hereditary. He was gloriously generous in his magnificence and many a dusky damsel learned that he could drive with one hand over the roads between Birmingham and its myriad suburbs: Bessemer, Ensley, Woodlawn, Pratt City, East Lake, Fairfield. . . . Each and every one of them sought to ensnare him with her feminine charms, but Florian was as frank as he was wary. " Me — Ise off of women absotively an' ontirely! "

Occasionally Florian condescended to collect a few dollars by wildcat taxicab work, thereby courting durance vile because of the lack of a commercial license. But even with that the car was an expense which Florian could ill afford. Florian's nature, fortunately, was such that worry of the morrow did not often disturb the tranquillity of today.

Not since the winning of the now famous Florian Slappey Gig in the Genuine lottery — paying him twenty-five hundred dollars for the one he had timidly invested — had Florian been so excruciatingly happy. His bliss was intensive. He received adulation and envy in great, luscious gobs.

But it was too good to last — and it didn't. The explosion occurred one Saturday evening while Florian was curled up in the driver's seat of his car, immersed in the column of negro news which appears once a week in *The Birmingham Ledger.* On the opposite page was a double-column headline and beneath the headline a story of considerable personal interest to Florian.

GEORGIA CHAUFFEUR IS
ROBBED OF HIS CAR BY
BANDIT NEAR ANNISTON

MASKED HIGHWAYMAN SUPPOSED
TO HAVE BROUGHT CAR TO BIR-
MINGHAM — POLICE ON
LOOKOUT

Instinct prompted Florian to a perusal of the

story. He waded through the elegant display of adjectivial reportorial imagination —

> Held up shortly before reaching Anniston while en route to Birmingham while driving a limousine belonging to Robert J. Barbour of Peachtree street, Atlanta; Beauregard Tuggle, chauffeur, was robbed of his car and severely beaten in a terrific battle.
>
> Tuggle was driving the car from Atlanta to meet his employer, Mr. Barbour, who arrived in Birmingham recently from Memphis and registered at the Molton Hotel. According to Tuggle's straightforward and graphic story he was held up by a masked bandit shortly before arriving in Anniston, and was relieved of his car and nearly two hundred dollars in cash. After the desperate battle he was left bound and gagged by the roadside.
>
> The car has a Georgia license, No. 1981763. A reward of $500 has been offered by Mr. Barbour for the return of the car and the capture of the bandit. Both car and bandit are thought to be in or near Birmingham.
>
> The fight with the bandit was a thrilling one, according to Tuggle's story. He was attacked—

Florian's brow wrinkled in perplexity. He had a haunting idea that all was not as it should be. He became suspicious of the fact that he had been trimmed, that he was a come-on, a receiver of stolen goods that were dangerous to possess. He knew, and yet he verified his knowledge. He alighted and walked to the rear of the car. The figures 1981763 blazed up at him mockingly from the license tag.

He climbed into the car and sank limply into his seat. He understood for the first time why the suave Mr. Selkirk Stiggars had been willing to pledge a fifteen hundred dollar car for a paltry two hundred dollars. He recalled the hard look of Mr. Stiggars' eyes, the belligerent swing to the Stiggars' shoulders. Florian had met more than one bad nigger in his time and he now realized that Mr. Stiggars was all of that — and more.

He figured it all out. One, Beauregard Tuggle, had been relieved of Mr. Barbour's car near Anniston. The highwayman, under the deceiving name of Selkirk Stiggars, had wormed into a poker game with the money he had taken from the heroic chauffeur and after losing that, had let his car go for two hundred. That the two hundred had followed the trail blazed by the first hundred and fifty did not particularly interest Florian.

He writhed as he envisioned the Stiggars chortle of glee in the knowledge that Florian had taken unto himself a property liable to land him in the county jail. He remembered the credence which had been given Sally Crouch's sceptical story. There were folks — coloured folks — who would rejoice to see him hoist by his own petard.

He shrugged. He was stung for two hundred dollars. Of course, there was a reward extant — a reward of five hundred. Florian wanted that reward. Five hundred dollars would leave a balance on the credit side of the ledger. The trouble was that while he would have little difficulty in returning the car, he fancied that there would be considerable opposition on the part of Mr. Stiggars should he happen to meet him and suggest that Mr. Stiggars submit to arrest.

A negro boy strolled northward on Eighteenth street, whistling. He paused near Florian's car and Florian fancied that his eyes were focussed on the license number. The boy resumed his walk. The whistling had ceased. Florian experienced a cold chill like the first touch of an annual malarial attack.

He saw a policeman on the corner, the blue coat — as usual — unbuttoned. He realized that the policeman at whom he gazed, in common with every other member of the city force, was on the lookout for Georgia license number 1981763. Fear of the police was a novel experience; a sensation far from pleasant.

Florian Slappey was worried. He banished all thought of the five hundred dollars reward and bethought himself ways and means of getting rid of the car. Obviously the first step was —

He was an ingenious man and a man of action. He started up his motor, let in his gears and sped down the alley bisecting the block between Third and Fourth avenues. He emerged on Seventeenth street, turned south and brought his car to a halt near the curb.

Dusk had merged into night. The arc lamp on the corner spluttered disconsolately. No human was in sight. A South Ensley car shot by the corner, out-bound . . . then all was quiet again. Florian worked swiftly. He raised the seat cushion, found a pair of pliers, and within one minute and ten seconds the damning Georgia license had splashed into the sewer. Then, without regard to speed limit, Florian swung into Third avenue and so back to the parking space from which he had started a few minutes earlier.

He was temporarily relieved, but far from satisfied. The situation was one requiring expert advice. It presented infinite possibilities — both for benefit and for harm. Florian did not tarry. He made haste to the offices of Lawyer Evans Chew and ten minutes later the dignified, be-spectacled coloured attorney was in possession of the facts. His first query was disconcerting: "How much you paid for that car, Brother Slappey?"

"Two hund'ed dollars."

"You done said eight hund'ed befo'."

Florian made an impatient gesture. "Co'se I did. What you 'spec' me to say? Might's well make 'em believe a plen'y. But I ain't come up heah to make talk 'bout whether I 'zaggerated on the price. I wants yo' legal 'pinion."

Lawyer Chew stared ominously at his vis-a-vis. "Brother Slappey — you is shuah in bad."

"Hmph! Guess I don' need no lawyer to tell me that."

"They is grave danger that you have hopelessly 'criminated yo'se'f both by telling an untruth regeardin' the original purchase price an' also likewise by th'owing away the Geo'gia license tag. Destruction of 'criminating evidence, Brother Slappey, has been held by all the Co'ts of the land to be constructive evidence of guilty knowledge."

"I is got the guilty knowledge all right, Lawyer Chew. So's all the p'lice in Birmin'ham. Question is: what is I to do?"

Lawyer Chew rose and approached his dusty bookshelves. He solemnly and absorbedly consulted a musty legal tome which Florian was fortunately unaware bore the title "Pomeroy's Equity Jurisprudence." Finally Chew delivered his decision.

"You is got to get rid of that automobile!"

"Pshaw! Is you had to do all that studyin' to tell me that?"

"I never risk giving advice," retorted the lawyer with dignity, "until I have reinforced myse'f with a p'rusal of the latest dicta an' decision."

Florian scratched his head. Lawyer Chew was too vague and impersonal for him. "All right," he said at length, "Ise got to git rid of the car. Now s'pose you read some mo' out of that they book an' tell me how I is to do it."

"You stands in the lights of a receiver of stolen propitty," intoned Chew, "an' as such you ain't got any right to keep it."

"Golly! We is been agree' on that fo' a half hour."

"The title of the man from which you bought the car was a bad title in the eyes of the law an' the fac' that you is an innocent thi'd pa'ty don' do you no good where the true owner is conce'ned at." Lawyer Chew believed in handing out a surfeit of undigestible legal axioms in return for a fee.

"'Bout that rewa'd, though —?"

"Ah! The rewa'd! O'dna'ily I'd say you should see Mr. Barbour of Atlanta — the on'y hitch thereto bein' that he's li'ble to think you is in cahoots with the highwayman."

"The feller what hel' up his shoffer?"

"Yes. 'Course we mought go up to the Molton an' take a chancst —"

"Of gittin' 'rested?"

"They's a chance, of course. But, on the other hand, they is the pos'bility that you will git back yo' two hund'ed an' maybe th'ee hund'ed dollars mo'. An' as we are 'greed that the car must be returned —"

Florian rose resignedly. "You go with me?"

"As yo' lawyer. . . ."

"Reckon I need you?"

"Reckon you do, Flo'ian. You is li'ble to tell too much truth!"

Within a half hour the two nervous negroes were at the Molton Hotel and the clerk had notified Mr. Barbour that two coloured men wished an interview with him regarding the missing automobile. They were sent up to his room and found themselves a bit reassured as they gazed into the quizzical grey eyes of an overlarge man whom they instinctively recognized as a Southerner born and bred. "Thank Gawd!" muttered the attorney to himself, "that he ain't no Yankee."

"What do you boys know about my car?" queried Barbour.

"A heap, Mr. Barbour," came Chew's ready answer. "Thisyer is Flo'ian Slappey; a chu'ch man an' one of the mos' respective citizens of our coloured c'mmunity."

"I shuah is," echoed Florian.

Barbour smiled genially. "And you?"

"Evans Chew, suh: an attorney licensed to practice befo' all the Co'ts of the sove'eign State of Alabama. Flo'ian has became my client in this matter under c'nsideration."

"I see. And your friend Florian is the man who knows all about my automobile?"

"Perzac'ly. In brief, Misto' Barbour, Flo'ian has yo' limmysine."

"Where is it?"

"Downstairs on the Fif' avenue side. I wants you to un'erstan', Mr. Barbour, that Flo'ian is an hones' man an' when he read in the *Ledger* 'bout the five hund'ed dollars rewa'd, he was all fo' retu'nin' it to you an' nev' sayin' nothin' 'bout being paid fo' his honesty. But I says to him, I says: 'Brother Slappey — I got a hunch Mr. Barbour is a lib'al man an' he'd sho' pay you the five hund'ed dollars reward if'n he knew you had been stung.'"

"Stung?"

"Yassuh. You see, suh, 'tis thisaway: Flo'ian was umfortunate enough to buy yo' car fum the highwayman what stold it fum yo' shoffer!"

"A-a-ah! Suppose you sit down and tell me all about it."

Lawyer Chew started the story. Florian interrupted. Chew resumed. Florian interrupted again — fearful that some vital detail tending toward the eventual return of his two hundred dollars might be omitted. And finally the harassed attorney with his ponderous phraseology threw up his hands: "If'n you think you can tell it better'n me, Flo'ian — go ahead."

Florian may not have told it better — but he certainly told more of it. His recital became an impassioned plea for the reimbursement of his two hundred dollars. He supplied details which the lawyer had never heard. He even insisted that he had known all along that something was wrong and that out of the natural honesty of his nature he had risked his two hundred dollars in the altruistic attempt to return the car to its rightful owner.

Robert J. Barbour of Peachtree street, Atlanta, listened with quiet, unsmiling amusement. He had lived his life in contact with the society city negroes of the south and he knew them and their eccentricities. Therefore, he knew exactly what portions of Florian's story to accept and what to reject. When the tale was finished he delivered his verdict.

"I believe you paid the two hundred dollars for the car, Florian — and I'll make it up to you if I find the car in good condition. As for the other three hundred — you can have that when you find the highwayman and deliver him over to me. Under the terms of my offer I am not bound to pay you a cent — but I'm not anxious to see you lose two hundred dollars through me."

Florian exhaled a sigh of infinite relief. He escorted Mr. Barbour to the Fifth avenue side of the hotel and a half-hour spin over the Norwood Boulevard convinced Mr. Barbour that the car was in exceptionally good trim. Whereupon the two hundred dollars which Florian had originally paid out was returned to him in full, with the doubtful promise of the additional three hundred in the event of the capture of the bandit.

The two negroes walked down Twentieth street together. "My fee," suggested Lawyer Chew delicately, "is ten dollars."

"Whut? Ten dolla's?"

"You heard me, Flo'ian."

"Fo' a half hour's wuk?"

"Perfessional services."

"Huh! Graft!"

"I have earned it, and I must insist —"

Florian sadly delivered over two five-dollar bills. "W'en a lawyer says he's got to *insist* on havin'

BACKFIRE 201

money, Brother Chew — I got more sense'n to think I c'n git out of payin' it."

"Thank you." Chew pocketed the bills. "And at any future time you require my se'vices: if you meet Selkirk Stiggars, for example —"

"I'll need you then to 'fend me fum a cha'ge of manslaughter," snapped Florian venomously.

Florian's psychic condition regarding a meeting with Mr. Selkirk Stiggars, bandit, were an admixture of boundless hope and abiding fear. Should he meet Mr. Stiggars and be able to hold him until the iron fingers of the law could grasp the Stiggars windpipe, he would be richer by three hundred dollars and a big winner on the deal — even counting the cost of upkeep.

Three hundred dollars was three hundred dollars; but, reflected the perturbed Florian — Mr. Stiggars was Mr. Stiggars. He fancied that Mr. Stiggars might register somewhat too strenuous objections should he undertake to hand him over to the police. To Florian's knowledge road-agents had a congenital antipathy to jails. Besides, Florian was far from sure that he was physically able to detain Mr. Stiggars, even should he care to make the attempt. He envisioned the colossal bulk of Mr. Stiggars and the baleful glare of the bloodshot Stiggars' eyes. Florian thought Stiggars and then he thought three hundred dollars. He couldn't decide. He had a hunch that he was destined to meet Mr. Stiggars before the passing of very many days —

He did. It happened Monday night while Florian was en route — afoot — to escort Miss Gussie Muck to the movies. A heavy hand fell positively upon Florian's shoulder and a shadow bulked ominously behind him.

"Mistuh Slappey!"

Florian knew the voice. He had heard it rumble from behind a dwindling stack of chips — "Raise you five dolla's. . . ." He was face to face with the practical necessity for the decision at which he had been unable to arrive in theory. The situation was, to say the least, annoying.

"Mistuh Slappey!"

Florian accelerated. "Ise busy —"

"Sa-a-ay! Lis'en heah. . . ."

He listened. Something in the other's nuance informed him that listening was strictly in order. He turned. His face broke into a warm, friendly, welcoming smile and his right hand came out in effusive greeting. "I'm dawg'd if'n tain't Mistuh Stiggars!"

"That's which," came the unsmiling retort.

"How you is, Brother Stiggars?"

"Tol'able. I wants to make talk with you."

"Tomorrow mawnin' at nine 'clock —"

"T'night. Now."

"You got to excuse me, Brother Stiggars, 'cause I is got a pressin' 'gagement with a lady."

"You is got a 'gagement with me — immedjit."

"But, Brother Stiggars —"

"— An' if'n you don' keep it chancsts is you won't nev' have no mo' 'gagement a tall."

"You don' understan'. . . ."

"Reckon I does. You c'mon!"

Florian parleyed. He looked Mr. Stiggars over and found his demeanour anything but reassuring. He thought of the chauffeur who had been beaten and bound and gagged. . . . Florian had no desire to accompany Mr. Stiggars into a dark alley. He had a premonition that it might not be beneficial to his health. "Reckon we c'n make discussion right heah, Mistuh Stiggars."

The big negro shrugged. The bad light was in his eyes. The bulge was evident in the right hip pocket. His opening shaft was a bit paralysing — "You done me out of my car over to Anniston las' week, Mistuh Slappey."

"'Twas business —"

"I ain't gwine make no talk with you 'bout the how-comes. What I is after is — I wants my car back!"

"Oh!" Florian subsided suddenly. The bandit wanted the car and the car was gone. Florian's last chance to placate his unwelcome companion had departed. "Y-y-you do?"

"I shuah does. An' I got money — r'il money. I wanna buy it."

Florian waxed suspicious. "Whar you git that money at?"

"Over to the Pool an' Ginuwine lott'ry. I bet th'ee dollars on the Washerwoman's gig an' out she come. I got six hund'ed dollars — cash money."

"Fo'—'leven — fo'ty-fo'," breathed Florian. Stiggars' statement rang true. Florian had that day heard of a stranger who had cleaned up six hundred dollars on the Washerwoman's gig. "Well?" he questioned.

"I on'y owes you two hund'ed an' twen'y-five dollars, Mistuh Slappey — but I is a hones' man an' I is ready to pay you two hund'ed an' fifty. I wants that car an' I wants it now, an' I'm adwisin' you not to make no talk about you done sol' that car because if you have, Mistuh Slappey they's li'ble to be action 'roun' heah an' you an' me will know all 'bout it."

" But s'pose —"

" I ain't keen on s'posin'. W'en Selkirk Stiggars wants sumthin' he mos' usually gits it. On'erstan'? "

Florian nodded. " I sho' does, Brother Stiggars. B'lieve me — I sho' does."

" Whar that car is at? "

The proposition was put squarely up to Florian. The decision had been forced upon him. He faced the disquieting necessity of trapping Mr. Selkirk Stiggars if he wished to save his own skin.

" Les' talk it over," he temporized.

" 'Tain't nothin' to talk over. Whar that car is at? "

" To the garage. I was thinkin' yo'd come to my room an' take a sociable drink —"

Mr. Stiggars' eyes glistened. " A sho' nuff drink? "

" Yeh. No white lightnin', neither."

They repaired to Florian's room and the bottle was produced. Further invitation was unnecessary. Whiskey and Selkirk Stiggars had quite evidently met before.

" 'Tain't that I ain't willin' to give you back that they car, Brother Stiggars —"

" Better not be. 'Tain't nowise healthy fo' no nigger to go contrariwise fum Selkirk Stiggars."

" I is gwine telyphone the garage."

" We c'n walk there."

"Woul'n't think of troublin' you, Brother Stiggars. Not a tall. 'Twoul'n't be p'lite. The car'll be heah in a few minutes."

Florian made his escape, leaving Selkirk with the fast emptying bottle. He sped to the telephone in Broughton's drug store and called Lawyer Evans Chew. "Lawyer Chew?"

"Yes."

"This Flo'ian Slappey."

"Uh-huh."

"I needs yo' 'sistance, Lawyer Chew."

"How come?"

"I is captured that bandit nigger!"

"*What?*"

"Sho nuff," expanded Florian. "He put up a pow'ful hahd fight but I landed him fin'ly. He's up to my room — locked in. What I wants you to do is hike to the Molton Hotel an' git Mr. Barbour. Also two or th'ee p'lice. Or fo'. W'en you gits to my room, don't knock — jes' walk in — see?"

"Yeh."

"An' so's they won't be no misun'erstandin', Lawyer Chew — yo' fee fo' this ain't gwine be more'n five dollars: that salisfact'ry?"

"Reckon so."

"Tell'm this, Lawyer Chew — this heah Stiggars is got six hund'ed dollars cash on his pusson. He won it to the lott'ry. An' say — Lawyer Chew — take a frien's adwice an' w'en you-all come in my room, see that you is las' in line yo'se'f."

Florian was in an emotional ferment when he returned to the bibulous bandit. "Car's on the way now, Mistuh Stiggars."

"Le's go down an' meet it."

"Better stay heah, Brother Stiggars. Boy'll come up an' let us know."

"We c'n go down —"

"No," negatived Florian firmly: "Don' look dignyfied."

Selkirk Stiggars wanted to get his hands on the automobile. But he didn't want to get his hands off the bottle. The latter won. He held on — and talked on, volubly extolling his physical prowess in dealing with various gentlemen of colour who had in the past made the mistake of doublecrossing him and who now slept peacefully beneath the sod of various Southern states. There was something sinister in his selection of a topic. And then there came the sound of footfalls on the stairway — and then more — and more.

"H-h-h-heah he c-c-c-c-comes, Brother Stiggars."

"Huh!" Stiggars rose threateningly. "That ain't no garage boy, Mistuh Slappey. Tha's a regyment."

The thumping ceased just beyond the door — paused menacingly. The fetid air of the room was surcharged with danger. Florian tensed the muscles of his skinny legs for a leap beyond the zone of fire. Knowing bad men in general, he had small doubt that Mr. Selkirk Stiggars would shoot — and shoot fast. The bulge in the right hip pocket appeared to expand. He hoped vaguely that Lawyer Chew was well out of range.

The door swung back and a policeman stepped into the room. He trained the muzzle of his service revolver straight — at Florian Slappey. That individual, teeth chattering, shrilled in terror —

"I ain't him, Mistuh P'lice: they's yo' man, yonder!"

But the bandit did not shoot. He did not even try to make his escape. He stared in very unbanditlike fashion over the shoulder of the policeman into the quizzical grey eyes of Mr. Robert J. Barbour of Peachtree street — Atlanta. His expression was that of a man who gazes upon an apparition. He was trembling visibly.

Slowly the lips of Mr. Barbour expanded into a grin: a very broad grin. The grin became a chuckle — and then grew into a laugh. He gave quiet directions to the officer. "That's all right. You can put up your gun."

Florian stared from Stiggars to Mr. Barbour in perplexity. He was even a bit resentful. Something was radically wrong. His nerves, keyed to battle pitch, were raw and jangling. Only Stiggars' terror reassured him. "Wh-wh-what's all this?" stammered Florian.

Barbour addressed the bandit. "I am pleased to meet Mr. Selkirk Stiggars," he chuckled. "Mr. Stiggars — as I understand that you have six hundred dollars in cash in your pocket, will you kindly hand over two hundred to me: which amount I paid for the return of my car. You may pay over three hundred more to Mr. Florian Slappey, yonder. That is his promised reward for capturing you."

"N-now, Boss-man . . ." stammered Stiggars.

"Do as I say!"

The money was paid over as directed. Florian pocketed the three hundred dollars. . . . "What's it mean?"

Mr. Barbour laughed heartily. "I thought I'd find you here," he said to Stiggars. "Honestly, Beauregard, did you think I swallowed that story about the masked bandit?"

"But — but, Boss," defended Stiggars, "it was a pow'ful good story."

"I — I ain't on'erstan'," gasped Florian.

"It is very simple," explained Barbour laughingly. "Selkirk Stiggars is my chauffeur, Beauregard Tuggle. He got into that poker game in Anniston and lost fourteen dollars of his own money and a hundred and fifty of mine. Then he pawned my automobile and came on here with his story of being robbed by a bandit. He supplied too many and too graphic details. I gave the story to the newspapers and you showed up and returned the car. And the way I knew that I had Beauregard is that Selkirk Stiggars is the name of my best friend's chauffeur. Beauregard was too lazy in his selection of an alias. I spotted him the minute I heard your story — which explains why you got my two hundred dollars so easily. As for you, Beauregard, you may pay me the other hundred you have and work out the additional fifty. I have an idea that this will teach you a lesson."

"Huh! I reckon it's done done it." Then his eyes met those of his employer and his lips expanded into a wide, white grin. "Golly, Boss-man," he said pridefully, "they ain't no nigger gwine put nothin' over on you, is they?"

Florian Slappey counted over his three hundred dollars. He reluctantly detached a five-dollar note which he handed to Lawyer Evans Chew. "They's yo' fee, Lawyer Chew."

"Huh!" deprecated the lawyer, pocketing the money, "on'y five dollars an' you th'ee hund'ed ahead of the game?"

"The diffe'ence bein'," withered Florian, "that I *earned* mine!"

A HOUSE DIVIDED

A HOUSE DIVIDED

A THIN, plaintive wail split the quiet of the night. For a few seconds it maintained a high, shrill pitch; then diminuendoed to a croupy pizzicato sobbing. Derry Moultrie sat up straight in bed, the glory of his lavender pajamas wasted on the blackness of the night.

"Dawg gawn! Narcissy, ain't that Chinners' baby never sleep?"

"Yeh — in the day times," snapped his wife viciously.

"Seems like they'd ought to have some 'sideration — Oh! Law — lis'en at that!"

That was a hoarse, croaky baritone which effectively drowned the infantile cries. The man's voice punctured the thin board partition which divided the Chinners and Moultrie sides of the two-family house and pounded on the eardrums of the harassed Moultries.

> O-o-oh!
> A jay-bird sat on a hick'ry limb,
> He wink at me an' I wink at him;
> I pick up a rock an' I hit 'im in the shin —
> He say: "Please, Mist' Chinners, don' do that ag'in!"

For perhaps fifteen minutes Truman Chinners bellowed discord into the night, faithfully chronicling the vicissitudes of the unfortunate jay-bird. Came a pause — and the Moultrie family listened hopefully. But the Chinners infant had no mind to end the concert and his tremolo squeal resumed the nocturne where the proud father had left off.

The baby cried: cried until it choked and then settled into a prolonged sobbing. The voice of Chinners *père* rumbled once again through the partition —

>O-o-oh!
>A jay-bird sat on a hickory limb,
>He wink at me an' I wink at him. . . .

It was too much strain for the jangling nerves of the overwrought Derry Moultrie. He left his bed in a bound and snapped on the electric bulb. He crossed the room and hammered on the board wall until it shook. The voice of Truman Chinners came querulously to his ears — a momentary relief from the infernal singing.

"Wha's all the row 'bout?"

Derry was choking with rage. His naturally chocolate complexion had taken on a greenish tinge and his voice quivered with passion. "Jes' wan'ed to know," he roared, "how long you runs on one windin'?"

A severe silence ensued. It intensified Derry's wrath more than a sharp answer. "If'n you cain't keep that baby quiet . . ."

That, evidently, was the baby's cue. He took advantage of it with a vengeance. The wailing which had gone before had been quiet and soothing in comparison with the squawks and squeals and choking grunts which echoed Derry's unfinished threat. Narcissy, draped now in an old-rose kimono — the gift of white folks for whom she had once condescended to cook — fancied that she heard a Chinners' chuckle. She apprised her husband of

"He crossed the room and hammered on the board wall until it shook."

A HOUSE DIVIDED

the suspicion and together they paced the floor, robbed of all chance for sleep.

The mantel clock cuckoo'd thrice. An A. G. S. train shrieked tauntingly as it rumbled through the city. The parental Chinners had settled to a crooning duet — the father's rancid baritone a full measure ahead of the mother's rich contralto.

Each sound from the Chinners' manse seemed intensified by its journey to the Moultrie home. The thin boarding which had converted a one-family cottage into a source of double rental, was evidently imbued with acoustic properties. Derry and Narcissy sat on the edge of their bed and shook with silent rage. Finally forbearance ceased to be a virtue and Derry smashed a clench fist into an open palm: " 'Tain't to be stood!"

" 'Tain't!" agreed Narcissy dutifully.

"Folks what is got babies don' have no 'sideration a tall."

"Not none," came the wifely echo.

"Jes' wait'll I gits to him — Ise gwine make him stop that racket!"

"How?" queried the annoyingly practical Narcissy. Derry whirled on her in a rage.

"How? How I know how? I ain't no cunjer-doctor, but Ise man enough to make 'im quit. Enough is too much. Ain't nobody gwine put nothin' ov' on Derry Moultrie. One month sencst that baby be'n bohn an' I ain't had a night's res' ontil yet. Seems like folks'd have mo' sense'n to have babies in a two-fambly house."

Narcissy shook her head commiseratingly. "Orpha Chinners was tellin' me yestiddy —" She

broke off suddenly and lifted her head expectantly. Something was wrong. Silence had occurred on the other side of the partition. The Moultries tiptoed to the wall and applied their ears. They heard sibilant mutterings, much cautious tipping about the room, then, in the voice of the father —
" Dawg'd if'n he ain't 'sleep a'ready! "

The qualifying adverb set Derry Moultrie a-quiver with a vast righteous indignation. It was the last straw. For thirty days and more he had lost his quota of sleep and Derry, in common with all others of his race, was over-fond of the Morphean embrace.

" They ain't gwine put nothin' ov' on me," he muttered vindictively, whereupon he raised his rich, clear tenor in the opening measures of a popular syncopated hit. It was balm to his soul to envision the petrifaction caused beyond the partition by this latest offensive manœuvre. Narcissy smiled with benign approval. There came an imperative rapping from the Chinners side of the house and the angry voice of Orpha Chinners.

" Quit that racket, Derry: you is gwine wake Wade Hampton up."

Apparently Derry did not hear. Certainly he did not cease his leather-lunged singing. Within two minutes his valiant efforts were rewarded by the startled screaming of Wade Hampton Chinners. Punctuating the infantile yells he could hear the fervent profanity of the father and the volley of threats which accompanied it.

War had been declared.

An engagement of outposts occurred at six-thirty in the morning after a night of bitter recrimination through the dividing wall. Derry Moultrie and Truman Chinners, both carpenters by profession, met on the common veranda as they sallied forth to work. Red eyes gazed hostilely into red eyes. Both men were physically exhausted by the labours of the night. Neither was in a fit condition for a day of hard work. Derry would have passed on without a word but the battle-spirit of fatherhood was rampant in Truman's blood as he placed himself deliberately in Derry's path and glared up into his eyes.

"Derry Moultrie — Ise warnin' you to be careful they ain't no repeatin' of las' night."

"What 'bout las' night?" inquired Derry innocently.

"That yowlin' you an' Narcissy was doin'."

"I reckon this is a free country."

"You done it to wake'n up li'l Wade Hampton."

"I ain't got no mind 'bout Wade Hampton. An' if'n I had — ain't he been keepin' me awake fo' a month?"

"I cain't help what he does —"

"Folks what cain't control they babies, Truman Chinners, ain't got no right to have 'em. If'n you c'n keep that bag of yells quiet I reckon they ain't no reason why us cain't git along pleasant like we useter."

"'Tain't my fault —"

"Hmph! Reckon you is gwine say Orpha makes you sing!"

"She does."

"You is some hen-pecked man, Truman. Nex' thing, Orpha'll be sewin' pink ribbons on yo' nightshirt to fool the baby!"

Truman flared. "What goes on in my house ain't no concern of your'n, Derry."

"Same to you, an' also ditto. If'n they ain't no law 'gainst a baby yowlin' an' you singin', I reckon us'n c'n have a concert any time we want it."

Truman squared up to his once friendly neighbour. He had half the size but twice the belligerency of Derry.

"Bet' not make me sore, Derry."

"Pfff! You ain't noways th'eatenin' me, is you?" And, as a complimentary afterthought: "You li'l runt!"

"I ain't th'eatenin'—I'se wa'nin'—tha's all!"

"Huh! W'en I gits wa'ned, I wants to git wa'ned by a man."

"You is gwine fin' out quick enough I is a man if'n you keep on like what you done las' night. 'Member that, Derry Moultrie. If'n you vallie yo' complexion, you jes' 'member that!"

The men separated without an actual physical clash, Truman Chinners strutting like a victorious bantam to his temporary job a few blocks away; and Derry Moultrie toward the car line.

Derry was angry. His mind was busy with a consideration of ways and means having as their objective the downfall of the Chinners household. The beauty of a perfect morning was wasted on his misanthropic mood. He swung into Avenue H with long, space-eating strides. His eye happened to light on a sign. He knew that sign. It had startled darktown's society set with its unheralded appearance three days previously. It was an ornate sign, grinning forth from the veranda of a one-family cottage in the centre of the residential section populated by the ultra-fashionable coloured citizenry.

PRINCESS RAJJAH
CLAREVOYANT EXTRIORDINARY
OCULTISM —   — CRISTAL GAZING
Find Out What Your Husband and
Sweetheart is Doing

DO YOU WANT TO GET RICH FOR
ONE DOLLAR
Sure You Do!
Then See The PRINCESS RAJJAH —
— Most World Famous and Cheapest

He perused the sign carefully. His lips curled scornfully back from twin rows of shiny white teeth. "Bunk!" he soliloquized sceptically: "an' they ain't 'ary one of these heah niggers ain't fell fo' it! 'Ceptin' on'y me!"

He boarded a trolley for the centre of the city and transferred to a suburban car marked "Westfield." In the trailer he found a jam of fellow-workmen, most of whom were bound for Westfield where five hundred cottages were being erected by a big contracting firm under rush orders. From the workers' standpoint the job was an excellent one; the wages large, the hours easy — and, until the birth of Wade Hampton Chinners the carpentering of Derry Moultrie had found favour in the eyes of all the foremen; white and coloured alike.

But the past month had effected a change. No longer did Derry come whistling to work refreshed by a long night of undisturbed slumber. He was the victim of vicarious insomnia. He dozed over his labours — and thereupon fell from grace. All of which had considerable to do with his rancour against the whole Chinners family.

Previous to the advent of little Wade Hampton, the Moultries and the Chinnerses had been the best of friends. The ladies found each other congenial as neighbours and fellow-members of The Lily of the Valley Club. The husbands spent their evenings together discussing professional matters. They were members of the same church and both held minor offices in the exclusive Sons & Daughters of I Will Arise.

The baby had changed it all. Friendship had been metamorphosed into enmity. The parents of the child — their first and only — resented the resentment of the childless couple. They could not understand that anything Wade Hampton might do could be otherwise than wonderful or universally pleasing. They considered it an honour that the Moultries were allowed to sacrifice a paltry few hours of sleep for the pleasure of listening to the lusty, precocious yells. The Chinnerses did not object: certainly the Moultries' protests were indicative of basest ingratitude and a lack of all sense of appreciation. It wasn't the Moultries' baby and it wasn't their house. The Chinnerses were not responsible for the very thin boarding which separated their homes.

Relations had been broken off in toto. But there was no gainsaying the fact that the Chinnerses were getting the better of what had rapidly developed into bitter warfare. It was inevitable that the Moultries would grow tired of remaining awake for the purpose of waking Wade Hampton when he drifted off to sleep. On the other hand: night wakefulness came natural to the baby.

Derry Moultrie developed, with desperate and somewhat devilish ingenuity, new methods of torture. He went to the expense of having a telephone installed. For obvious reasons, the instrument was placed in the kitchen, out of Chinners' earshot. The Chinnerses had a telephone and for many nights after the installation in the Moultrie home, the dropping off to sleep of Wade Hampton was the signal for a violent jangling of their telephone bell. Truman Chinners would leap for the 'phone, hoarsely whisper a "Hello!" only to hear the mocking click of a receiver at the other end — which he fortunately did not know was the Moultrie home — and the cool, calm voice of Central inquiring "Number, please!" Inevitably Wade Hampton waked, squalled — and was trundled by his father.

But despite Derry's best efforts victory perched on the Chinners' banner. Derry and his now haggard wife realized poignantly that they had lost the fight and that they were destined to spend the remaining eight months of their leasehold in a nightmare of sleeplessness.

The diminutive cause of all the trouble continued to howl his nights happily away. The fond parents took it all as a matter of divine course, and the carpentering of Truman Chinners became even more expert than it had been. He was in the grip of proudest fatherhood and each nail driven developed a finer technique under the inspiration of his lusty-lunged son and heir. Truman had even been emboldened to a flyer in independent contracting which, unfortunately, had driven him close to the ragged edge of disaster. But even that professional debacle had been salved by the pudgy brown fingers of his son.

Derry Moultrie had no such balm. The condition — trifling enough at the outset — had been magnified a thousandfold by the long period of enforced sleeplessness. The tempers of himself and his wife had been utterly annihilated. They became crabbed and rowed with one another.

The warfare between the two sections of the divided house became merciless. Chinners more than half-suspected the source of the many-times-nightly telephone calls and muttered overt threats having to do with the complete and sudden extinction of the Moultrie family. But by the end of the second week it had become patent to the Moultries that things could not remain as they were. Even their temporary triumphs were too dearly bought. Whereupon, after a heavy-eyed consultation with his consort, Derry presented himself before Goodrich Carroll, agent for the house in which he lived. He explained to Mr. Carroll that he wished the Chinnerses removed and removed quickly. Mr. Carroll shook his head.

"They have a lease, Derry."

"Sho'— don' I know that, Cap'n? But what good's a lease if'n white folks cain't bust it?"

Mr. Carroll smiled. "You must have a reason."

"Sho' is."

"What is it?"

"Jes' trouble," answered Derry evasively. "You see, Cap'n Carroll, us'n the Chinnerses don'

A HOUSE DIVIDED

git 'long so well like what we useter. Mis' Chinnerses is got pow'ful uppity 'long with my wife an' they is rowin' all the time. An' w'en wimmin gits to rowin' Cap'n, they ain't nothin' to put between 'em but distance an' lots of it. An' of co'se me'n Truman ain't frien's like what we useter be, an' Ise pow'ful skeered they's gwine be trouble between him an' I."

"Why don't *you* sublet?" inquired the real estate agent. "I'd agree if you secured a reliable tenant."

Derry shook his head. He had no mind to end the vendetta by a Moultrie evacuation. "Guess'n I could if'n I had to, Cap'n; but to tell the hones' truth, this heah job which I is got over to Wes'fiel' ain't li'ble to las' so long on account they ain't like my work so much as they useter. An' besides they ain't no mo' houses 'roun' where I lives at an' seein' tha's the bes' resydential section fo' coloured folks what they is I sort of hate to move out of it."

"Doesn't it strike you that the Chinnerses might feel the same way about it?"

"Them? Naw! They is got a baby, Cap'n Carroll, an' w'en folks has babies they don' keer no mo' 'bouten sassiety. I been rentin' fum you th'ee yeahs, Boss-man, an' I knows good an' well they ain't nobody gwine git nothin' fo' nothin', so I kinder thought if'n I was to pay you 'bout twen'y dollars you might fin' out some way to bus' that lease — eh?"

Mr. Carroll chuckled. He liked this tall, slim, clean negro whom he had found an honest, reliable tenant. And he knew there was some compelling motive behind the unusual request, especially since it was backed by a proffered bribe of twenty dollars — cash.

"I really don't believe I can do anything, Derry; but I'll take the money and try. If I fail, I'll return the twenty."

"You could fin' 'nother tenint easy, coul'n't you?"

"That's the very easiest part of it, Derry. The rub comes from Truman Chinners. If he doesn't care to move, and continues to pay his rent — I can't put him out."

"G'wan, Cap'n," retorted Derry with glorious, grinning confidence, "they ain't nothin' you coul'n't make a nigger do if'n you sot yo' min' to it."

But after three days of intensive diplomatic effort, Mr. Carroll reported that he was unable to influence Truman Chinners to vacate his home. "Sorry, Derry — but there wasn't a thing stirring. Here's your twenty —"

Derry waved it wearily aside. "You hol' on to it, Boss-man. You is good as a bank, anyways. An' they ain't nev' no tellin' w'en sumpin' will come up."

"I'm afraid nothing will," was the cheerless answer, "unless you bring it about yourself."

Derry looked up suddenly. "Onless I — Boss-man, you sho' spoke a mouthful that time."

"Meaning what, Derry?"

The beginnings of a thought were agitating Derry's brain. He answered vaguely. "I — I ain't know yit — 'zac'ly — Cap'n. Not 'zac'ly. But I sort of feel's if I was gwine have an idee."

He left the office of the real estate agent and walked homeward with long, easy strides. And

A HOUSE DIVIDED

the idea which had been begotten of Goodrich Carroll's casual remark, matured rapidly. Derry's brow wrinkled with a tumescence of thought as he swung into Avenue H and paused before the sanctum of The Princess Rajjah — Clarevoyant Extriordinary — Most World Famous & Cheapest. For perhaps ten minutes he studied that sign intently. Then his lips expanded to a broad, red smile and the smile became a chuckle.

"Golly!" he murmured, "Ise gwine take a chancst. They ain't nobody superstishuser'n Truman an' Orpha Chinners. Not nobody a tall."

The noon hour had not yet chimed and by the delay in answering his eager ring, Derry correctly judged that the clairvoyanting business was on a temporary decline. He was pleased with the idea, but not a little surprised.

From the day of the Princess's arrival, darktown had been stirred to the roots over her undeniable soothsaying prowess. Much wisdom had dripped sonorously from her supposedly East Indian lips in a dialect suspiciously Afro-American. She had discovered lost jewelry and brought about more than one marriage. She had foretold commercial successes and traced the past with a vague generality which carried specific meaning to the gullible listeners. In short — The Princess Rajjah had become quite the society rage.

But dollars are dollars, and even a clairvoyant who sticks consistently to the silver lining in her prognostications must discover that negro pocketbooks are not elastic. Having one's fortune told was a luxury which few could afford at all, and none often. At the hour of Derry's arrival Mr.

and Mrs. Princess Rajjah were deep in discussion of removal to new and more fertile fields.

A quick glance through the curtained window, and Mr. Princess Rajjah postulated that a new worshipper was come to the shrine of the infinite. He swiftly donned a gaudy bathrobe and a tall headgear resembling a be-starred dunce's cap, whilst Mrs. Princess slipped out of her kimono and into the robes of state: a glass-jewelled seance costume. She placed herself in a cheese-cloth booth behind a small table on which rested a crystal globe. She deftly summoned a rapt expression and plastered it on her face.

As Derry entered the room he was impressed in spite of himself. A few Chinese joss-sticks burning in the rear blended with the odour of breakfast onions in extremely oriental fashion. More — the Princess was exceedingly restful on discriminating masculine eyes in her soothsaying regalia: a fact which Derry noticed and the Princess noticed that he noticed. Derry planked down his dollar and followed directions to gaze into the crystal sphere.

The Princess gave a full dollar's worth. She was unable to call Derry's name but she told accurately that he had been born in the South, that he was a workingman, married (a rash guess but a good one), that he made substantial wages (which fact she adduced from his clothes), that he held a good position and would continue to hold it, that he loved his wife but somehow was not disinclined to admire the pulchritude of women more beautiful than Mrs. Derry, that his prospects were bright, that he would achieve his heart's desire . . . and, in brief, everything in the patter of the fake fortune teller which is Delphic in substance. And the more she talked the surer Derry became of his ground. When she subsided he gave a phlegmatic "Thanks" and struck straight from the shoulder.

"If'n you c'n tell all that fo' a dollar, Princess, I reckon you'd spout a pow'ful fine fo'tune fo' 'bout twen'y — woul'n't you?"

The subliminal mind of the clairvoyant snapped quickly out of tune with the infinite. Here was earthly, material talk which she understood and she made a record journey back to mundane levels.

"Twenty dollars?"

"You said it."

"Cash?"

"Spot."

She clutched his hand but he jerked it away. "Not mine," he explained.

"Oh!"

"They's a man in this heah town name of Truman Chinners. I wants you to git him heah an' tell his fo'tune."

"When do I get the money?"

"In adwance. On'y I ain't want you to tell him no fo'tune like what you is jes' been tellin' me. If'n I shell out this heah twen'y dollars I want him tol' *my* kin' of a fo'tune."

Professional ethics fought a brief battle with the crying needs of the royal larder and the latter was returned victorious.

"Splain yo'se'f, Mistuh —"

"Nev' min' my name. It mought slip out. What I wants to know is — does you think if'n this heah Truman Chinners, which is married an' has a baby also — if'n he come heah could **you** skeer him so's he'd move away fum the house where he is livin' at now? P'efe'ably away fum town so's I woul'n't be bothered with him no mo'? He's pow'ful s'perstishus, Miss Rajjah, an' if'n you c'd wuk it —" He produced his wallet significantly.

The Princess sighed profoundly. She knew that the tall, good-looking man before her was no disciple of Karma and she talked plain English. "I reckon I could do mos' anything hones' fo' twen'y dollars."

Derry hitched his chair closer. "This heah thing ain't not on'y hones', Miss Rajjah — it's a pos'tive cha'ity. Lemme staht at the beginnin'—"

A half hour later he reached the end. His eloquence had swayed the hungry Princess and she promised to excel herself in bringing about the result which Derry so passionately desired. The two ten-dollar bills, binding the bargain, passed from his hands to hers — a ceremonial which Mr. Princess Rajjah witnessed gleefully through the portiers. Business was decidedly picking up and he envisioned a Rajjah feast of succulent pork chops and tender, crisp apple fritters.

Narcissy Moultrie was not as spontaneously enthusiastic as the Princess over the news of the twenty. "Ain't you reckon she'd of did it fo' less'n that, Derry? Not that I ain't sayin' but what 'tis a good idee, but twen'y dollars —"

"Huh!" retorted Derry loftily, "Princesses ain't no pikers, Narcissy. 'Tain't possible to git 'em to wuk fo' you fo' a cent less'n twen'y dollars."

"Mebbe come she ain't no Princess."

"Sho' she is. She say she's a reg'lar Hindu fum Hindustanee. But if'n she is or she ain't don' make no diffe'ence if'n she gits them Chinnerses away fum heah. It has became a matter of p'inciple with me. If'n we was to pack up an' lef' heah Truman Chinners'd go 'roun' tellin' ev'ybody 'bout how he run us off. . . ."

The wifely jaw squared. "That bein' the case," she said grimly, "I reck'n we c'n affo'd to spen' that twen'y, 'specially if'n Cap'n Carroll gives you back the twen'y what you give him to git rid of Truman off'n his lease."

Meanwhile the nocturnal jangling of the telephone was temporarily discontinued and an armistice of a sort declared between the Chinners and Moultrie households. Little Wade Hampton howled pæns of victory in the stilly hours of the night, but somehow he had lost his power to enrage the Moultries. They realized that they now held eleven of the trumps and they patiently awaited developments from the realm of the supernatural.

Thus far Truman Chinners and his wife had battled heroically against the temptation to visit the seeress on Avenue H. They were both steeped in superstition and fiercely attracted by anything which savoured of glimpsing the future; but they had taken unto themselves the first member of a second generation and their parental duty was plain. They could not afford two dollars and it was romantically unthinkable that one should go without the other.

It had been a hard battle, but conscientiousness and the necessity for economy had won out. Truman had given in most grudgingly. The future did not look entirely roseate for Chinners *père*. He had recently, in the glory of fatherhood, and the certainty of accomplishment — essayed the contract for the building of a small house on Seventeenth Street. Things looked bright at the outset, but two of his best workmen had accepted more attractive offers elsewhere and in order to get new men in a hurry Truman was compelled to advance the wage scale upon which his bid had been based. Then bad weather took a hand — a contingency which was not provided against in the contract. The day for the completion of the job found it still unfinished, and the following week saw the paper profits melting slowly away, until, when the task was finished and his accounts straightened, Truman found that he had been paying the owner of the little house seventy-two cents a day for the privilege of working for him.

Thereupon he decided unanimously that the contracting business was not what it was cracked up to be. He had been hoist by the petard of his ambition and received a severe setback. He accepted five days' work at union wages and was glad to get them. At the end of that period he faced the necessity for securing anything which happened to present itself. From Orpha he received little encouragement. Orpha was too absorbed in the temperamental eccentricities of little Wade Hampton Chinners to hear the not too distant howlings of the wolf.

The night after Derry's conversation with the Princess Rajjah, Mr. and Mrs. Simeon Broughton called upon the Chinnerses. Simeon — big, bluff and hearty — was good-naturedly tolerant of the effervescence of his radiant young wife. As for Pearl, she was fairly bubbling over with excitement inspired by the brummagem display and convincing chatter of the Princess.

"We is jes' come fum the Princess Rajjah's," she exclaimed, "an' she's sho' the wonderfullest 'ooman. . . ."

Truman squirmed. "Reckon she is," he returned wistfully.

"She done tol' me an' Simeon all 'bout ourselfs, an'— an'—" She paused impressively. "She done call yo'all's name right out."

Mr. Truman Chinners stiffened. "*What?*"

"Sho' nuff! Ain't it the truth, Simeon?"

The giant of a man, who made an excellent and steady living as community gardener for fashionable white folks in the summer months and furnace chaperone in winter — nodded his head. The fact that Simeon was impressed had a two-fold effect on the naturally credulous Truman.

"She — she said sumthin' 'bout *us?*"

"Yeh. . . . She say: 'I see two figgers flyin' 'roun' a house on Eighteenth street,' she say, jes' like that. 'One of them they figgers is name' Opportunity an' one of 'em is name' Trouble.' Hones', Mistuh Chinners, she say it jes' 'zac'ly like that. Ain't that the Gawd's truth, Simeon?"

"Yeh — jes' thataway."

"An'— an' what else?" quavered Truman Chinners.

"She say: 'I see a name — name of Chinners. An' two figgers — one name' Opportunity an' one name' Trouble. They is flyin' 'roun' the Chinnerses' house. Whar this heah Mistuh Chinners is at?' Then she kinder stop an' git ghosty: 'I must see Mistuh Chinners,' she say. 'Is Mistuh

Chinners in the house right now at p'esent?'"

Truman had turned a pale green. " You — you ain't makin' fumadiddles with me, is you, Mis' Broughton?"

"Co'se I ain't. I ain't no jokin' gal whar sperrits is consarned at."

"What else she say?"

"Nothin'."

"Not nothin' tall?"

"Nary 'nother word."

After the Broughtons had departed Truman paced the floor. His psychic condition was pitiable. He was infinitely worried — but not too worried to kill two birds with one stone. Since his emotional seethe commanded that he walk, he carried Wade Hampton Chinners in his paternal arms, much to that young gentleman's delight.

The Infinite had spoken through the lips of the Princess Rajjah — lips which were even at that moment smacking most unethereally over the juicy pork chops purchased with Derry Moultrie's money. Had Derry been gifted with occult powers he would have revelled in the knowledge of Truman Chinners' mental turmoil.

Truman fought it out by himself. The Princess Rajjah could not have hit upon two words more calculated to hopelessly intrigue his interest. Opportunity: — he was seeking Opportunity as no man seeks it until he faces a period barren of work. And the trouble omen . . . he cast a wild glance at the cherubic face of his now sleeping son. Trouble meant Wade Hampton — he was quite sure of that. He discussed the matter with Orpha but Orpha could not see things his way. She knew little of his foggy business vista and to her a dollar expended upon the Princess Rajjah was a dollar spent for selfish, inexcusable indulgence. "Fo' a dollar," she expounded, "we c'n pay the fust installment on that carri'ge down to the fu'niture man's, an' Wade Hampton is jes' nacherally got to have him a carri'ge. 'Tain't decent not to."

Truman gave in. He did it reluctantly, stubbornly, and with an ill-will. But he gave in.

But when, on the following night Florian Slappey — wealthy mentor of the younger social set, breezed in on them with news that once again the prophetic figures had appeared to the gaze of the Princess Rajjah as floating over the Chinners' home, and that she imperiously demanded the presence of Truman Chinners if he was to be saved disaster to "some one in that they home what is got the initials W. H. C.—" Truman Chinners went and he went fast.

His chest was heaving and his forehead beaded with cold perspiration as he presented himself before the Princess Rajjah. She dismissed two waiting disciples and cannily accepted his dollar. He was vastly impressed by the tawdry glitter. He watched her as she focussed her eyes on the polished crystal and slipped promptly into a thoroughly efficient and impressive trance.

She started speaking. Sure of her ground — thanks to the exhaustive biographies furnished by the foresighted Derry Moultrie — she spoke with perfect assurance. No generalities crept in to mar the convincing effect. Her nuance was deep and throaty and not unmusical. With the finely developed theatric instinct of her race she swayed her lithe, shapely body, rolled her eyes until the whites showed terrifyingly and intoned her spirit message.

"Yo' name is Chinners — Chinners — lemme see: Tru — Truman Chinners. You is got a wife name' Orpha — tha's it — Orpha Chinners. Tha's yo' wife's name. You lives on Eighteenth Street 'tween Avenues G an' H: tha's whar you lives at, Truman Chinners. You lives right they. I see a thi'd member of the fam'ly — ve'y small an' tiny — a li'l bitsy baby. Name'— name'— is it Wade Hampton Chinners? Is that the name, Truman Chinners?"

"Yeh . . . yeh. . . . Tha's my baby. Tha's him."

Truman was in a pitiful condition. Every muscle in his short, heavy-set body was tensed. He was leaning forward in his chair, hands clutching the table-edge, eyes popping from their sockets. He was the type of subject to warm the cockles of a good soothsayer's heart. And the Princess Rajjah was not slow in responding to his flattering gullibility.

"They is a figger floatin' 'roun' yo' home, Truman Chinners — a figger — a figger. . . . Figger name' Opportunity. It is talkin'— talkin'. . . . It say: 'Truman Chinners, you mus' leave off fum livin' whar you is at!' It say: 'Truman Chinners, they is a chancst fo' you to make a heap of money — a heap of money — away — west — west. . . . Fo' you to make piles of money — west. . . .'"

"Wes'fiel'?" breathed Truman.

"Westfield. An' they is 'nother figger a-flyin' 'roun' 'longside ol' Opportunity, Truman Chinners, an' his name is Trouble — Ol' Trouble flyin' 'long with Opportunity. An' Trouble is talkin'— talkin'. . . . Trouble is p'intin' down th'ough the ruf of yo' house, Truman Chinners, p'intin' to a li'l baby — a li'l baby. . . . Baby name'— name' Wade Hampton Chinners. Trouble p'intin' to the baby — to that they baby. . . .

"Trouble lookin' pow'ful dahk on that baby, Truman Chinners . . . it's trouble fum nearabouts — trouble fum yo' neighbors. . . ."

Truman shook as with ague. "That'll be Derry an' Narcissy Moultrie!"

"Trouble ain't mention no names," continued the medium craftily, "ain't mention no names — 'ceptin' on'y he is lookin' west an' smilin' . . . sayin' if you leave off fum livin' whar you is livin' at an' go t'wa'ds the settin' sun they ain't gwine be no mo' trouble. But w'en he looks east or st'aight down —'specially st'aight down — he's frownin' sumpin' terrible. Trouble, Truman Chinners, trouble fo' the li'l baby less'n you move fum livin' whar you is at!"

Truman's spine was all marrow when he reached home. The incantations of the Princess Rajjah lost nothing in the retelling. He passed an apprehensive night within easy reach of a revolver, his eyes fixed menacingly upon the thin board partition which separated his home from the Moultrie domicile.

To say that he and his wife were convinced of impending danger is to display rank conservatism. They were fairly petrified with terror and at dawn of the next day they started preparations which were more hasty than thorough.

It was a red-letter day for the Moultries who sat grinningly in their dining-room and harkened to the sweet music of preparation for the exodus. "Twen'y dollars," breathed Derry. "It's cheap at twice the price!"

That afternoon the Chinners evacuated the ill-omened Eighteenth Street house, their belongings piled high in a rickety one-horse dray. The family boarded a street-car and disappeared from the neighbourhood. The Moultries relaxed in supine bliss. Then they prepared for a fitting celebration.

They were too happy to be satisfied with their own society. Informal invitations were telephoned and by nine o'clock P. M. the revelry was in full swing. It lasted until two in the morning: a hodge-podge of dancing and soft drinks and peanuts and popcorn and ten-cent-store candies. For a spontaneous affair it was a signal triumph.

And, free from the yowlings of the Chinners heir, Derry and Narcissy slept as they had not — not since the next-door visit of the stork many weeks previously. They slumbered the sleep of the wholly righteous and utterly exhausted. When they waked the sun had already mounted brilliantly to mid-heaven and their breakfast doubled as lunch.

It was too late for Derry to consider working and he and Narcissy declared a holiday. Derry robed himself in his best suit — a black-and-white checked affair which had long been the pride of his social hours. Narcissy was radiant in a blue-plumed white hat, a gorgeously embroidered crepe-de-Chine waist, a blue serge skirt and a shiny, crimson belt. They made an attractive picture as they strutted townward, and, once in the centre of the city, Derry turned eastward.

"Whar you is gwine, Derry?"

Derry chuckled. "Ov' to git that twen'y dollars back fum Cap'n Carroll."

The real estate agent greeted them genially and burst immediately into words. "I have some mighty good news for you folks," he said.

"Yassuh?"

"I got rid of the Chinnerses."

"You got'n rid. . . ."

"Surest thing, you know. Truman Chinners happened up in my office yesterday morning and I grabbed him. I didn't mince matters. 'This is your last chance, Truman,' I said positively: 'Will you or will you not take twenty dollars for your lease?' Trust Goodrich Carroll not to give him a chance to raise the ante. 'Answer yes or no,' I said, 'and be quick!'"

Derry felt slightly ill. "I — I — reckon he didn't hahdly consider it ve'y long, did he, Cap'n?"

"Nope!" cheerfully. "He snapped me right up. 'Where's the twenty?' he asked, and I forked over your two ten-dollar bills. I was going to ride by this afternoon to tell you the good news."

"Thanks. . . . Say, Cap'n, reckon you didn't happen to ast him what fo' he come up to see you 'bout, did you?"

Mr. Carroll shook his head. "Why, no. Now that you mention it, I don't think I did."

"Thought not," murmured Derry dully.

"Why?"

"Nothin'."

"You must have had a reason for asking —"

"Ain't no reason —'ceptin' on'y I got a hunch Truman was comin' heah to offer you money fo' lettin' him git out of the lease."

"Don't be foolish, Derry."

"Cain't help it, Cap'n Carroll. Guess'n I was bohn foolish."

He and Narcissy turned sadly away. That his twenty dollars had been unnecessarily paid over to Truman Chinners put a thorough damper on their jollity. Now that Wade Hampton had departed and his wailings become mere memory, he loomed less formidable and the forty dollars much larger. The angle of perspective was changed. Derry and Narcissy found themselves looking through the reverse end of the telescope.

"Got another tenint?" queried Derry apathetically.

Carroll rubbed his hands. "Certainly have. They'll move in tomorrow."

"Name' which?"

"Preston, I think. Not sure, though. Anyway, they're paying me two and a half more per month than Truman Chinners — so I really owe you a debt of gratitude."

"Huh! Ise shuah glad somebody owes me sumthin'. It's a pow'ful strange feelin' these heah days."

Sleep did not come easily to Derry Moultrie that night. The farther away his forty dollars, the more attractive they seemed. Narcissy sensed his mood and refrained from nagging — too much. But she nagged sufficiently to make Derry glad when morning came and he could depart for his day's labours in Westfield.

A HOUSE DIVIDED

At two o'clock that afternoon he reappeared. But he was not empty-handed. His right fist clutched the workbox containing his tools. He was a-tremble with fury and there was blood in his eye. He flung into the house without a word and slammed his tool-box down on the best rug. There was no hint of apology accompanying the act.

Circumstance and instinct combined to warn Narcissy that this was no time for fault-finding. She bided her time, awaiting the inevitable opening of the verbal floodgates. It came in a single fervid expletive:

"Damn!" spat Derry.

"What — what you doin' home this heah time of day, Hon?"

"Ise home an' Ise gwine stay home! They's some things no se'f-respectin' man c'n stan'!"

"Sumthin' wrong?"

"Sumthin' *wrong?* Jes' heah that 'ooman! Sumthin' wrong? Huh! Whyn't you ask me is sumthin' *right?*"

Narcissy waited patiently. She knew her husband. "Yeh?" she suggested.

"It's that they Princess Rajjah — what you think she done did?"

"What?"

"She's went an' sent Truman Chinners ov' to Wes'fiel' lookin' fo' a job."

"To Wes'fiel' whar you wuks at?"

"Whar I *did* wuk at!"

"Did he git him a job?"

"Did he? Trus' a feller like him to lan' right. He goes out they an' tells them white-folks he's a contractor an' gives the name of the feller he done b'ilt that house fo' what he botched up so bad. They call the man up an' he gives Truman a reccomen' . . . an' they goes an' hires him —" he paused and fairly shot out the final words: *"As a foreman!"*

"Foreman?"

"An' that ain't the wo'st of it," continued Derry bitterly. "They makes him foreman ov' the job what I is workin' on. Jes' like what I is said — they is some things which is too much fo' any se'f-respectin' man to stan' . . . an' I quit! Quit col'! Tha's better, I says to myse'f, than waitin' twell Truman Chinners fires me!"

A pregnant silence ensued. It jarred on the nerves of Derry Moultrie. He looked up and met his wife's eyes.

"What's eatin' you, Narcissy? You ain't look so happy yo'se'f."

"I ain't."

"'Count of which?"

"Them new tenints — them Prestons which moved in nex' do' this mawnin', Derry."

"Well . . . what 'bout 'em?"

"Nothin' . . . 'ceptin' on'y that they is got twins th'ee months old!"

POPPY PASSES

POPPY PASSES

ELLICK PINCKNEY sank twin rows of glistening teeth into a crisp, juicy winesap. He relaxed luxuriously in the moth-eaten upholstery and allowed his eyes to dwell with infinite appreciation on the curvy, marvellously garbed figure of Poppy Blevins.

Poppy was extremely restful on the eyes. She was considerably shorter than the elongated Ellick but nature and applied science had conspired to make of her a creature desired by men.

She was a woman of culture, of poise and of fascinating *élan*. Her complexion was a rich chocolate, her wealth of hair a bewitching blend of inherited kink and carefully cultivated straightness. She had wide-open, flashing eyes and a vampirish art in using them. Every move was harmony to which her rich contralto voice played obligato.

Ellick sighed. "You sho' is a woman to do any man proud, Poppy."

"Huh! Ain't you men never think of nothin' new to tell a gal?"

"I reckon others is tol' you that befo', ain't they?" he inquired jealously.

"Reckon so." She smiled with satisfaction and placed one laced boot carefully atop its mate while she shamelessly angled for further flattery. "I ain't see what's so 'tractive bout'n me."

"I does," returned Ellick wistfully, "an' I reckon either I ain't the on'y one."

She raised her eyes swiftly. "Meanin' which?"

"Acey Upshaw!" The name spewed from between his lips with a nuance of intransigent distaste.

Poppy Blevins shrugged. "Mebbe so he does."

"I ain't like that man, Poppy."

"Neither he don' like you."

"If'n you an' me was engage'—" hopefully.

"We ain't."

"We was built fo' one 'nother, Poppy. We likes the same things, an'—"

"Coul'n't git 'em if'n we *was* married," she retorted practically. "W'en I marries, Ellick, I marries fo' love; but also I is gwine marry a man which c'n s'phot me in the way I been use' to. You know puffec'ly well. . . ."

"My business is goin' good." He envisioned his tiny shoe repair shope with its antique equipment and its perturbing cloudiness of title. "Goin' good . . ." he echoed with less confidence.

"'Tain't yourn!" flashed the girl.

"Will be."

"You ain't never paid Acey Upshaw that last 'stalment, is you?"

"Not yet."

"When you gwine pay it?"

"Pretty soon," he answered vaguely. "Soon's I git the money. If'n 'twas anybody 'ceptin' ol' Acey I woul'n't min', but that ol' secon'-han' immytation of a wore out firecracker woul'n't give his own mother a 'stension on a note. He ain't good fo' nothin' 'ceptin' on'y c'lectin' dollars."

"They's worser faults than what that is, Ellick,"
"I was a bohn idjit to buy that shoe shop offen Acey. On'y I wan'ed to git a business of my own so's you woul'n't half to marry no man what hel' a job. An' I'd own it, too; come him to give me a sixty-day 'stension. I been soht of thinkin', Poppy — soht of thinkin' — mebbe you — him — mebbe if'n you ast him —"

The radiant butterfly shrugged with vast indifference. She had as little real interest in Ellick's business affairs as she had understanding of them. "Ise got troubles of my own, Ellick."

"Soht of which?"

"I got a hearin' from my sister today. She 'lows my ol' man gotten eight hund'ed dollars from the railroad count'n they cut his lef' han' off an' they's comin' out heah to make visit with me."

"All of them?"

She nodded. "Whole crowd: Mom an' Pa an' Lithia. Letter said they was leavin' Sat'dy, gittin' heah Sunday night an' fo' me to 'range so's they c'n boahd whar I is at."

"Whar they livin' at now?"

"Cha'leston."

"South Ca'lina?"

"Uh-huh! An' they ain't gwine do nothin' 'ceptin' on'y be in the way, Ellick. I jes' ain't need 'em. Nor neither they ain't gwine like it heah count'n they is from Cha'leston."

"What that got to do with it?"

"They is two kin's of niggers," the girl answered profoundly, "Cha'leston niggers an' niggers. Cha'leston niggers is diffe'ent from other niggers an' they never fit in nowheres else 'scusin' on'y w'en they is caught young like what I was. They ain't country nor neither they ain't city. They ain't much of anythin'. They ain't got no style. They talks funny. I reckon they is gwine 'barrass me sumthin' terrible while they is heah, Ellick; less'n my frien's he'p me out by takin' them off'n my han's."

"You ain't shame' of yo' folks, is you, Poppy?"

She shook her head impatiently. "I ain't shame' of them s'long's they ain't heah. But w'en they is heah I is in bad. I an' them don' move in the same soht of sassiety. How you reckon they is gwine look 'longside by sassiety wimmin like Pearl Broughton an' Cha'ity Driver an' Imigene Rush an' Ione Segar an' Gussie Muck an' Mallissie Cheese an' Narcissy Moultrie an' Vistar Goins? How you think my folks is gwine ac' 'long with them ladies? Cha'leston niggers ain't got on'y one idea, Ellick, an' that is how long ontil the nex' meal is. What they ain't got is no soul. An' they's more'n a few of these heah wimmin in this town, Ellick, which would be pow'ful glad to sneer at me 'cause my folks ain't swell like what theirs is. I reckon my fambly stahted back jes' bout'n far as theirs done."

"Even if they ain't travel so fast sencst, huh?"

"Tha's it." She paused and glared a challenge at Ellick. He plunged hopefully. "Now, if'n you was married to me, Poppy —"

"I ain't an' I ain't aimin' to be. Guess a father an' a mother an' a frowsy ol' sister is 'nough for one gal without she takes a husban' too."

"Mebbe they ain't on'y gwine stay a few days,"

he encouraged, sensing the depths of her misery over the impending visit.

"You ain't know my ol' man," she gloomed. "He c'n do nothin' better an' longer'n any man I knows. He is gwine remain heah ontil that money is all gone an' then mos' likely Mom'll be doin' washin' an' Lithia'll have a job somewheres an' he won't want to go back. An' as fo' Lithia — she's 'bout as bad. You ain't never saw no gal like what she is, Ellick. All she wears clothes for is to keep from goin' nekkid. She ain't got no mo' style'n a fried oyster. She sho' is diffe'ent from what I is."

Ellick gazed appreciatively at the exquisite Poppy,— fashion plate of the coloured social set. Poppy's wardrobe was as much of an eight-days' wonder as its source was a mystery. No one understood quite how she did it. True, she hired out as nursegirl and for her undeniably efficient services received four dollars each and every Saturday night. But the wages didn't tally with her wealth of crepe-de-Chine and Georgette waists, her gloriously plaid skirts, her high, laced boots, her sheer silk hosiery.

The general public did not know that Poppy's shibboleth was clothes. It didn't understand that she bought her garments second-hand from the young unmarried daughter of the household wherein she worked nor that she cheerfully did much extra labour for the possession of beautiful and one-time expensive garments. Poppy's passion for pretty clothes took the form of miserliness carried to the ultimate, and their attainment the only goal toward which she was willing to expend effort. In all other things in life she was supine: too jellyfishy even to be described antagonistic. Of course with her rainbow raiment was the inevitable perquisite of social recognition . . . and beyond that twin triumph she had no thought.

Poppy was vividly aware that she was perhaps the prettiest girl in the city's Afro-American younger set. She set an immense value on her looks. And she had deliberately planned to capitalize her beauty by mercenary marriage.

Had Poppy been governed in the slightest degree by the dictates of what passed muster as her heart she would long since have returned an affirmative answer to Ellick's constant and passionate avowals of love. But at best her affection for him was shallow — albeit it was as deep and unselfish a love as she was capable of harbouring. Of other suitors she had at least two score but they were ambitionless men who worked as elevator boys, second assistant janitors, salaried taxi drivers, delivery men . . . with weekly wages ranging from four to eight dollars. They were automatically beyond the pale. Only Acey Upshaw remained with Ellick on the eligible list.

Acey was rich. Acey's dear departed father had owned a small farm adjoining one from which a few drops of oil had been squeezed some three years previously — Acey at that time being the proprietor of the Star Shoe Repairing Parlour — We Fix Them Good While You Wait: — a one-man establishment with possibilities and little else.

The process of producing a little oil from the innards of the farm adjoining the Upshaw property had been negotiated by a promoter who was a past master in the gentle art of fooling all of the public some of the time. In the enthusiastic rush which followed, Acey's father sold out for five thousand dollars. Some said the shock killed him. Certainly he became entirely defunct.

He was buried with pomp by the Over The River Burying Society of which he was past president. The funeral was quite the longest which the quiet little country town had seen in years. Acey did his ex-parent proud by generously furnishing a full brass band and refreshments for more than two hundred joyfully earnest mourners. After the brief formalities attendant upon settling the cash estate, Acey returned to the city of his choice and branched out as part owner of a flourishing taxi-cab business.

For awhile he clung to the shoe shop, his motives being part sentimental and part practical — he had difficulty in locating a purchaser. Five months previously Ellick Pinckney had nibbled — then fallen. Ellick signed a contract which had been drawn up by a keen negro lawyer, made a small first payment, paid again at the end of a two-months' period, made still another contribution toward the purchase price when four months had elapsed and now faced the grim necessity for final payment at the termination of the sixth month — distant some thirty days.

The original contract had been drafted in the days when Acey and Ellick were pals, before the sinister influence of rivalry had builded a barrier of hatred between them. Ellick now knew that Acey desired nothing so much as the opportunity to retain both The Star Shoe Repairing Parlour and the money paid out by the unfortunate Ellick.

From the standpoint of the frankly mercenary Poppy, marriage to Acey was a very good thing indeed. True, insofar as her personal preferences were concerned, she favoured wifehood to the easy-going, good-natured, society-loving Ellick. Ellick was a city product, born and bred. Acey was congenitally provincial and had resided in a metropolitan atmosphere for less than five years.

But he was hopelessly enmeshed in the mesmerising spell of Poppy's radiant personality and promised to be a good thing as a husband. Certainly there was no doubting his ownership of the ducats necessary to supply her with the sensuous comfort of clothes and ease and social eminence which constituted her paramount desires.

Poppy was canny. She was sufficiently fond of Ellick to content herself with a little less affluence as his wife, and so she had cleverly kept the two men dangling whilst she cold-bloodedly weighed them in the balance. She knew that either man was hers on the moment's asking. She reduced them both to the state of mental seethe where each imagined that he was pledged to her while understanding clearly that she was in no way committed to him. Meanwhile she was content with the joint and several adoration and smugly cognizant of the fact that their voluntary servitude enhanced her social prestige.

So she had drifted on in a state of blissful lassitude, worrying little about today and less about tomorrow, enjoying herself hugely and content to let her destinies shape themselves . . . and now this had come!

Poppy was exceedingly peeved over the impending visit. She was frankly and thoroughly ashamed of her family. Of her sister she knew little: Lithia had been a wild-eyed, skinny-legged street urchin when Poppy departed the ancestral homestead in Kirkland Lane, but she knew that her parents were uncouth and destined not only to remain out of the picture of the city's negro society set — but to destroy her prestige as well.

Background was essential to Poppy. She was entirely superficial herself and a single false note was certain to beget clanging discord. She affected regal airs and had boasted of her family. She was thoroughly detested for the superiority which she assumed and there were many society matrons eager for a chance to lop off her social head. She knew that her bubble was about to go bust which meant, of course, that in order to save her face she would be forced into immediate matrimony with Acey Upshaw — a state which she did not particularly desire despite the obvious and manifold benefits accruing from such a match. There was, in her two-bit soul, a wee mite of a spark which impelled her to hesitate before relinquishing all hold on the faithful and enraptured Ellick.

As to the inevitability of the family visit — Poppy knew that there was nothing to do and she did it. When the Southern train from Atlanta wheezed under the shed of the handsome terminal station, Poppy was there to meet it; and with Poppy were Ellick Pinckney and Acey Upshaw.

Poppy, grim-jawed and angry-eyed, had bedecked in raiment of such glory that it promised to dazzle

her unwelcome family into immediate and complete
subjection. Her hat was a Copenhagen-blue velvet
affair with a red turkey wing and a vermilion ro-
sette. Her coat suit was a rich maroon serge,
braided with navy. Her belt was wide and shiny
and crimson. Her waist was the flesh colour of
white folks. Her stockings were grey silk, embroidered in white, and her twelve-inch laced boots
were mouse-coloured. She carried an ornate bag
made of brocaded ribbon and a jangling vanity set
of silver plate.

Nor were her cavaliers lacking in sartorial elegance. They stood nervously beside her, wary of
her captious mood: Ellick, rangy and powerful;
Acey, short, slender, and, in the matter of complexion, the least African of the trio. The men
wore pearl grey hats, spats to match and carried
suede gloves and polished canes.

The passengers streamed through the under-
ground passage and up the wide concrete stairway
to the exit gates. Poppy watched with anxious,
staring eyes. Acey saw them first and discreetly
fought back a chuckle. " Heah they comes," he
announced positively.

Lithia Blevins led the way and the combination
of a long and tiresome day-coach journey and poor
electric lights didn't give Lithia any the best of
the deal. She was about the height and general
dimensions of her sister and the contour of her
face was pleasing. But she was more than a little
haggard and worn and was wrestling earnestly with
two sagging, battered suitcases. Her costume was
absurd enough for a stage version of the Yankees'
idea of the Southern negro. Her hat was a ridicu-

lous ante-bellum, dun-coloured affair made utterly grotesque by what had once been a feather. Her waist and skirt formed a nondescript combination mercifully concealed by a frayed coat. Her hosiery was of cotton and her shoes enormous and too fondly worn.

The parents — "Huh!" diagnosed Ellick privately, "they ain't nothin' but jes' on'y niggers!"

The visiting Blevinses were properly awed by their daughter's elegance and Lithia shied nervously from the two resplendent escorts. They passed through the coloured waiting-room and emerged on Twenty-sixth street where, at a grandiose signal from Acey, Clarence Carter whirled his taxi to the curb and they piled in.

The distraught Poppy, terrorized by the certainty that the realization was destined to be even worse than the nightmare of anticipation, took them to her boarding establishment where she had arranged to house them during their sojourn so that she might have them more completely under her thumb.

Once at the house Lithia grabbed a suitcase, excused herself and begged permission to "wash up a li'l bit." The Blevins parents seated themselves in dumb resignation and Ellick and Acey stood nervously by a window. Ellick winked. "That Lithia — she ain't spoke ontil yet, is she?"

"Nope."

"An' the ol' folks: reckon they is dumb, too."

"They ain't never rode in no autymobile befo', I'm bettin'," snapped Acey. "They ain't got no call comin' to a real city."

They turned their eyes toward the dazzled parents: Mrs. Blevins unconscionably portly and superlatively black; Blevins *père* shrivelled and wizened and topped with a nap of close, kinky hair. Into the mind of both leaped the same thought: these were the persons from whom the incomparable Poppy was sprung. For the first time they were struck with the idea that Poppy might be something less than divine. They were awakened to the fact that she might have human faults, not the least of which was exaggerated ego.

Poppy slammed into the room, seized her parents' luggage and tossed it unceremoniously into their room. "Ain't you better go tidy up, Mom?"

"Hah!" Mom's heavy jowls quivered with merriment. "Reckon yo' ol' Mammy don' need no tidyin' up."

"If'n you want to change yo' dress —"

"Whuffo', Chile? Reckon dis dress been good enough."

"Lemme take off yo' hat. I 'clare, Mom, you is still wearin' yo' winter hat."

"G'wan, Gal. I been wearin' dat hat fo' five yeahs. Ain't nothin' wrong wid dat hat. If dey was it would of done wore out befo' dis. Miss Farrington what lives on Tradd street gimme dat hat — an' her's quality folks. Reckon I is gwine *be* wearin' dat hat fo' 'nother five yeahs."

She might have rambled on indefinitely but Poppy impatiently cut her short. She heckled her mother and she snapped at her father until finally Mom Blevins could stand it no longer: "Lis'en heah at what I is sayin' Poppy Blevins: yo'd better keep a civil tongue 'tween dem lips o' yourn or dey's gwine be plen'y action 'roun' whar you is at

an' you sho' gwine know all bout'n it. I ain't 'low
no nigger gal to talk to me like what you is been
doin' . . . an' if'n my own daughter tries it —
huh! 'twouldn't be de fust time I tanned you!"

Poppy flounced from the room. She wanted to
think things over. Obviously she had started off
on the wrong tack. Her strategy needed altera-
tions. She sat moodily on the edge of the bed —
and meanwhile Lithia re-entered the parlour.

The two men sat up and gasped audibly. Lithia
had undergone a transformation. She was wearing
a clean gray skirt and a white shirtwaist which
was alluringly open at the throat. Her hosiery was
cotton and her shoes brogans . . . but somehow the
men forgot that: they were looking at the newly-
brushed, crinkly hair and the — the — Oh!
Lithia was smiling . . . that was the keynote of
the transfiguration.

Lithia had a way of smiling: it seemed to lift her
in a trice from the commonplace to the ethereal.
And with the change of clothes she had acquired
an ease of manner just sufficiently tinged with modest diffidence to intrigue Ellick Pinckney's interest. She was a new and interesting type to him.
Too, she was sufficiently like Poppy in face and
figure immediately to pass as a beautiful woman.
But the beauty of her face was different. There
was an unsophistication, a softness, which Poppy
did not have.

She carried a pillow from the sofa and placed
it behind her mother's head. "Feel comfortumble,
Mom?"

Mom sighed. "That shuah is good, Lithia.
Mebbe yo' Pa. . . ."

Pa glanced nervously about the room. "Kin I?"

"Shuah," laughed Lithia encouragingly. "Heah!" She fished into his pocket and produced a reeking corncob pipe and a sack of granulated tobacco. She filled the bowl and tamped it expertly. Then she held the match and he puffed contentedly. Lithia turned toward the men. "Pa ain't hisse'f without he ain't got his pipe," she explained.

"I — I bet you is a good cook," commented Ellick without understanding what prompted the remark.

The girl laughed musically. "Reckon I is — kind of. Mos' Cha'leston niggers cooks good."

"Y'ever work out?"

"Co'se. I is cook fo' some quality folks down to de Batt'ry."

Ellick sighed. "Poppy ain't much cook. She's mostly sassiety."

"Ain't she beautiful?"

"Kinder — like what you is. An' they say she's a good nu'se. But cook! Huh! on'y think to eat she ev' made fo' me was some wonder san'wiches."

"Wonder san'wiches?"

"Yeh!" he grinned. "You wonder whar the meat is at."

Lithia threw back her head and laughed ringingly. Ellick liked to hear her laughter. He wracked his brain for something else funny. He glanced around for Acey and found that gentleman deep in conversation with Old Man Blevins. As for himself, he didn't particularly miss Poppy.

"Ain't nev' been to no big city befo', is you?"

"Nope."

"Reckon I is gwine half to show you the sights. This is a pow'ful fine town. How 'bout gwine to a movie with me tomorry night?"

Lithia glanced apprehensively toward Poppy's door. Ellick intercepted and interpreted the look. "Tha's all right with her. Me'n Poppy's sich close frien's it's sorter up to me to show her sister a good time."

Lithia accepted the invitation with alacrity and when Poppy returned to the room fifteen minutes later she found her sister cosily ensconced in the corner with Ellick Pinckney. She shrugged with regal indifference and attached Acey Upshaw unto herself. If her plan of campaign was to inspire Ellick with jealousy she failed miserably — at least insofar as outward appearance was concerned.

Ellick and Acey departed at the same time. They walked together to the corner because their paths happened to lay in the same direction and not because they liked one another. But when Acey would have passed on, Ellick stopped him.

"Acey!"

"Yeh?"

"Bout'n that money I owes you on the shoe shop —"

"What 'bout it?"

"I needs a sixty-day 'stension."

"Huh! Reckon 'stensions ain't my business, Mistuh Pinckney."

"But if'n I ain't got the money —?"

"Tha's yo' lookout, Mistuh Pinckney. I is got plen'y good s'curity — *an'* a contrac'."

"But you is a'ready been paid mos' all what is due."

"Mos' all ain't all. You is got thutty days to pay the rest of the balance an' you take my adwice an' do it. Tha's all what I is got to say bout'n it. Good night, Mistuh Pinckney!"

Acey turned away and Ellick watched his departing figure forlornly. Ellick was decidedly up against it. It was of course patent to him why the needed extension was refused. Sans business, Ellick would be placed with the matrimonial also-rans and Acey left alone on the eligible list, and of the fact that Acey wanted Poppy there was no doubt — nor did Ellick blind himself to the certainty that Poppy was the sinister motivating influence in Acey's detestation of him.

Ellick, too, coveted Poppy for better or worse; he was enthralled by her exotic radiance and had aspired to her for so long that it had become a habit. More, Acey's dislike was reciprocated with interest and therefore the winning of the delectable Poppy would constitute a personal triumph of no mean proportions.

On the other hand Ellick's little shoe business meant much to him. He was an expert shoe repairer and had long been ambitious to own his own business. The following morning he carried his troubles to the office of Lawyer Evans Chew in the Penny Prudential Bank Building, the nine-story office structure which was the pride spot of Darktown's civic centre.

Lawyer Chew listened attentively, a portentous frown on his face; long, slender fingers toying with a writ of garnishment which lay on his desk.

"You say you is got a contrac', Brother Pinckney?"

"Uh-huh!" Ellick produced from an inside pocket a frayed and thumb-marked document. "Heah 'tis."

Lawyer Chew arranged horn-rimmed spectacles on his nose and perused the paper meticulously.

At length he laid it aside and cleared his throat. "You — er — a — is in a bad way, Brother Pinckney."

"Ain't it the truth?"

"I sispec' this contrac' was drawn up by Lawyer Artopee Gaillard, wa'n't it?"

"Sho' was."

Lawyer Chew *tchk'd* commiseratingly. "Too bad — too bad!"

"Wha's too bad?"

"This heah contrac'. Ise afraid you is in a bad way, Brother Pinckney."

Ellick passed a red handkerchief across a perspiring forehead. "Lis'en heah at me, Lawyer Chew: I ain't come to you foh to heah I is in bad. I come to learn how I c'n git out."

"W'en a 'torney ain't got no more conscience than what Lawyer Gaillard is got —"

"You mean they ain't no way outen that contrac'?"

"None whatever."

"But Lawyer Gaillard said —"

"It don't make no diffe'ence what he said, Brother Pinckney. In — er — a — contrumversy in which a written instriment is concerned they ain't no oral testimony allowed to be intrumduced to modify or explain that which is wrote, same bein' a provision of the Statute of Frauds cal'clated to 'liminate to a minimum all chancst of persons bein' *particeps criminis* when they is a mutual and seve'al desire to break said contrac' as hereinbefo' mentioned."

Ellick shook his head dazedly and came up for air. "W'en you c'lects a fee, Lawyer Chew, they ain't no client gwine say you ain't gave 'em enough words."

"What I mean is," explained the counsellor with dignity, "that what any one said when this contrac' was drawn don't make no diffe'ence whichsoever. What is wrote an' duly attested therein is all which you is interes' in, an' said contrac' which I now hol's in my hand says that you is in a bad fix."

"But s'posin' I don't raise that las' payment: does he git his business back an' all what I is paid out to boot?"

"Unfortumlately he does. Ordinary he woul'n't, but you is had the wrong procedure from the staht. What you should have done was to transfer title to yo'se'f an' give a mor'gage; 'stead of which you is done contrariwise."

"Contrariwise how?"

"You signed that contrac' of yo' own free will an' unblemish' volition, Brother Pinckney; an' thereby you is gwine half to stan'. The money what you is paid out stan's in the light of an option, said option being forfeited autimatically an' *in toto* case'n all payments ain't fo'thcomin' on the day which they is due on."

"Oh! Lawdy . . . an' they ain't *no* way out?"

"No. Not onless fo' a c'nsideration properly

wrote an' inserted into this heah document, Mistuh Acey Upshaw'd be willin' to exten' . . ."

"If'n Acey Upshaw owned all the gasoline in the world, Lawyer Chew, he woul'n't even give me a smell."

"You mean you an' him ain't friendly?"

"I an' him is lovin' the same lady, Lawyer Chew. I reckon that makes you on'erstan' it somewhat better now, huh?"

Chew nodded sagely. "It is clea'er; much clea'er. I see it with infumately greater cla'ity. Could you borry this money elsewhere?"

"Not hahdly, 'specially like if what you says the title on the shop ain't mine. Ol' Semore Mashby might lemme have it ordinary, 'scusin' the other day w'en I was laughin' at him on account what 'Rias Nesbit done to him bout'n that di'min' ring of Elzevir's: you know, him an' Cass Driggers bought a autymobile—"

Chew grinned broadly. "I've heard about it. How about Flo'ian Slappey?"

"He'd mos' prob'ly loant it to me in a minnit, but he ain't heah. He's went to N'Yawleens fo' a month. Now, if'n you had some extry cash—?"

"I is a lawyer, not no money-lender, Brother Pinckney."

Ellick rose abruptly. "You ain't so durn' much of either. W'en I come in heah to see you I ain't had much hope. Now I ain't got *none!*"

Ellick was supremely gloomy during the balance of the day. Business was returning expenses and a small profit, more than enough to provide a fairly comfortable living for himself and an economical wife, but somehow he was unable to get sufficiently ahead of the game to raise the cash required within thirty days by the adamantine Acey Upshaw.

Acey was always a hard man to deal with, but never harder than in this particular instance where the grande passion had entered the game. The encumbrance against Ellick's business was a handful of trumps which Acey was playing expertly, secure in the knowledge that nothing but cash and plenty of it could save Ellick from business disaster. Nor was Acey particularly worried over the fact that the girl of his choice preferred the rival — other things being equal. He knew that other things were not going to be equal, and realized that with Ellick reduced to a job he would have a clear road to her hand. And Acey desired Poppy as he had coveted few other things in his life.

He took her to the movies that night and swelled with triumph when, in the lobby, he nearly collided with Ellick Pinckney and Lithia Blevins. The contrast between the sisters was striking. Lithia looked pretty — no denying that — but she lacked the style, the poise, the urbanity of Poppy.

Ellick experienced a slight twinge of jealousy at sight of Poppy on Acey's arm, and was surprised that the jealousy was not stronger and of longer duration. Perhaps, he thought, it was because the surest road to Poppy's heart at present was by way of taking the unwelcome and hopelessly provincial sister off her hands. Perhaps . . . well, dawggone it! Lithia was Poppy's sister and the sister of such a glorious creature as Poppy couldn't help being interesting.

Across the creamy crests of ice-cream sodas, the

deliriously happy Lithia and the surprisingly contented Ellick chatted. "You is sho' a pretty gal, Lithia."

"Huh! Poppy's the pretty one."

"Oh! she's swell, of co'se. . . ."

"Poppy is change' considerumble, Misto' Pinckney."

"If'n she was ever like you, she sho' has."

"She ain't like the Cha'leston niggers no mo'— not a tall."

"You ain't got no call castin' spurchuns on Cha'leston niggers, Miss Lithia. Not if'n you is like them."

"Dey is a'right, I reckon. Co'se dey ain't high-tone' like what Poppy an' her frien's is . . ."

"High-tone' ain't ev'ythin', Miss Lithia. They's other things which counts. Bein' willin' to work an' a good cook an' not too-'stravagant an' all like that."

"Mebbe you is right, Mistuh Pinckney . . . but I an' Poppy sho' is diffe'ent."

"Bless Gawd!"

"What you mean?"

"Nothin'—nothin'! On'y if'n they wa'n't no diffe'ence in folks, Miss Lithia, they woul'n't be much interestin'—tha's all what I means."

"Tha's sho' the truth, Mistuh Pinckney." She drained her glass and rose. "Ise got to be goin' home."

He arched his eyebrows. "Home? A'ready?"

"Yeh — y'see, sencst his accident Pa ain't much able to do things fo' hisse'f an' Mom, she's so fat, he don' like her foolin' 'roun' him, so I sort of looks after him."

"Ain't that a heap of trouble?"

"Trouble ain't no wuss'n what you thinks it is, Mistuh Pinckney. It's thinkin' makes it hahd."

Lithia was prominent in Ellick's dreams that night. And the following evening when Acey Upshaw — at Poppy's suggestion — took Lithia under his wing, leaving Ellick to the more resplendent sister, Ellick discovered to his surprise that he was discontented. And as, on alternate nights, he escorted Lithia to movies and dances and municipal band concerts, he became more than ever impressed with the striking variation in type which may exist in a single family.

In brief, Ellick discovered that he was not only liking Lithia more, but Poppy less. Lithia was broad figuratively as well as literally and she had a fine, noble conception of the husband's position in the domestic realm. She realized, for instance, that the wife should work and contribute her earnings to the general fund; that no matter how affluent the husband, the wife had no right to squander his money for worthless clothes and fancy fol-de-rol. She believed that a wife was created for the sole purpose of ministering ceaselessly to the creature comforts of her chosen man . . . and into Ellick's mind there seeped the idea that it was Lithia and not Poppy in whose arms he could find contentment.

He longed to go to Acey and relieve that gentleman of the alternate evenings which Poppy forced him to spend with Lithia. But he didn't do it — and Ellick's evenings with Poppy became things of torture to him; first because he had plumbed the depths of Poppy's selfish nature and secondly because he writhed with consuming jealousy at every thought of Acey's bland, smiling face close to that of the adored Lithia — and he was afraid that his request might result in open hostilities in case Acey exhibited a disinclination to agree.

"I ain't min' takin' Lithia out mo' evenin's," he informed Poppy one evening. She flashed him a sharply suspicious glance.

"Reckon you don't. Not by the way you ac's, anyways."

"Now, Poppy — you is the 'sinuatinest woman. They ain't nothin' atween I an' Lithia. On'y I kind of thought mebbe yo'd rather be with Acey Upshaw."

"Huh! I ain't sayin' I would an' I ain't saying I woul'n't. But I'll say this much fo' Acey — he ain't fickle like what you is. Acey would ruther be with me than with Lithia. She's ignorumt an'—"

"I reckon you is gwine say Acey is smaht enough to see that an' I ain't, huh?" he said testily.

"You is at libbity to take what I says any way you likes, Mistuh Pinckney. This heah is a free country. You an' Acey is diffe'ent kin's of men. He ain't havin' his haid tu'ned jes' cause'n a gal looks at him sof' an' tender. Lithia is went to you' haid, Mistuh Pinckney —"

"I ain't kickin' at you goin' with Acey Upshaw, is I?"

"'Twoul'n't do you no good if'n you did."

"Reckon you'll be sayin' nex' you is gwine marry him."

"I ain't sayin' I ain't."

Ellick felt that he should be broken hearted.

But instead he was surprised by the feeling of relief which surged over him. " You always has loved Acey more'n you has me."

" I ain't got no respec' fo' a man which is done what you is done."

" Meanin' which? "

" Went an' forsook me fo' a country nigger like Lithia jes' cause'n she makes cow-eyes at you."

" Tha's yo' own bohn sister what you is stradoosin', Poppy."

" If'n I cain't talk against my own sister, who c'n I talk against? I asts you that, Mistuh Pinckney. What I was gwine say is that Acey ain't never lost his haid."

" Acey ain't got so much haid to lose," retorted Ellick angrily. " An' furthermo' an' also if'n you p'efers Acey to me I reckon I ain't gwine raise no howl."

" I does p'efer him! " she flashed. " An' if'n yo'd ruther be with Lithia. . . ."

He rose slowly. " Reckon I would."

" Ise gwine marry Acey — so there! "

" Reckon I ain't cryin' over that, Poppy Blevins. Lithia's the kin' of wife I wants."

" You go an' git her, then," raged Poppy. " Go on an' git her — you no-'count, fickle, wuthless nigger, you! What you think I cares bout'n a man like what you is, anyways, when I c'n git one like Acey Upshaw? You an' Lithia is two of a kin'— y'orter be raisin' cotton on a plantation 'stead of livin' in a city. They ain't enough sperrit in the two of you to run a kerosene lamp. Ise wishin' you good day, Mistuh Pinckney — an' w'en you sees Acey jes' tell him Ise waitin' fo' him: that's all — jes' tell him I wants him."

Ellick Pinckney made his exit with as great dignity as was possible under the circumstances. Once outside, he threw back his shoulders and inhaled a great breath of relief.

For the first time in three weeks, Ellick Pinckney was happy. For the moment he almost forgot the imminent fall of the Damoclean sword which hung suspended over his little shoe shop.

He had admitted for many days that Lithia Blevins was the woman with whom he wished to share the joys and sorrows of the balance of his life . . . but thought of Poppy had terrified him. Poppy, he fancied, was in love with him and would, perhaps, insist on marrying him whether or no. He now felt that he was free.

The sensation was exquisite. He had effected a miraculous escape from a life of servitude to a shallow, selfish, vain woman.

There was also more than a little satisfaction in Poppy's genuine anger for by it Poppy had shown plainly that she did care for him! Acey was a good enough second choice . . . but he smiled sardonically as he recalled her bitter request: "W'en you see Acey tell him I wants him!" Grandstand stuff. . . .

Suddenly Ellick Pinckney stopped short. His lower jaw slowly sagged. His eyes opened wide. His lips expanded into a grin and a chuckle issued from between his lips. And finally he slapped one broad palm resoundingly against his thigh.

"Dawg-gone!" he chortled. "Ise bettin' fo'

bits 'gainst a hole in a pair of shoes it'll work! Ding-bust. . . ."

The idea was inspirational and splendidly logical. Ellick strode down the street with shoulders swinging triumphantly and an interminable chuckle agitating his cheeks.

The more he thought it over the funnier it was and the more certain of success. There wasn't a flaw in the scheme. Acey wanted Poppy, did he? And Poppy — spurned by Ellick — desired Acey? And Ellick needed Acey's good will? The circumstances dovetailed into a perfect whole.

Acey Upshaw rose hurriedly as his dark and particular aversion breezed into the office and slammed the door. "What you want?" demanded Acey curtly.

Ellick forcibly banished from his face all semblance of happiness and in its stead summoned a visible lugubriosity which had more or less effect on the man opposite. Then Ellick sighed. He was an artist at sighing, was Ellick. "Acey," he opened, "me'n you ain't been lovin' one 'nother much lately, is we?"

"No," shortly, "we ain't."

"We useter be good frien's, Acey."

"Useter ain't is."

"Frien'ship is the Lawd's noblestes' gif' to man — Rev'end Arlandas Sipsey say that in Chu'ch yestiddy."

"I don' 'ten' his Chu'ch."

"Now, Acey. . . . Anyways, I been thinkin' what a shame 'tis we is done discomtinued from bein' frien's like what we useter be."

POPPY PASSES

Acey was vaguely impressed — but suspicious.
"What all this mean, Ellick?"

"It means," sighed Ellick, "that I is done saw the error of my ways, Acey, an' I is came to you with the han' of frien'ship outstretch' in forgiveness. I is came, Acey, cause'n we is 'lowed a woman to bust in between us —"

Acey stiffened. "I ain't 'scussin' wimmin with you, Ellick Pinckney."

"Lis'en heah to what I is sayin', Acey; you an' me is been lovin' the same gal, ain't we?"

"Yeh."

"An' us both jes' wants to see her real happy, don't we?"

"'Pendin' on which —"

"'Pendin' on nothin', Acey Upshaw. I says to myse'f, I says — if'n I loves a lady I wants to see her happy an' if'n she c'n be happier with you than what she c'n with me — why, I reckon I woul'n't be much man if'n I ain't tell you: ain't it the truth?"

Acey gasped. He was beginning to get the drift of Ellick's conversation and was astounded by the display of magnanimity. "You — you is been talkin' to her?"

"Yeh," sadly. "I lef' her no mo'n fifteen minutes ago."

"Why you is come to me?"

"Acey Upshaw — that they gal don' no mo' love me than she loves Semore Mashby. The man what she is lovin', Acey Upshaw — is you! It's done busted my hea't to tell you this, Acey — but we useter been frien's an', like what I done said, if'n it'll make her happier to be yo' wife I guess Ise man enough to let you know that she is waitin' to home fo' you to come an' ast her will she marry you."

Acey's head wobbled. He braced himself more firmly that this epochal display of altruism and self-sacrifice might not fell him. "You — you is comin' heah to tell me — she loves me — an' I is to marry her?"

"Uh-huh!"

"You is sho'— sho' bout'n that, Ellick?"

"Ain't she done tol' it to me less'n fifteen minutes ago?"

"Geeemanety!" Acey's hand shot out. "What you is said bout'n frien'ship sho' is the truth, Ellick Pinckney. It's the noblestes' thing what man is got an' Ise proud we is frien's again."

"Bless Gawd!" intoned Ellick fervently as their hands met and clasped.

"Amen!"

"Jes' like ol' times, ain't it, Acey?"

"You is a noble frien', Ellick Pinckney. An' I is mean an' small. I is shame' of myse'f w'en I thinks of how I was gwine squeeze you outen that shoe business—"

"Don' you worry bout'n that, Acey. Even if you takes my shop away from me like what you is got a legal right to do, I ain't gwine raise no howl. 'If'n yo' brother paste you on one cheek, give 'im a shot at 'tother.' Tha's my motter where my frien's is concerned at, Acey."

Acey brushed one hand across his eyes and seated himself at the desk. For a minute he wrote busily and then extended a paper to his friend. "I is learn' my lesson, Ellick. They is a 'stension on the business fo' ninety days marked fo' val'able considumration. 'Tain't gwine be writ in the Heavumly book that Acey Upshaw wa'n't man enough to meet a frien' halfway."

"You is a good man, Acey. An'," glumly, "they is yo' hat. Go an' make that gal happy, Acey. Make her happy, an' my blessin's go with you."

Acey departed swiftly and Ellick followed him to the street with his lips parted in an unholy smile of triumph. He almost convinced himself that he had done a noble and generous act. And it had worked— Ye Gods! but it had worked! He was rid of Poppy, repossessed of Acey's invaluable friendship, held a ninety-day extension on the business and — last and most important — had cleared for himself a path to the hand of the divine Lithia with its promise of matrimonial bliss.

Ellick walked slowly down the street toward the house where the Blevinses boarded. He was feeling very, very much at peace with himself and the world. He was positive that by this time Lithia would be at home. . . .

He turned in at the gate which hung limply on a broken hinge. The door, opening from the tiny veranda into the living-room, was ajar. Ellick tiptoed across the porch and pushed the door gently. He entered the room.

Then he started back. For the room was already occupied. It was occupied by a man and a woman and the woman was tightly clasped in the arms of the man.

The man was Acey Upshaw!
The woman was *Lithia!*"
And Acey joyfully welcomed the unfortunately

successful matchmaker, who gazed in pop-eyed horror at the illuminating tableau. " It's fitten you should be the fust to congratumlate us, Ellick," he said, " because they never was no nobler deed than what you done in sendin' me to Lithia w'en I knowed you was lovin' her yo'se'f."

" You — you mean — you an' *Lithia* is engage'? "

" It was you done it, Ellick. If'n you hadn't of tol' me 'bout her bein' in love with me I never would of had the nerve to prepose. Ain't you gwine be happy with us, Ellick? "

Ellick nodded slowly, vainly striving to reconstruct a shattered cosmic scheme. " Yeh! Ise happy . . . on'y, My Gosh! Acey — you sho' does work fast! "

PAINLESS EXTRACTION

PAINLESS EXTRACTION

THE patient was exquisitely miserable. He lay tensely in the chair, popping eyes focussed on the plump hand of Miss Corena Clemmins, trained nurse. Miss Clemmins' fingers were wrapped competently around a pair of shiny cow-horn forceps recently rescued from the steamy depths of the sterilizer. She stood by in efficient silence, waving the forceps gently and professionally deaf to the gurgling protests of the prospective victim.

Dr. Brutus Herring, Dentist, glanced in a brief and satisfied manner toward his trained assistant; tested his hypodermic and slowly sucked into its innards the local anesthetic which he was about to inject. Then he turned calmly toward the patient.

"Open yo' mouth, Brother De Lee."

"Wh-what you gwine do?"

"Jes' on'y a little nerve blockin'. One jab an' it's all over."

"With me?"

Dr. Brutus Herring nodded to the nurse, who placed a strong, capable hand on the patient's forehead and forced him back against the headrest. The dentist inserted his needle and jabbed. Mr. De Lee promptly responded with a wiggle of agony and a long-drawn whooshy howl. Then he relaxed. "That don' hu't no mo'," he admitted.

Dr. Herring stepped back. "Co'se not. Ain't

I done said it wa'n't gwine hu't on'y fo' a secon'? Now we'll wait ontil it gits 'nesthetized tho'ough."

Two minutes later he relieved Miss Clemmins of the forceps and turned again toward the chair. Cold beads of perspiration stood out on the chocolate forehead of Mr. De Lee. "D-Doc, you shuah it ain't gwine hu't?"

"Not a bit — not a bit. Open yo' mouth."

The mouth opened slowly — reluctantly. Then it closed again and the man in the chair sighed with prayerful relief. "Doc, they is some one rappin' at yo' do'."

The knocking sounded again: an insistent, nervous tattoo. Miss Clemmins crossed the room and the door swung open.

The man who stood in the doorway teetering on the balls of enormous feet was very short, very thin and unbelievably black. Small as he was, his clothes fitted him a trifle soon. He wore large, gold-rimmed spectacles and a portentous frown. His voice, startling in its volume, boomed across the room.

"Mawnin'— mawnin'. Busy, Dr. Herrin'— busy?"

The dentist nodded. "Mawnin', Dr. Atcherson. Yes, I is ve'y busy."

"Doin' what? — what?"

"I is about to puffo'm a extordonta."

Dr. Elijah Atcherson, M.D., snorted. "Huh! Nothin' on'y a tooth-pullin'. Nothin' tall but that. Guess you don' require Miss Clemmins' service fo' such as that."

Dr. Herring stiffened to the full of his six magnificent feet of light-brown manhood. "Reckon

I is the bes' judge of that, Dr. Atcherson, an' I judges I needs her."

"Simple little thing like —"

"If'n you was a dentis', Dr. Atcherson, yo'd mebbe know that a extordonta is a se'ious operation. I needs Miss Clemmins an' I is gwine have her."

"Fumadiddles!" bellowed the little man. "What you need her fo'?"

"S'posin'," clinched Herring, "s'posin' my patient should get a fractured jaw — what then?"

"Yo'd call in a M.D.— tha's what."

Mr. De Lee sat up very straight in the chair, a light of inquiring horror in his eyes. "Oh! my Gawd! Doc. . . ."

"Lay back down, Brother De Lee. I ain't gwine hu't you — but I hires a perfessional nu'se to insuah my patients the bes' intention what is possible case'n things goes wrong." He turned huffily toward the little man in the doorway. "I is got to ast you to escuse me, Dr. Atcherson. I ain't holdin' no clinic."

"But I need Miss Clemmins — now. I is got a compoun' fracture case out near Potterville, an'—"

"I employs Miss Clemmins much as you does, Dr. Atcherson. W'en I completes with her se'vices you c'n have her, an' not befo'."

Dr. Elijah Atcherson banged the ground-glass door and puffed into his own handsomely furnished office. He slapped himself down in a swivel chair, cocked his big feet on the desk, lighted a panatela and puffed great clouds of smoke into the room.

From this point of vantage Dr. Atcherson gazed

through the open door of his office into the large ice-cream parlour on which the suite of offices occupied by himself and Dr. Herring abutted. Behind the marble-topped fountain a tall, slender, yellow negro concocted fizzy drinks with an expert hand and two energetic little coloured boys scurried from crowded table to crowded table waiting on the press of coloured humanity which sought solace from the sweltering heat of the July day in the delectable, cool specialties obtainable only in The Gold Crown Ice Cream Parlour.

Visible evidence of the prosperity of The Gold Crown, which was owned jointly by Dr. Atcherson, Dr. Herring and March Clisby, the tall soda dispenser, was too much for the ebony physician. He bounced his skinny, wizened figure from the chair, shoved his hands into trousers pockets and strolled magnificently forth to inspect the cash register. March Clisby greeted him with a genial grin: " The Ol' Gol' Crown been cashin' in th'ough the hot spell, Doc."

"That so? That so?" The huge voice rumbled through the store and customers looked up hastily to seek its source. Many bowed to the great physician, but he condescended to return only a few of the obeisances — and those thus noticed swelled with pardonable pride. Dr. Elijah Atcherson, leading coloured surgeon of the state, was the acknowledged bell-wether of the city's Afro-American flock.

A large, throaty yell, emanating from the office of Dr. Brutus Herring, split the buzz of conversation in the Gold Crown. Dr. Atcherson shrugged and minced back toward his office for hat and Boston-bag. "Call it tooth-pullin' or call it extordonta," he philosophized, "Ise bettin' they ain't no diffe'ence in the way it hu'ts."

The door of the dentist's office swung back and Mr. De Lee, sadly the worse for wear, staggered weakly into the hall and out through the side door. Behind him came the cool, competent Corena Clemmins. She presented herself before Dr. Atcherson. "You want me to go with you into the country, Doctor?"

"No," roared the great man testily. "I was jes' aimin' to take you joy-ridin'. Tha's all. Get yo' hat an' get it quick!"

Miss Clemmins got it. Five minutes later she seated herself beside him in the high-powered, expensive roadster. He let in his gears and they rolled away into the heat.

The city sweltered in the merciless blaze of a midsummer sun. It was such a July day as can only come in the South after a cool, pleasant June. The heat waves danced crazily above the steaming road; the sidewalks received the rays of the sun, intensified them, and radiated them back into the heat saturated atmosphere. The big office buildings, rising high in the air, were peopled at every window by clerks seeking the zephyrs which were that day non-existent.

Corena Clemmins relaxed in the luxurious upholstery and closed her eyes. It was an immense relief after the strain of maintaining a semblance of neatness in the stuffy offices. Unconsciously her body inclined toward the skinny little doctor. The heat — the arduous labours of the past few hours — the exhaustion begotten at a barbecue the previous night — the natural drowsiness of the day: they conspired diabolically and Miss Corena Clemmins dozed. And, dozing, she slid closer to the doctor and her head rested lightly on his right shoulder; lightly enough to fail to disturb his preoccupation.

And with that tableau in the car they passed a slow-moving, city-bound trolley. On the street car was an exceedingly ample, flamboyantly dressed lady of colour who saw the automobile. More, she glimpsed the contented smile which played about the lips of the doctor and the blissful expression of the nurse. She did not know that at the moment the doctor was exultingly rehearsing a recent and eminently successful operation for ruptured appendix nor that the nurse was asleep. She saw only the beatitude of the couple. She cared to see nothing else. The fire of a vast and righteous wrath flamed in her eyes.

The Amazonian creature was Mrs. Dr. Elijah Atcherson!

For seventeen miles Dr. Elijah Atcherson headed into the country. He passed through two or three scattered suburbs resplendent with cosy bungalows nestling behind green, velvety lawns. Children romped about in defiance to the humidity. Even the stately pines seemed to have wilted before the vicious attacks of the sun, and only a few grey clouds hovering over the crest of Red Mountain to the south gave any faint promise of relief.

The doctor and nurse reached the home of their patient, a drab, unpainted, ramshackle cabin perched precariously on the side of a steep, rocky hill. The unfortunate, a little negro boy twelve

PAINLESS EXTRACTION

years of age, screamed with terror at sight of his visitors and the doctor forced his distracted parents from the room. Then he seated himself beside the bed and conversed quietly with the pain-wracked youngster. The rumble remained in his big voice but the quick querulousness was gone.

At length the compound fracture was set, the arm in splints and the boy smiling brightly. In his palm was a bright, new half dollar — gift of Dr. Atcherson. The man of medicine and his nurse stepped onto the tiny veranda and just as they did so a clap of thunder reverberated across the valley.

A pale grey haze had come over the sun. The fleecy grey clouds had blackened ominously. A jagged lightning flash punctured the grey pall and Corena Clemmins instinctively sidled closer to the doctor. That individual shrugged philosophically, put up his curtains, roared instructions to the grateful parents and signalled Miss Clemmins to a place at his side.

They had gone little more than two miles down the valley when the storm broke with a fanfare of heavy thunder and blinding lightning. Then the heavens opened and the rain came down — heavy, swishing sheets which transformed the red clay road into a sea of slimy mud and battered in through the slit between the two halves of the windshield. The car skidded dangerously from one side of the road to the other. One curtain ripped loose with a noise like the cracking of a blacksnake whip and the torrent poured in, drenching the nurse to the skin.

Dr. Atcherson handled his car in grim-jawed silence. Then without a word, he swung in from the road and braked down in the lee of a little cabin. He alighted and knocked. There was no response. He tried the door, it yielded to his touch and he entered. The cabin was deserted. He beckoned to the nurse and she joined him.

"They ain't no use tryin' to git home in this," he commented loudly.

She shook her head. "We'd git bogged shuah."

One hour passed: two — three. Heavy dusk settled swiftly into black night. At six o'clock Dr. Atcherson took his place at the wheel, started his motor and tried to move the car. But the machine had other ideas regarding the propriety of driving under such adverse conditions. It refused to budge. The motor roared and the rear wheels whirred angrily as they kicked up a stream of red clay. The doctor alighted and rejoined Corena Clemmins.

At eight o'clock the rain stopped as suddenly as it had started. The clouds scudded from the face of a brilliant full moon and the skies became peppered with bright, twinkling stars. By nine o'clock the doctor had put on his chains and extracted the car. But the going toward town was slow and heavy. At half past ten they pulled up before the Gold Crown Ice Cream Parlour.

The Gold Crown was ablaze with light. The crowd within was dense and extra help had been impressed to wait upon the voracious patrons. The bedraggled doctor and nurse crossed the sidewalk. Then, with his hand on the screen door the doctor paused suddenly and would have turned away. But he was too late.

His wife had seen him!

PAINLESS EXTRACTION

She swept grandiosely toward the door from the rear of the Gold Crown, rendolent of cheap perfume, a-jangle with ornaments, and with an expression of uncompromising venom on her heavy, black features.

"Lustisha looks like trouble an' heaps of it," soliloquized the doctor weakly.

The crowd was willing to scent good sport. There was a sudden cessation of chatter and a general craning of necks toward the scene of the impending domestic drama. No one knew exactly what was coming but there was no mistaking the ample militancy of the little doctor's large wife.

Elijah Atcherson stepped within and strove vainly to summon to his aid the ponderous dignity with which he subjugated every one in the world with the single exception of his consort. But it was no go. He was too small, too skinny, too bedraggled, too woebegone. His clothes were plastered with wet, sticky mud; his spectacles awry, his huge feet mud-coated and resembling a pair of ditch-digging instruments after a hard day's work. The voice of Mrs. Lushtisha Atcherson cut nasally through the crowded store.

"Is you have a good time on yo' joy-ride?"

Dr. Atcherson gazed beseechingly into the eyes of his wife. "Now, Lustisha . . ." he wheedled.

"Don't you staht 'Now-Lustisha-in'' me, 'Lijah. I asts you again an' fo' the secon' time: is you have a good time on yo' joy-ride?"

"I been out on a perfessional call."

"Huh! Pow'ful funny perfession you is got. Where you go to?"

"Two miles this side of Potterville."

"How long was you at yo' patient's house?"

"'Bout —'bout an hour."

"An' you been five hours gittin' back — huh?"

"The sto'm, Honey. . . ."

"Don' you go tellin' me no malorna bout'n you got stuck in the mud 'cause I is been married to you too long to stan' fo' any sech a story as that."

"The roads was slipp'y —"

"So was you. I is had enough of these heah goin's-on, 'Lijah Atcherson. I is bringin' all these folks to bear witness I is stood my las' insult at yo' han's."

"What you mean: insult?"

Lustisha struck an attitude: clenched hands resting on that portion of her anatomy possessed of greatest beam. "If'n 'tain't a insult fo' a married man to go traipsin' 'roun' with a yaller hussy —"

Corena Clemmins, up to this moment a passive — if angry — spectator, stiffened. She shoved between the harried man of medicine and his gloriously angry spouse. "Tha's enough of *that*, Mis' Atcherson!"

The crowd eddied closer about the prospective combatants.

"'Nough of which?"

"Stradoosin' me."

Lustisha sniffed her disdain. "I ain't got no words fo' you, gal."

"Yo'd better have words fo' me, Mis' Atcherson, an' lots of 'em," snapped Corena firmly, "because if'n I ain't git a 'pology quick Ise gwine have you 'rested fo' criminal liable."

"You is on'y jes' talkin' with yo' mouth."

"You is the one been talkin' with yo' mouth, Mis'

PAINLESS EXTRACTION 285

Atcherson, an' less'n you 'pologizes quick you is gwine be mighty sorry you done same."

Lustisha gazed first at Corena, then at the cowering figure of her husband — then at Corena again. There was no hint of leniency in Corena's attitude and Lustisha experienced a vague doubt as to the wisdom of her public diatribes. She hedged. " I ain't on'y said my husban'—"

" You done call me a hussy. 'Pologize an' 'pologize quick! "

" Well . . . I'll admit I ain't *know* it."

" You is gwine admit I is a lady."

Lustisha tossed her head angrily. " All right, be a lady if'n you wants. You cain't make me mad."

With that she turned away, signally defeated in the first open clash with her husband's office assistant and keenly conscious that she had become a laughing-stock. Corena, smiling triumphantly, sailed through the store toward the offices in the rear. Elijah Atcherson followed fearfully in her wake. In the sanctity of his office he faced her: his expression a masterpiece in concentrated lugubriousness.

" We is done played hell now, Miss Clemmins."

" Mebbe so you is, Dr. Atcherson. Me, I ain't got nothin' whichever to do with yo' dimestic affairs."

" Yes, you is."

" How come? "

" You is done make a fool outen my wife —"

" The Lawd done that."

" I ain't 'sputin' with you. But what you done out they in public she is gwine git revenge fo'."

" I ain't skeered of her."

"But I is," he postulated dolefully. "She is gwine take it out on me w'en we gits home."

"Hmph! If'n I was a hen-pecked man like what you is — which I ain't, bless Gawd! — I'd puffo'm a operation fo' the removal of a weddin' ring."

"Not a chancst to d'vohce her."

"How come not?"

"She won't let me."

Once in the bedroom of their pretentious home on Eighteenth street, Lustisha opened fire. Elijah, stripped of his pomposity, sank supinely into a chair and listened limply. Lustisha said everything about him she could think of and many things regarding Corena Clemmins which she dared not say in public. Finally, however, she ran out of breath. Elijah looked up meekly.

"That all?" he inquired.

"No —'tain't."

He sighed resignedly. "Go ahead. Might's well finish 'count you got such a good staht."

"You is got to make public respitution."

"Fo' what?"

"Fo the insult you an' that hussy made on me t'night."

"How we insulted you?"

"Nev' min' how: fac' is, you done it. An', like what I is said — you is got to make public respitution."

"How? How?"

"You is got to decharge that woman."

He sat up straight in his chair, the one surviving spark of belligerency flaming. "Won't!"

"Will!"

"I say I won't."

PAINLESS EXTRACTION 287

" You got to."

" Cain't! " he clinched.

" What you mean: cain't? "

" Ain't got no cause."

" Joy-ridin'—"

" I is tellin' you I ain't hahdly knowed she was with me —"

" Lis'n heah at what I is sayin', 'Lijah Atcherson: I seen that gal ridin' with you — seen her with my own eyes — an' she had her haid on yo' shoulder. An' don' you go tellin' me a man don' know w'en a good-lookin' gal has her haid on his shoulder."

" You is all wrong."

" I seen it from the street car."

" You is the seein'est woman, Lustisha," he exclaimed impatiently. " You sees things which ain't never was."

" That they woman is got you fooled, 'Lijah Atcherson. Ev'y man an' woman in our sassiety set is laughin' at you."

" Whaffo' they laugh at me? "

" Fo' how that woman is makin' a monkey outen you. She's a nachel-bohn wampire an' you ain't got sencst enough to see it. She is wampin' you on account you is rich an' pretty soon they is gwine be some blackmail."

" Huh! Lustisha — you is been gwine to too much movies."

" What I sees I knows," she retorted hotly. " An' what I knows I knows, an' I knows she ain't nothin' 'ceptin' on'y a pe'fessional wampire."

He laughed heavily. " Haw . . . I is a swell specimen fo' a wampire to pick on, ain't I? "

"Skinny little no-'count runts like what you is, is the easiest pickin's what they is fo' wampires, 'Lijah."

He waved his hand shortly. "They ain't no use makin' no mo' talk 'bout'n it noways, Lustisha. Corena Clemmins is under contrac' with me an' Dr. Herrin' ontil nex' April an' I an' him ain't gwine th'ow away no eight hund'ed dollars by lettin' her go even if he was willin'."

Her lips compressed into a straight red line. "An' he ain't?"

"No."

"He likes her?"

"Shuah does."

"Hmph! An' him a engage' man!"

"My Gawd! Lustisha, ain't you nev' gwine believe us'n don' regahd her noways 'ceptin' on'y as a nu'se?"

"I ain't nev' gwine disrumgahd the fac' that a man c'n git all the medical degrees which is an' they ain't no guarantee wrote on his diploma which says he is gwine be blind to a pretty face an' a good figger. Ise jes' tellin' you this — you is got to get rid of her or they is gwine be trouble a-plen'y. Heah me?"

"Heahin' you is the easiest thing they is."

"All right. Now I is th'ough."

Elijah Atcherson nodded. "Bless Gawd!" he said under his breath.

For several days thereafter Mrs. Lustisha Atcherson maintained a strange and unnatural silence towards her spouse regarding the radiant trained nurse. Elijah was at first darkly suspicious, and finally philosophically reconciled to the temporary peace. He was not given to anticipating the tomorrows of his domestic life. Too well he knew that they were certain to come, and come kicking. His wife was a veritable genius at discovering new reasons for, and methods of, household torture. But the seed of doubt had been planted and Dr. Elijah Atcherson did a little watching on his own hook.

Thinking it over in the light of the recent ultimatum, he decided unanimously that Corena Clemmins was entirely too pretty a person for the workaday world. He decided further that there might — only might, mind you — be some ulterior motive in her assiduous attention to duty. She was always willing to hold private confabs with the doctor or his dentist friend. True: they were no exceptions — she was popular with all men. She seemed to strive for such popularity. She even spent a great deal of her time in the company of the sartorially perfect Mr. March Clisby, manager of The Gold Crown Ice Cream Parlour, and owner of a one-third interest therein.

Dr. Atcherson knew considerable about medicine and surgery but his ideas of vampiring were hazy. He fancied that all vampires worked this way: having many men on a string — men of money and influence. Men whose standing in the community was a commercial asset. Of course it was ridiculous that she could see anything attractive in his shrivelled self, yet it was undeniably true that she never shirked an opportunity to be with him. Ergo: she must have an ulterior motive. Or two or three of them.

Personally Dr. Atcherson wanted nothing to do

with her or any other woman. He desired nothing so much as the complete elimination of the sex — starting with his wife. His experience with woman had been in the singular number, possessive case — and productive of a large, gloomy gob of unrelieved misery. Still, until his wife's tongue again dripped vitriol he was content to let well enough alone and went his way with such contentment as he could summon — not however, entirely free from doubt of Corena Clemmins' motives.

But if Elijah succeeded in hypnotizing himself into the belief that because his wife had suddenly become tight-lipped on the subject of vampires in general and Miss Corena Clemmins in particular, she had forgotten her humiliation in the Gold Crown Ice Cream Parlour or her hatred of Miss Clemmins — he was wrong.

Lustisha Atcherson became a snooper. And she did her snooping usually around the Gold Crown Ice Cream Parlour where from her vantage point at a certain seat at a certain table she could see much of what transpired in the offices at the rear.

Lustisha, too, quickly learned that Corena was a charmer of men. It was she who noticed two important things: first, that Corena was openly striving to ensnare the affections of Dr. Brutus Herring and, second, that she was not unwilling to practice on smaller fry: the potential victim in this case being the immaculate March Clisby.

Finally Lustisha's patience was rewarded. Early one sultry July afternoon she swept indignantly out of Dr. Herring's office and made her way with all the speed her bulk permitted to the

PAINLESS EXTRACTION

home of Miss Mayola Kye, fiancé of Dr. Herring.

Mayola's demure little face, and tiny, rounded figure gave no hint of the battle spirit which smouldered within her. At heart she was a fiery little thing; intensely in love with the handsome, debonair, Herculean Dr. Brutus Herring — and insanely jealous. At sight of her visitor Mayola experienced a qualm — and then another qualm. She didn't like Lustisha because Lustisha's visits invariably boded trouble of some sort. And trouble was something which Mayola avoided whenever she saw it first. Now, however, there was no escape so Mayola made the best of a bad situation.

"Evenin', Mis' Atcherson."

"Evenin', Miss Kye. How you is this evenin'?"

"Tol'able — tol'able, thank you. How you is?"

"Mis'able!" snapped Mrs. Atcherson in her nasal, high-pitched tones. "Jes' plain mis'able."

"'Count of which?"

"Men!"

"Meanin'—?"

"All men, an' mos' pertickeler my husban'."

"Sho' now, Mis' Atcherson; they ain't nothin' wrong with yo' husban'."

"Lot you know bout'n him."

"Don' he treat you good?"

"He'd better!"

"I is sho', Mis' Atcherson, that you is misundumstood sumthin'."

"I is been a innercent, trustin' fool, an' w'en I fin's out what I fin's out today, Miss Kye, I says to myse'f, I says: 'Us wimmin is got to stan' together.' Tha's jes' 'zac'ly what I says."

Mayola had no desire whatever to stand together with Mrs. Atcherson, but she nodded approvingly. "Ain't it the truth?"

"So I come right to you, Miss Kye, 'cause you is the one pusson ought to know bout'n it even if it hu'ts to heah it. I feel it's my bounden duty, Miss Kye —"

"You nee'n't go worryin' yo'se'f —"

"I knows it. But I is a cha'itable woman, Miss Kye, an' I woul'n't go seein' no lady —'specially a Lodge Sister, git into sech a fate. An' seein' as you is a'ready engage' to him —"

Mayola grew rigid. Her eyes dilated. "Engage' to which?"

"Brutus Herrin', ob co'se. Who else?"

"Wh-what 'bout Brutus?"

"Him an' that woman."

"I ain't quite on'erstan', Mis' Atcherson."

"That nu'se which him an' Dr. Atcherson is got down to they office. She is a'ready ruint my husban'— ol' wampire!"

Mayola's lips came together firmly. "I cain't 'low nobody to talk 'gainst my fiansay, Mis' Atcherson: not nobody."

"I ain't said nothin' ag'in him, is I?"

"You has 'sinuated —"

"I ain't 'sinuated nothin' I ain't know is fac'."

Mayola was impressed in spite of herself. "What you is drivin' at?"

Lustisha rose. "If'n you ain't interes' . . ."

"I is. 'Deed I is. Set down — please."

Somewhat mollified, Mrs. Atcherson re-seated herself. "They ain't nothin' I is sayin' bout'n him I ain't sayin' bout my own husban'. That wampire nu'se — that Corena Clemmins — is wampin' them men. . . ."

It looked like mere spiteful conjecture to Mayola and she could not, in duty, sit idly by while this stout creature traduced her beloved. "You know what the poeck says in Latin, Mis' Atcherson — *Honey swat key molly pants?*"

"I ain't interes' in what no poeck says in Latin, Miss Kye. I is interes' on'y in what niggers says in English. An' what they does! An' w'en a good-lookin' young man gives a han'some woman a solid gol' ring of eighteen carrots, I reckon they ain't no poecks gwine make me think they ain't sumthin' mo' to it than jes' on'y plutonic frien'ship."

"Who give which a gol' ring?"

"Brutus Herrin' give Corena Clemmins one. Nor neither that ain't all, Miss Kye. 'Twas a ring he made his ownse'f outen gol' which he had in his office an' jes' fo' the pussonal sediment of it — he set it with a beautiful false tooth, 'stead of a di'min'."

It was too much for Mayola. Some things she might have overlooked but not this infamy. The idea that her dearly beloved had with his own hands created a ring and by way of exquisitely delicate sentiment set it with a false tooth, prostrated her. Her trim little figure grew tense and she leaned forward in the chair: hands tightly clenched. "You c'n prove that, Mis' Atcherson?"

Lustisha shrugged indifferently. "Ain't got to prove it. You go ast him."

Mayola was galvanized into action. She rose determinedly. "I is gwine do jes' that!" she snapped, and vanished within the house. When she emerged, dressed for the street, Lustisha had disappeared.

Mayola went immediately to the offices in the rear of the Gold Crown Ice Cream Parlour. March Clisby beamed at her from behind the fountain. "Evenin', Miss Kye."

"Evenin', Mistuh Clisby," came the frigid answer. "Where Dr. Herrin' is at?"

"In his office."

"Alone?"

"Uh-huh."

"Where Miss Clemmins is?"

March Clisby glanced at her peculiarly. "In the office with Dr. Atcherson. Why?"

Mayola's tense nerves jangled. She swung on the unoffending soda king. "I knows a heap of folks, Mistuh Clisby, which makes a good livin' by mindin' they own business!"

What display of lovers' passion there was in the meeting between Dr. Brutus Herring and the desirable Mayola, had its source within his breast. She was frigidly aloof. And she came to the point with a directness that fairly flabbergasted him. For a minute he was too startled to reply. She stamped her foot impatiently: "Did you or di'n't you give her a gol' ring which you made yo' ownse'f an' set with a false tooth?"

"Why — why — Mayola. . . ."

"Is or ain't?"

"It — it wa'n't on'y jes' a trifle."

"Then you did, huh?"

"Jes' a li'l' trifle, Mayola. On'y jes'—"

She was perilously close to tears. "I is th'ough an' done with you, Brutus Herrin'," she railed passionately. "You an' that no-'count 'Lijah Atcherson, both. Ain't you got sense enough to see that woman ain't nothin' on'y a plain, common, o'dina'y, ev'yday wampire which is came heah to work you an' 'Lijah Atcherson on account you is rich? Ain't that plain? Sho' 'tis — an' you is done fell fo' it . . . tha's how come you come to give her that ring which you made yo' ownse'f. I reckon I is been a fool, Brutus Herrin'. But I ain't gwine be no fool no longer'n what I is a'ready been. Heah —" she ripped from her finger the handsome diamond engagement ring he had presented to her a few months previously. "Give Corena Clemmins this heah ring, too. Reckon it'll look pow'ful good 'longside of the one you made."

She swung toward the door but he stopped her.

"Mayola!"

"I ain't gwine make no mo' talk with you."

"Lemme 'splain."

"'Splain to her. If'n you ever wants to 'splain to me, Brutus Herrin', the fust thing you is got to staht off with is to tell me you is done fired her."

For perhaps five minutes after the door slammed behind the girl of his heart, Dr. Brutus Herring stood staring at the mute, mocking panels. The ring . . . of course he had given Corena the ring. Corena was a good scout — at least he had always so thought. She had assisted wonderfully in his work. She — why, dawg-gawn it! — she was the first nurse with whom he had ever worked who was able to give gas successfully. And the ring had been an innocuous token of his professional esteem. Just because she had helpd him. . . .

Corena — why, dad-blame it! the woman was a ha'nt. He realized suddenly that she was the shoal upon which Dr. Elijah Atcherson's bark had foundered. Into the mind of Dr. Herring there leaped an old saying: "Where smoke is at they is boun' to be a blaze!" What if — well, both Mrs. Atcherson and Mayola Kye had unqualifiedly dubbed Corena a vampire.

Dr. Herring sank weakly into a chair. He felt ill. In a second his well-ordered cosmic scheme had gone flooie. Down the hall a door opened, closed again, and he saw the fair Corena cross the hall and enter the Gold Crown. March Clisby edged ingratiatingly around the counter and Brutus plainly saw the dazzling smile with which she greeted the elongated man of business. There was no misunderstanding that smile. It was the smile which a woman reserves for the man she desires to bewitch. Brutus recalled distinctly the number of times she had bestowed such a smile upon him. Was there no limit to the perfidy of a vampire? He knew that she must have made capital of the ring he had given her: else how did Mayola know about it. The woman — first skinny, bloodless Dr. Atcherson, then himself — and now March Clisby. Decidedly the vampiring business was on a boom.

He felt an impelling urge to talk it over. And as co-employer of the pulchritudinous Corena he sought Elijah Atcherson.

The doctor looked up testily as he entered. "Busy doin' nothin' as usual," he roared in greeting. "You dentis's is got a graf'."

Brutus swelled with such mite of pride as he was able to muster. "I is got a patient comin' in

PAINLESS EXTRACTION

half a hour," he retorted. "Epocoectomy an' orthodentia case both."

"If'n you got all that on yo' min'," discouraged the M.D., "what you come botherin' me about? I is a busy man. Git out!"

Brutus sank forlornly into a chair. "Atcherson," he opined gloomily, "sumthin' is got to be did."

"Right — fust off. An' that sumthin' is you is got to git outen my office while I is busy."

"This is impo'tant."

"I guess I is got sumthin' mo' impo'tant than what you is got."

"I is mentionin' Corena Clemmins!"

Dr. Atcherson abruptly laid aside the microscope slide he had been preparing. His narrow-lidded little eyes glittered. "What 'bout her?" he bellowed. "What 'bout her?"

"She's a wampire!" returned Brutus with all the courage of his new-found conviction.

"Now lis'en heah at me, Brutus Herrin'; if'n you is come in heah to dip yo' oah into my pussonal an' dimestic affairs —"

"This heah is my own affair, Atcherson. Mayola Kye is done bust up our 'gagement skallyhootin'."

Elijah chuckled with unholy glee. "Guess'n you ain't gwine laugh at me no mo' 'cause of what Lustisha done that night, huh?"

"I 'pologize," returned Brutus humbly. "To you an' Mis' Atcherson both."

"Huh! Wha's that: what you is sayin' now? You 'pologize to Lustisha, too?" Atcherson was roaring bellicosely and waving his skinny arms in violent defense. " I is tellin' you now, man to man, Brutus Herrin', what I is tol' you heahtofo'— I ain't nev' looked at that woman no other way than —"

" 'Tain't how you looks at wampires, Atcherson; it's all in how they looks at you," and Brutus plunged into a detailed and heart-rending recital of the circumstances leading to the ruination of his might-have-been matrimonial bliss. " The result of all of which is," he wound up, " that fo' our own sakes an' fo' our dimestic peace an' happiness, we is got to fire that gal."

" Contrac'," raved Atcherson. " She is got a contrac' ontil nex' April."

" We could offer a bonus —"

" All right — offer a bonus then. I ain't said nothin' 'gainst it, is I? It's wuth a hund'ed dollars to me to have a li'l' peace in my home oncet in awhile. Give her a bonus an' let her go."

Brutus glanced nervously around the office. " You is gwine help? "

" Not me."

" I is skeered to make talk with her alone. I is li'ble to git comprimised."

" Huh! Seems like you cain't git comprimised no comprimiser than what you is a'ready. But," valiantly, " if you insis's. . . ."

Dr. Brutus Herring timidly summoned Corena from the Gold Crown, and in a still, small voice offered her two hundred dollars cash in exchange for her copy of their written contract.

Corena listened in tight-lipped silence. Absolutely innocent, she was bulwarked with the fighting sense of outraged virtue. She swung on Bru-

PAINLESS EXTRACTION

tus. "How come you to make me this heah proposition now, Dr. Herrin'?"

"Jes' happen so."

"Sho'?"

"Absotively."

"Miss Mayola Kye — yo' fiansay — wa'n't she in heah a few minutes ago?"

"Uh-huh."

"What she said bout'n me?"

"Nothin'."

"Not even mention my name?"

"No. That is — not perzac'ly."

"Hmph! I reckon she is been joinin' in the chorus of the song which Mis' Atcherson stahted, ain't she?"

"Now, Miss Clemmins —"

"Whyn't you fen' me when she said things 'gainst me, huh? Ain't neither of you men got no gumption? Whyn't you 'fen' me when Mayola Kye talked 'gainst me jes' now?"

Brutus tumbled into the trap. "How you know she said things 'gainst you?"

"I know it now. An' I might's well tell you both sumthin' so's they ain't gwine be no misundumstandin'. W'en Mis' Atcherson stahted in on me that night I been out in the sto'm with Dr. Atcherson I knowed she was gwine try git rid of me. An' I knowed if I quitted I'd say good-bye to my reppitation as a lady. So I done saw Lawyer Evans Chew an' showed him that contrac'. He says that contrac' cain't be busted, an' that because of its perfessional nature you is not on'y got to keep on payin' me my salary but you is also got to keep me workin'."

The eyes of the unfortunate pair met and held. Corena's attitude confirmed their worst fears. She had them in her power — just how and why they didn't know — and she had no intention of releasing them. "Two hund'ed dollars bonus?" tempted Brutus.

"Th'ee hund'ed?" dared Atcherson, the bellow gone from his quivering voice.

"No! Not th'ee hund'ed n'r neither a thousan'. Yo' wimminfolks is set out to ruint my reppitation an' they ain't gwine do it. I wants you both to undumstan' I is a lady an' I is a nu'se also an' I is got a contrac' which says I work heah ontil nex' April. Tha's all. If'n you wan's me, gen'lemen, on a *perfessional* matter, I will be findable in the Gol' Crown Ice Cream Pa'lor."

The door closed firmly behind her. For five minutes there was nothing to be heard in the room but silence and very little of that. Finally Dr. Elijah Atcherson sighed. It was a deep, fervent, harried sigh which rattled the window-panes. "Wimmin is plumb hell," he remarked.

"Admittin' that," rejoined Brutus argumentatively, "we is still got to consider how this heah wampire is to be got rid of."

"Ain't you jes' heah her say she ain't gwine got be rid of? Ain't you?"

"What she say ain't got nothin' to do with it. She's plumb mad now an' she is got sumthin' up her sleeve which we ain't want her to perduce. We is got to get rid of her — like a wisdom tooth which is decayed."

"You do it then — you is a dentis'."

"You claims you is got mo' brains than what I is got."

"'Tain't no lawyer brain. An' even if 'twas, they ain't no lawyer gwine help us out."

Brutus cogitated. "If'n she'd on'y lef' of her own accord —"

"If'n I ain't nev' had no su'gical cases 'ceptin' simple appendectomy my reco'd would look awful good."

"Even wimmin like her falls in love — or sumthin'."

"Mos' usuamly sumthin'. Co'se we is got to git her to lef' us."

"How? If'n we on'y had one good frien'. . . ."

"We is, but he coul'n't be no help."

"Name which?"

"March Clisby."

The men looked at one another. Then they both started to speak.

"March is pow'ful han'some —"

"— An' him an' her is good frien's —"

"— They been knowin' each other sencst befo' she come to work fo' us —"

"— An' he'd do a heap if'n we ast him."

They waited until Miss Clemmins had completed her day's labours and departed for the sacred precincts of her boarding house on Seventeenth street. Then March was summoned into conference. He eyed askance the fragrant perfecto which Elijah forced upon him and shied from Brutus's eagerness to light it. After much verbose preamble they got down to brass tacks.

March listened popeyed to their tale of woe, puffing great clouds of smoke into the room and shaking his head from side to side as though it was too heavy for his long, thin neck. Finally the collaborated story was completed and the professional men eagerly awaited March's decision. It came hesitatingly.

"Ise bettin' you gen'lemen is all wrong," he declared.

"Mebbe one of us'd be wrong," answered Atcherson in a voice as free from a roar as nature permitted, "but never both ob us. Not never both. It jes' coul'n't happen."

"But I been knowin' Corena —"

"So is we: tha's the trouble."

"She must of had some reason fo' refusin' to quit."

"My Gawd! March Clisby — ain't that what we is been tellin' you fo' the past half a hour? Co'se she is got a reason an' the reason is us. She ain't nothin' on'y jes' a wampire."

March's eyes narrowed. "An' you claims to be my frien's?"

"We is yo' frien's."

"Yet you is wishin' me onto a woman which you says is ruint you both?"

"You ain't engage'— neither married."

"I — I — know that. . . ." March hesitated — and was lost. Brutus and Elijah opened a verbal bombardment before which better men than March would have fallen. They fairly overflowed with persuasive logic. According to their arguments, March Clisby would assure himself a private little golden throne in heaven by this act of charity; he would become a benefactor to the human race by setting up as an eliminator of vampires.

"B-b-but," stammered the dazed March, coming up for air, "what they is in it fo' me?"

"Oh!" There was a sudden letdown in enthusiasm. "Sumthin'," answered Atcherson vaguely.

"What?" persisted March cannily. "Co'se — pervidin' I succeeds."

The bare mention of success proved the Open Sesame to their wallets. "How much you want, March?"

March Clisby hesitated. He knew that these men needed his help — yet, understanding the soreness of their straits, he hesitated to voice his demands. "I is a young man," he opened timidly, "an' I ain't got nothin' befo' me on'y a future —"

"Yeh . . . yeh. . . ."

"An'— an'— well, I was thinkin' if'n I c'n do this heah thing fo' you gen'lemen you-all ought to be willin' to give me another thi'd of the Gol' Crown Ice Cream Parlour so's I'd own the cumtrollin' interes'."

The price was steep but not sufficiently steep to beget any great amount of hesitation. The Gold Crown was a good paying proposition as such propositions go, but both doctors were too well fixed in the goods of the world to require the little which they received as a two-thirds share of its revenue.

"Tell you what we'll do," compromised Elijah. "T'morrow mawnin' we'll go down to Lawyer Artopee Gaillard an' draw up a contrac' which gives you cumtrol as gene'al manager no matter what we says an' also gives you two-thi'ds of the profits s'long's you stay with the business. That gives you all what you wants an' pertec's us case'n you ev' got sore an' wan'ed to sell us out."

March Clisby beamed beatifically. He extended both hands comprehensively. "You is both gen'lemen of the fust water," he proclaimed, "an I is proud to sacrifice myse'f on the altar of my frien'ship fo' such."

By noon of the following day Elijah and Brutus were all smiles. There was no gainsaying the fact that March had no intention whatever of shirking his end of the bargain. He spent every available minute in the immediate vicinity of Miss Clemmins, smirking and smiling ingratiatingly: a fish angling for the bait. He brought to the reception-room — when it was vacant — foamy, frothy, ice-cream sodas, samples par excellence of his own handiwork. That night he begged off and, leaving his assistant in charge, escorted Miss Clemmins to Champion Moving Picture Theatre Number Two — Coloured Only — where they sat tensely through the ninth blood-curdling episode of The Hounding of Hattie.

During the days which followed March intensified his efforts. Nor did Corena Clemmins register any violent objections. Her attitude toward Brutus and Elijah, however, was cold and aloof — much to the delight of those gentlemen. She was icily professional and stonily distant. The doctors attributed it all to March's effective work and gave that earnest young man due and liberal credit.

Brutus made two attempts to get back into the good graces of Mayola Kye. Both times the door was slammed viciously in his face. As for Lus-

PAINLESS EXTRACTION 305

tisha Atcherson, she maintained her menacing attitude of potential belligerence. The doctors waited impatiently for concrete developments. And the developments were not long in materializing. Twelve days after the original conversation, March Clisby drew them into conference in Brutus's office. He reclined luxuriously in the dentist's chair, lighted a Turkish cigaret and made his report.

"Gen'lemen," he announced, "you-all shuah did han' me out a tough job."

"Huh? You ain't mean —"

"— I mean I is tried 'suasion an' ev'ything else what they is to try an' 'tain't no use."

"Oh! Lawdy, March — you ain't quittin' on us, is you?"

"No-o: not perzac'ly."

"What you mean: not 'zac'ly?"

"They ain't on'y one way to remove Corena away fum heah?"

"Come which?"

"I is got to marry her!"

Brutus looked at Elijah and Elijah looked at Brutus. Their consciences were suddenly troublesome. It was plain that March had succumbed to the lure of the siren, and also patent that the trustful young man little understood the halter which he was calmly proposing to place about his own neck.

"Marry her?"

"Uh-huh."

"But, March — they sho'ly must be some other way."

He shook his head in positive negation. "I been

knowin' that gal longer'n what you has, Doc. An' w'en she's sot on a thing she's sot on it tho'ough an' complete. They ain't no movin' her a tall. An' if'n I is any jedge she is sot on remainin' where she is at ontil she is married."

Brutus sighed. He was a tender-hearted man and hated to guide his friend to the slaughter. But his own happiness meant much. He spread his hands wide in a gesture of grudging consent. "Well — go ahead an' marry her."

Elijah cleared his throat and bobbed his head. "Guess you is got to, March."

March Clisby unctuously rubbed the palms of his hands together. "That brings on mo' talk —" and he hesitated modestly.

"Which?"

"A gal like what Corena is — she ain't gwine stan' fo' no six-bits weddin'. She is gwine deman' all the trimmin's an' a reg'lar sho'-nuff honeymoon."

"Ain't it the truth?"

"An' I cain't 'ford it!"

"Oh!" Elijah was beginning to see a light. "We is gave you enough a'ready, March."

March started to rise. "If'n tha's how you feel bouten it, Dr. Atcherson, I reckon I ain't got to marry her, is I?"

Brutus forced the victim back into the chair. "Yes, you is," he grated. "How much this heah swell weddin' an' honeymoon gwine cos'?"

The prospective bridegroom set his figure at a minimum: "Th'ee hund'ed dollars."

"Make it two hund'ed an' fifty."

"Th'ee hund'ed is the rock-bottom price an' I is

PAINLESS EXTRACTION

losin' money at that, genl'lemen. Remember, I is the one got to live with her all my nachel life."

Elijah sighed ponderously. "Bein' a married man, March, I know sumthin' bouten what that means. S'far's I is concerned at, the th'ee hund'ed is satisfactory." He tentatively produced his checkbook. "You is shuah she is gwine marry you?"

"Soht of."

"Soon as the 'gagement is publicly announce', March, you gits the th'ee hund'ed. We'll write the cheks an' hol'n 'em ontil then."

"Tha's easy," grinned March. "I is bettin' I c'n cash in by t'night."

And he did! Immediately on the heels of the announcement Brutus was received once again into the arms of the adoring Mayola — thoroughly contrite now for the manner in which she had treated him. As for Lustisha, she actually beamed upon her husband across their dinner table and just before his departure after the evening meal, she implanted a warm, moist kiss upon his unwilling lips.

The wedding, which occurred three weeks later, marked a social epoch. Even Lustisha Atcherson, who could not have been kept away by a team of wild horses, admitted that the bride presented a thoroughly entrancing picture. Mayola Kye, intoxicated by the festive atmosphere, unbent so far as to kiss the bride.

A large portion of unalloyed bliss had settled upon the shoulders of each of the guests. Supreme hilarity held sway and raucous humour ran rampant. Professor Alec Champagne's string-and-reed orchestra furnished an amplitude of raggy, itchy dance music. Even Elijah Atcherson allowed a corner of his mantle of dignity to slip as he circulated through the crowd, his bellicose basso rising triumphantly above the din.

And finally the midnight hour approached and the blushing bride retired to her boudoir to don travelling garb. Brutus Herring and Elijah Atcherson cornered the bridegroom in the hallway and pressed a thin envelope into his willing hand.

"They's fifty dollars, March. Tha's over an' above what we is a'ready gave you. You is sho' done yo' work tho'ough an' we wants you to know that we 'preciates it."

March was overcome with emotion. "You is both too good. Doin' what I is done did ain't nothin' tall fo' such fine fellers like what you-all is."

"Hmph!" grunted the pessimistic Elijah. "Jes' wait ontil you is been married a yeah!"

Meanwhile, in the sanctity of her room, the bride had divested herself of veil and bridal gown. She stood proudly before the dresser mirror in all the pristine glory of white satin ribbon and fluffy lingerie. There came a light tap on the door and it cracked open tentatively. "C'n I come in?"

Corena looked up into the tiny, contrite face of Mayola Kye. There was no resisting a penitent Mayola. "Shuah, Miss Kye — you is mos' welcome."

Mayola entered the room and stood uncertainly before the other woman. "I is done you dirt, Corena," she blurted, "an' I is sorry."

Corena impulsively kissed her. "Tha's all right, Mayola; tha's jes' all right. You — you —"

she cast about for some symbol of forgiveness: "You c'n he'p lace up my travellin' boots!"

From her post of honour at the feet of the bride, Mayola glanced up. "It took me all of a heap, Corena."

"Which?"

"Yo' weddin'— comin' sudden like it done."

The bride shook her head. "They wa'n't nothin' sudden 'bout our weddin'."

"But — but you ain't hahdly knowed March Clisby real well fo' more'n th'ee or fo' weeks."

Corena's lips expanded into a broad grin. The grin became a chuckle and the chuckle a full-blown, throaty laugh. "Sho' now, Mayola — you is plumb wrong there. Why, me an' March Clisby is been engage' sencst even befo' I went to work fo' the doctors. Co'se 'twas a secret 'gagement, but we was on'y waitin' ontil our feenancial affairs looked brighter." She paused briefly — then smiled again: "An' believe me, Mayola — things is shuah been comin' March's way right recent!"

THE END